Dying of Desire

A McCall / Malone Mystery

Glenn Harris

Dying of Desire is a work of fiction. Names, characters, places and incidents either are the product of the author's imagination or are used fictitiously. Any resemblance to actual persons, living or dead, or events is entirely coincidental. Portland, Oregon, of course actually exists. Major landmarks like Pioneer Courthouse Square and the Justice Center are where they belong, as are the streets and neighborhoods, but I have moved a few buildings around, put restaurants where none exist, erased houses that do exist, and generally wreaked minor havoc with reality for the purposes of my story.

Dying of Desire

CHAPTER ONE

Plastic wrap? She wanted to put plastic fucking wrap down there? How was he supposed to enjoy muff-diving if the muff was covered in plastic wrap?

Stupid bitch.

Morgan Klodpusser had too many stupid bitches in his life, in his opinion, not least among them Mrs. Klodpusser.

And now this brain-challenged young twit was really beginning to piss him off. What was her name? He didn't remember her name. Never mind that. Morgan wasn't a big fan of names, anyway.

"You want to do what?" he asked her incredulously.

She looked at him like he was the slow one and explained patiently. "If you wanna go down on me, I'm gonna cover it with plastic wrap first. I found a wad of gum stuck down there one time after a guy got through and that was it. Really gross. Plastic wrap from then on. That's the deal."

The whore looked to be in her twenties, he thought, which was good. Tall, a couple of inches taller than him, and that was fine. A little too thin with hair that was a little too mousy, not really good fantasy material, but what the hell? It was his experience that Portland, Oregon, didn't have the best-looking prostitutes in the world. She did have a nice face.

He would do something about that if she didn't stop dumping this stupid crap about plastic wrap on him. He felt his stomach churning, his fist clenching, and figured it might be time for a lesson. He hardly ever got the chance to teach his wife any more. She'd finally learned pretty much all the lessons.

He glared at the young woman sitting next to him on the motel room bed. She hadn't even taken her panties off yet and they were arguing about what he could or couldn't do down there. Unbelievable. "You're chewing gum yourself, right now, you stupid cunt."

She shrugged. "I ain't planning to go down on me. If you are,

1

that's the deal."

That was it. He got a good grip on her arm and jerked her clos-er. "Listen, you little...."

She thumped him in the chest with the palm of her hand and pulled back. "Hey! That hurts! You don't want to fuck with me!"

Which was so funny it almost broke through his rage. "That's exactly what I want to do, you dumb little whore, but first I'm go-ing to have myself a nice meal. Without any goddamned plastic wrap. Now get your panties off and...."

He felt an adrenaline surge like nothing before in his life when the door of their room suddenly crashed open. Jesus Christ! Was it the cops? The hideous embarrassment of appearing in court, in the news, flashed through him. What would the women back at the home office think? He would be ruined. Jesus Christ!

He had just enough time to see that it was a nasty-looking guy with hard features and empty, bulging eyes. No uniform but a very big gun. Just enough time before the universe exploded in a horri-ble noise and Morgan Klodpusser's whole chest went cold as ice.

He knew he was on his back on the bed and that someone was screaming, knew that he had to fight off the blackness that wanted to close in tight around him.

"Shut the fuck up!" he faintly heard a rough male voice shout. The screams stopped then. "Why'd you shoot this cocksucker, Jew-el?" the same voice asked more quietly. Morgan could hear the ar-rogance in it, the cruelty, and he wondered for a moment...did she? No, it was....

Then he thought, *Jewel...that's a nice name....*

And the blackness was complete.

CHAPTER TWO

Between having killed a man in cold blood and declaring my lust for Devon Malone, I hadn't been sleeping well lately.

The man was a rogue international spy and the most evil son of a bitch I'd ever encountered. I had no regrets about blowing his brains all over the wall but I did harbor some dismay that I had no regrets.

Devon Malone is my partner in the McCall-Malone Detective Agency in Portland, Oregon. She used to be a Portland cop. A detective in their missing persons unit, she went private and then agreed to combine her agency with mine. In her mid-thirties, she's a woman of olive-toned skin and sharp features, not a classic beauty but I certainly like her looks. At about five-six, she gives most people the impression of being a little delicate, but she may be the toughest woman I've ever encountered. Certainly the toughest to establish an intimate relationship with. The fact that I still didn't know her exact age was good evidence of that.

My exact age is fifty-three, by the way. I'm a stocky, reasonably fit guy with thinning hair who sometimes fears that he might be too old for his partner.

Our office is located above the Previously Owned Books Store at the corner of 3rd and Stark on the edge of downtown Portland. On the same floor with us are Eleanor Ivory (our bookkeeper and accountant as well as Internet expert and a fellow black belt), Sam Bitterly (our attorney), Ray Witkowsky (our insurance agent), and a small telephone survey operation for which we have no need. It was an excellent location for all kinds of reasons, as even Malone had to concede.

But on this day, three weeks after both the occurrences that were still disturbing my sleep, she was pissed.

"How many voicemails did you have this morning?" she inquired after getting her first cup of coffee and settling down on her side of our partners desk. She eyed the blinking light on her own phone with a slight shudder. She wore her standard uniform this morning, snug white tank top, form-fitting jeans, and black boots. Her shoulder-length brunette hair was carelessly tousled and her leather jacket was hanging on our hall tree. She could have stepped right out of a Hollywood movie featuring a female private eye, which didn't help reduce the media attention we'd been getting.

The old cliché is that there's no such thing as bad publicity. I would have agreed until recently. Ever since setting up my original agency I'd found myself in the middle of cases that got extensive news coverage—mostly thanks to my buddy-cum-nemesis Alison Roberts of our local independent TV channel. It was, I often thought, the primary reason the agency had continuing success.

But somehow being an agency comprised of a middle-aged man and a sexy younger woman, associated as we were with spies, murdered prostitutes, and gun fights in downtown motels, had pushed us over the edge into Crazy Land. Between media inquiries and potential clients who wanted to tell us all about the conspiracies we could help them expose, we were swamped with calls we didn't want and had, if anything. fewer legitimate jobs than usual.

"Six," I answered. "One sounded like a good prospect, a husband who thinks his wife's supposed bridge club meetings might involve hands of something other than bridge."

"Huh," she said and picked up her own phone. We could answer one another's phones if we had to, but we maintained separate numbers and voicemail, each with our own set of clients—always willing and able to back each other up. So far.

As she listened to her own messages, I pretended to do some typing while watching her expression out of the corner of my eye. It took a while and didn't look promising. She hung up with a sour expression.

"Eight," she announced. "Six media and two nutfucks." She checked something on her monitor. "So I'm working three skip traces and a cheating husband, the latter all wrapped up except for writing the report and preparing the bill. You've got the hardware store employee who might be ripping them off and now maybe a cheating wife. Good times."

I wanted to reassure her that things would soon get better but there were two problems with that. One was that I felt no such assurance myself and the other was that my phone rang.

"McCall and Malone Detective Agency. Clint McCall speaking," I answered pleasantly. You never know.

"Hey Clint, it's Veronica."

"Hey, kiddo, what's up?" Veronica Fortune, owner of the Pen and Pastry café, best-selling author of a book about her former life as a prostitute, and my very first client back in the day. She sounded a little stressed.

"I need you to come by as soon as you can." Definitely stressed.

"Trouble?"

"Maybe. I'm not sure. I need a favor. The favor isn't really for me, but she probably won't want.... Oh, it would take too long to explain it on the phone. You need to talk to one of my girls and make up your own mind. Could you get here sometime later this afternoon?"

Given the time of day, she had to be calling from the Pen and Pastry and "one of my girls" had to mean one of her waitresses, all of whom were also former ladies of the evening. It was Veronica's own private social welfare program not to mention good PR for the café.

"This afternoon shouldn't be a problem," I said. "Maybe even later this morning."

"Excellent. We'll be here whenever you can make it."

We hung up and Malone tossed me an inquiring look. "It was Veronica," I explained. "One of her employees has a problem, apparently, that she wants to discuss with me."

Slight grimace. "Ah. More pro bono work. Just what we need."

"Well, I can't ignore a friend asking for help. You're really in a bad mood this morning, you know that?"

Another grimace. "I know. Sorry. Just ignore me while I work on pulling the stick out of my ass."

"Will do." I would also continue trying to ignore the fact that my partner seemed to be having trouble relaxing with me ever since I'd told her I was interested in something more than a partnership. She hadn't categorically rejected the idea and she'd never been a go-ing-with-the-flow type anyway, but she was making it very difficult to establish even a tentative intimacy. Which maybe was the point. *Give her time*, I kept telling myself. Ignoring the fact that three solid weeks was already a lot of time.

Fortunately, a knock on our door derailed what was too often my train of thought lately.

CHAPTER THREE

"Come on in," I called out, and the door opened to reveal a young guy that I didn't recognize. Ah ha! Perhaps an actual client. At least he looked both sane and worried, a good combination from my point of view. Mid-twenties, around my height of five-ten but weighing probably thirty pounds less than my one ninety. Full head of unkempt dark brown hair giving rise to mild follicle envy on my part, wire-rimmed glasses and medium complexion. He was wearing dark dress slacks, blue shirt with the collar open, and a Navy blazer. Yuppie Time.

He scanned the two of us and settled on me. "Clint McCall?"

"That's me," I said. I gestured at my partner as our visitor approached the desk. "This is Devon Malone."

"Hi," he said to her and she nodded back as he sat in the visitor's chair on my side. Looked like he was going to be my client—if he was a client.

He again looked from one of us to the other. "Are you two...?"

"Partners," Malone spoke up when he hesitated. "We're partners."

"Ah, okay. I'm really here to talk to Mr. McCall, but...."

"We have access to a conference room," I interrupted, "if you feel we need privacy." Our insurance agent across the hall let us use his conference room when we needed to talk separately with clients. But the young man shook his head.

"No, no, this is fine."

"Then I'll just get on with my own work," said Malone, "and let you two talk." She turned to her monitor and began scrolling through something or another—though I was sure she wouldn't miss a word.

My visitor stuck out his hand. "I'm George Heatherly," he said as we shook. He glanced around, a little uncomfortably. "Nice office. Classic."

Which was true enough. From the '40s-era partners desk that I'd found at a yard sale to the old couch that had preceded Malone and the extra-large table-top fridge that had come with her to accommodate a snacking obsession, the space gave off "private eye" vibes that clients seemed to get a kick out of.

"What can I do for you, George?" The clock is ticking. Busy, busy, busy.

He took a breath and launched in. "I need your help. I work for *The Portland Bulletin*. Are you familiar with it?"

"It's a weekly, right? Lots of ads, mostly local business and neighborhood news? Pick it up for free at your local grocery?"

The breath came out in a sigh, almost of resignation. "Yeah, that's it. It's a good paper, for what it is, and we're trying to make it better. I was hired to bring some investigative journalism to the table and maybe eventually write a column as well." He paused. "Which is why I'm here. I need help on a potential story."

Okay, that was a little weird. "You want me to help with the investigation of a story you're working on?"

He actually blushed, putting a hand to his cheek as if trying to stay the crimson from creeping upward. "I know it sounds unusual but, yes, that's what I want you to do."

"Must be a big story. Tell me more." Heatherly might be a wet-behind-the-ears journalist for a paper that was handed out free in the downtown area and struggled to survive on advertising, but he also seemed to have a great deal of money. I was dressed as I often am in chinos and short-sleeve knit shirt even though it was early March. My somewhat threadbare sport jacket hung next to Malone's leather on the hall tree in the corner. Unlike mine, my potential client's clothing was expensive and his watch a genuine Rolex. No harm channeling some of that treasure into our own cash flow.

His mouth twitched in a momentary rueful smile. "It could be very big for me. And I came to you because of your background in journalism."

"How did you know about that?" I'm no Internet search expert

8

—I had somebody for that down the hall—but I doubted you could just plug "private investigator who used to be journalist" into the average search engine and come up with me.

"One of my professors at U of O recommended you," he explained. "You're kind of famous in local academic circles. Not many j-school faculty have gone on to become private detectives. You were at Portland State, right, and *The Oregonian* before that? And you have a black belt as well? You teach martial arts?"

"I was a working reporter for only four years," I said. "I went back to PSU to get my Master's and then joined the faculty. I taught journalism for a number of years, then moved into the private detective business. I don't teach taekwondo anymore, either. I did, under Master Young at his studio downtown, until he retired and then I set up a private studio with a few friends. We don't take students. But let's get back to what I can do for you." Hopefully.

"I've been getting anonymous tips," he said finally.

"About?"

"About a problem on the board of a local charity." He raised his eyes to mine. "You've heard of the Lifestream Foundation?"

"Don't think so."

"They recently built a big new homeless shelter on Burnside, supposed to be 'full-service'—food, shelter, medical referral, counseling, job placement, GED preparation, you name it. There's a six-member board, all from wealthy local families, that has been raising the money and now oversees the operation."

"And you're being told that something's going on besides charitable works."

"Yes, exactly, 'something.' I get the impression it has to do with the finances, but my caller hasn't been too specific."

"That's what you want me to do, find out what the something is?"

He compressed his lips for a moment as if he didn't want to answer. "First, find out if there's anything at all. I don't have a lot of experience with anonymous tips, but I know I can't assume

9

they're valid."

"Not to put too fine a point on it, but isn't this exactly the job of an investigative reporter?"

He sat back and sighed. "My job, you mean."

"Yep, that's what I mean."

This time he paused for almost a full thirty seconds, looking down at the floor, his face expressionless. Finally he straightened his shoulders and looked up.

"Mr. McCall, I've wanted to be a journalist since I was a little kid and thought Peter Jennings was the coolest guy on TV. Everything I've done, all through school, has been directed toward this work. I got good grades and I've written some good stories, I think, since I got out in the real world. I know the *Bulletin* isn't much, no competition for *The Oregonian* certainly, but it's not tabloid journalism either. We cover the business community downtown in addition to neighborhood news and generally do a better than competent job of it. I like to think I'm a pretty fair investigative reporter —or could be...but not when it comes to my wife's family."

Well, it took a while but here we were. "Ah ha," I said.

CHAPTER FOUR

"My wife's uncle is chairman of the Lifestream Foundation's board," Heatherly went on. "Norman Albright. The Albrights are one of Portland's most prominent families."

"I've heard the name. Is your wife involved?"

He flinched. "Involved? In the Foundation? No! Shanna's a librarian. She works at the central Portland library. She's close to her uncle, but has had nothing to do with the Lifestream Foundation. I just don't feel comfortable asking the kinds of questions that would have to be asked, especially if the story comes to nothing. If there really is a story there...then I'll have to decide what to do."

"You mean whether to publish it or not."

"I guess I mean whether to continue being a journalist or take up some other line of work. I hope to hell it doesn't come down to a choice between my family and my career."

"You could still do other stories even if you didn't do this one."

He shook his head sadly. "Call me an idealist or a fool or whatever but, no, I couldn't."

"Okay, I'll accept that. What exactly has this caller of yours said? How many times has he called? If it is a he."

"Yeah, it's a guy. He's called three times in the last two weeks. Very cryptic calls. The first time he said there was some hanky panky on the board...."

"He used that term, 'hanky panky'?"

"Yes."

"And that's all he said?"

"That time, yes. The second time he said I should look at the board's financial records. No hint what I should look for. The last time he called, he asked what I'd found and sounded grumpy that I hadn't done anything yet. Said I was the only reporter he was talking to and it was up to me. Then he hung up."

"Interesting. How long ago was the last call?"

"Just yesterday."

"And you don't recognize the voice?"

"No."

"Can you tell me anything else? Is he young, old, educated, foreign...?"

"He's well spoken, American English, and he doesn't sound like a young man." Heatherly shifted uneasily in his seat. "His voice is very soft. I had the impression he might be gay."

Oh, here come the homophobic stereotypes. "Because he speaks softly?"

"I guess. And because he says things like 'hanky panky.' Just something about his voice, his delivery, gave me that feeling." Apparently, Heatherly was beginning to hear himself. He swiped it all away with one open hand. "Forget it. I could be entirely wrong about that."

So I let it go. "And as far as you know, it's true that he's called only you—not any other reporters?"

"As far as I know. I haven't seen anything in the papers or on TV. No rumors about the board being investigated, but that doesn't mean it isn't happening."

"Doesn't it strike you as odd that this tipster would call the *Bulletin* rather than the city's major daily or one of the TV stations?"

"Yes. I'm not sure what to make of it."

"Has it occurred to you we could be dealing with somebody who wants to disrupt your family rather than uncover a news story?"

"Jesus." He contemplated for a few seconds. "No, I didn't really think of that." Silence, then a sharp look at me. "You said 'we.' You'll help me out then?" He cocked an eye over at Malone as well but she just kept working at her monitor.

I opened a desk drawer and pulled out a standard contract form and rate schedule. "If you still want my services after you've looked these over, I'll do what I can," I said as I handed the papers to him.

I swung my nicely padded swivel chair around so I could pretend to watch the traffic on Stark Street while he made up his mind.

I turned back with some relief when he cleared his throat and put the papers on my desk.

"This looks fine," he said. "First week in advance?"

"That's right," I said, "subject to partial refund if I'm on the job less than a week."

"No problem." He pulled out a checkbook and smiled a little sheepishly. "I don't make much writing for the *Bulletin*, but I married money." *And good for you*, I thought to myself. He filled out the check, tore it loose, and handed it across the desk. Meanwhile, I filled in the blanks on the contract and traded it across for him to sign.

He paused with pen above the signature line. "It probably goes without saying, but I'll say it anyway. I need you to be extremely discreet about this. I don't want Shanna's uncle to know I'm having him investigated."

"Don't worry," I replied. "It may be necessary for him to know there's an investigation, but he won't know it has anything to do with you. Not from me, anyway. Does your wife know you're here?"

He grimaced. "I'm afraid not. I haven't even told her about the calls. I didn't want to worry her...and I didn't know what to say, anyway." He signed the contract and handed it back. "Do you think you'll need to talk to her?"

I was not happy to hear that I might have the added complication of dealing with marital deception.

"Could be," I said. "It would be better if you went first."

He sat back, looking equally unhappy. "I'll talk to her," he finally said. He didn't sound committed to the idea.

We wrapped up a few final details, including the names of the rest of the Lifestream Foundation board and more information about Norman Albright; then I wished George Heatherly a good day and escorted him to the door.

13

"Well," Malone said as I returned to the desk, "that one sounds more interesting than your average cheating spouse. Good for you."

"Good for us," I replied. "I'm going to want your help with it if you've got time. Lots of people to talk to and bases to cover. Plus I have to go check out Veronica's problem."

"I always have time for you, Clint," she purred, laying on the phony sweetness.

"Right," I said, and left it at that. I'll confess that I've read some popular romances and am familiar with the idea that the supremely confident guy is supposed to just go ahead and make a move on the woman who is resisting only to provide him with the opportunity to conquer her. But oddly enough, they never talk about the woman who might unholster her Glock and blow your balls off if you did that. Could be it's a sub-genre that I've missed.

CHAPTER FIVE

The Hawthorne district of Portland is reminiscent of Berkeley's Telegraph Avenue back in the early sixties, before the love children discovered hard drugs. Lots of small shops featuring used books, records, retro clothing, rugs, and incense, a wide variety of food and drink. Veronica Fortune's café, the Pen and Pastry, is almost precisely in the middle of the main shopping area, just around the corner from my house where I'd left my car in the driveway.

It's a little larger than the average coffee shop, twenty tables that each seat four patrons—a successful operation both because of the excellent pastry kitchen and the locally famous owner. Even in the middle of a Tuesday afternoon almost half the tables were occupied. I did a quick scan looking for my daughter Colleen who often hangs out here but didn't see her.

Veronica saw me, however, as soon as I entered and greeted me with a peck on the cheek, then led me to a table at the back, her long red hair shifting and shining in the glow of the overhead fluorescent lighting. At forty-five she managed to keep looking better, her pale complexion and delicate features becoming more classic every year. Today she was downright spectacular in a colorful peasant blouse and full ankle-length skirt.

Somehow we had never gotten beyond the detective-client relationship. She was gorgeous and single and incredibly sexy but the tingle just wasn't there. She's been a good friend, though, and no question her escape from the street was not only complete but pretty impressive.

We sat down and one of the waitresses brought us our usual, espresso black for me and decaf with sugar for Veronica. I noticed that the young woman's hand was trembling slightly as she set the cups down. I looked up to see that her expression was tight with concentration, as if it were taking all her strength to maintain even that much control. She wouldn't meet my gaze and fled toward the kitchen the second her chore was done.

I turned to Veronica. "What's going on?"

"I have a new girl," she said.

"The one who just brought us our coffee?"

"Good guess. Her name is LeAnn."

"Okay. Is she the problem?"

"She's not the problem...but she has the problem."

"Okay."

"My problem is that she doesn't want help with her problem."

"This is beginning to sound complicated."

She smiled a little. "It is. LeAnn's just now trying to get off the street. Her pimp was Malcolm Guth. You've heard of him?"

The name wasn't familiar to me and I told Veronica so.

"He's not a major player and I don't know him personally," she said, "but from what I hear he's a nasty piece of work. Showed up in Portland a couple of years ago and started recruiting girls, mostly runaways he picked up at the bus station. He deals some drugs, but that's not what he uses to control the girls. This bastard uses pain. Beatings, even torture. He usually runs about a dozen girls out around 82nd and I guess they're all scared to death of him, even scared to try to get away because of what he might do if he caught up with them."

"But LeAnn was one of his?"

Veronica nodded. "Yes, though I didn't know that until today. When she first came in a few weeks ago, she led me to believe she'd been working on her own. But she got a call this morning and Maureen heard this end of it. Maureen said LeAnn was talking to somebody she called Malcolm and that he was threatening her."

Maureen Loori was Veronica's chief baker and assistant mother-figure to the staff, a fortyish black woman with rock-solid common sense.

"We sat LeAnn down for a little talk," Veronica continued. "The kid's still not being entirely straight about where she's coming from, but she did admit it was Guth on the phone and that he was

16

giving her some kind of trouble. Sounded to me like he might be showing up here."

"And that's when you called me?"

"Yes."

"Why didn't you tell me what was going on? I could have asked Malone to cover the office and come on down right then. Has Guth shown up?"

"No sign of him yet." She hesitated. "I didn't want to impose on you."

I reached over and patted her hand. "It's not an imposition. I sure as hell don't want to see any trouble come to you or the Pen and Pastry." Not least because I wouldn't want Colleen caught up in it.

She firmed up, then, and leaned a little closer. "Well, good, because what I really wish you would do is talk to Malcolm Guth. Check him out, see if you think he's a real threat to LeAnn or the shop."

"And, if he is, see if I can talk him out of it."

Which brought a wry little grin to her face. "That would be good."

"Consider it done."

She nodded with satisfaction. "Thank you."

I looked around the café. "First I'd better have a talk of my own with young LeAnn. Is she hiding in the kitchen?"

Veronica glanced around. "Probably. I don't know if you'll learn much, since she won't admit she needs help."

"Well, let's see."

"I'll go get her."

CHAPTER SIX

I downed the rest of my coffee as I and most of the other men in the room watched Veronica progress to the kitchen. Considering that many of them were no doubt in attendance not only for the excellent pastry and coffee but to entertain a few vicarious fantasies about reformed prostitutes, they probably wondered what might be going on between the famous owner and the balding guy in his mid-fifties. She disappeared for thirty seconds and returned with the young woman who'd served us.

LeAnn looked to be in her early twenties. Tall, probably close to six feet, and very thin with shoulder-length mouse-brown hair. Her complexion was ruddy, though apparently from emotional distress rather than outdoor exercise. She had what would probably be a pretty face when it wasn't contorted by anguish: well-balanced features, generous mouth, dark hazel eyes.

Those eyes were focused intently on me all the way across the room as if I might be a rattlesnake rather than your friendly neighborhood private detective.

Veronica pulled back the chair across from me and waited patiently until her younger companion reluctantly sat down. "LeAnn," she said as she took her own seat, "this is Clint McCall."

LeAnn's eyes were brimming with tears now. Her voice was soft but taut, stretched almost to the breaking point: "I don't need any help."

No hello; just right to it. Okay. Her tone thoroughly contradicted her words. Maybe I'd try a little contradicting of my own.

"I'm not here to help you. I'm here to help Veronica. We don't want any old friends of yours coming around to make trouble."

She jerked back and her eyes narrowed. "He's not my friend."

"If you don't need help, why did you come to Veronica in the first place?"

Her mouth opened and she unfocused for a second as she tried

19

to change direction again. "I...I needed a job. That's all."

"Tell me about Malcolm Guth."

"There's nothing to tell."

"What did he want this morning?"

"Nothing."

"Why isn't he your friend?"

Another shudder, her hands flat on the table as if to steady herself. "What?"

"LeAnn," I said as firmly as I could, "I'm not here to cause you any problem, no problem at all...unless you don't answer my questions. If you want to keep this job that you need, for instance, I want to be reassured that your past isn't going to come storming in the front door. You understand?"

She was in fact looking a little bewildered. Finally she turned to Veronica with a plaintive question. "Can he do that?"

Veronica knew I was just poking around, looking for an opening, and she went with raised eyebrows and a little shrug. "Clint does what he needs to do."

The young woman's face began to collapse into even greater despair.

"I can't go back," she wailed softly.

"You don't have to go anywhere you don't want to go," I said as gently as I could. "Just tell us what Guth wanted. You never know, I might accidentally help you a little if I'm helping your boss."

A slight frown as she worked to put that together, lips trembling. "I was his girl, you know."

Not "one of his girls." His girl. Could this child be so naïve as that? I nodded. "Okay," was all I said.

She looked around as if searching for words. "He wants me back, I guess."

"Did he threaten you? Did he say he was going to come down here after you?"

She shook her head. "He won't come here. He...he says I have

20

to come back on my own."

Veronica spoke up. "You wouldn't do that, would you?"

LeAnn turned to look at her, tears streaming freely now. "I don't want to." Her voice had risen and begun to quaver.

Veronica and I agreed with a glance that the kid had had enough for now. She put her arm around LeAnn for a moment. "Go clean up, catch your breath, and then get back to work," she said. "We'll see what we can do about Mr. Guth."

The young woman abruptly pulled away and stood up, her face and voice suddenly fierce. "No! You can't do anything about Mal. That would just make it worse. I want to stay here. I do. If you hassle him, he might.... I have to do this on my own. Please!"

Veronica raised both hands as if in surrender. "Okay, okay. We won't do anything to make it worse. Don't worry. We're on your side. Go on to the kitchen now and I'll be there in a minute."

My friend and I looked at each other as LeAnn hurried across the café toward the kitchen.

"Wow," I said finally. "There is some complicated shit going on there. I wonder what Guth has on her?"

Veronica looked after the fleeing figure. "I have no idea. The poor kid seems to be torn right down the middle. She's as scared of our trying to help as she is of Guth himself."

"See if you can find out a little bit more before I go chatting with Guth. I don't want to walk in blind."

"Okay. Now that we've broken through a little bit, maybe she'll share something else. I'll let you know."

We both stood up. "And I'll do some checking around on the street to see if there's anything unusual about our young friend's past life. You don't suppose she was really Guth's special girlfriend."

Veronica grunted in a ladylike manner. "No, I don't suppose that. She might have believed it. She's a sweet girl, but not the sharpest knife in the drawer."

"So I noticed."

I took a couple of steps toward the door and then had a

thought. I paused and looked back over my shoulder. "LeAnn is her real name?"

"Yes. LeAnn Hannaford."

"What was her street name then?"

"Oh, right. Jewel. Her name was Jewel."

CHAPTER SEVEN

Devon Malone stuffed the report and bill for Martha Wyman into a manila envelope and sealed it. When she called Mrs. Wyman earlier, the woman had not been too surprised by the results of the investigation; wives who trust their husbands rarely hire detectives to follow them. But still.... Probably she had had some hope she'd turn out to be wrong about hubby Milton taking a little extra time on the way back from his weekly meetings in Olympia to cruise for company on the streets of Portland. Company that he was usually able to find. And here were the photos to prove it, included with the report, as requested.

Devon addressed the envelope and tossed it into the outbox, then swiveled a bit to her right and leaned forward to look out the window at the hustle and bustle on Stark Street.

It looked a little blustery out there but the temperatures weren't too bad, in the forties, and there was (of course) a chance of rain in the forecast. Typical late-morning foot and vehicle traffic, the two about equal here on the edge of downtown. A good location, Devon thought, better than her old one on the Park Blocks, and she was almost used to it now.

She wondered idly what was going on with Clint's friend Veronica. That was a bit weird, that relationship, and she speculated not for the first time that there was or at least had been more to it than friendship. A guy like Clint McCall being "just friends" with a gorgeous sex professional who also had the brains to write a best-selling memoir? Devon didn't think so, regardless of Clint's claims to the contrary.

Relationship. Now he wanted a "relationship" with her. First that out-of-the-fucking-blue impulsive kiss and then his awkward declaration a few weeks ago. Jesus, he was her partner. Didn't he know that partners shouldn't be romantically involved? Did *she* know that? She hadn't cut him off, but she sure as hell was avoiding as hard as she could. Was it time? Was it really time to try to move on?

The weather wasn't the only thing unsettled around here.

A quick knock on the door interrupted her reverie and she almost reached for a weapon when it opened without her invitation —then relaxed when she saw it was Eleanor Ivory. As much as she ever relaxed around the woman—yet another really attractive female who'd been in McCall's life for a long time.

The agency's financial and computing expert had recently turned forty, a few years older than Devon, five-nine with long blond hair and the body of a fitness magazine model. Her lips are slightly too full and her nose slightly too small for classic beauty but they worked well enough together with the wide violet eyes. She wore a low-cut knit top and knee-length skirt and had some sort of magazine in her hand. She had recently sustained some pretty severe injuries at the hands of an ex-boyfriend who turned out to be a crazed killer, but it appeared to Malone that she was recovering just fine.

"Clint's not here?" she asked, looking off to her left down the hall toward the communal bathroom.

"Nope. What can I do for you, Eleanor?"

She hesitated for just a second, then came on across the room and set the magazine in front of Devon. It was the current issue of *Private Detective* ("the magazine for *professional* private detectives"). "I just wanted to ask him why we don't subscribe to this?"

Devon registered the "we," perfectly aware that Eleanor liked to think of herself as a junior detective in the agency, but chose to ignore it.

"It could be," she replied calmly, "because this is tripe published for dweebs who dream of being a private detective rather than real women like myself who actually are."

She would swear that Eleanor almost pouted. "Well. That's kind of mean."

Devon shrugged and shoved the magazine back toward

24

Eleanor. "Sorry."

Eleanor reached out and picked up the magazine, looked at it a little sadly, and then sank into Devon's visitor chair. "We should be girlfriends," she announced.

Devon gave her a deadpan expression. "I don't do girlfriends."

Eleanor literally threw up her hands. "But we work together, almost every day. I'm your accountant, your Internet expert, your...hacker! We...we're two women!"

"It's true. I've noticed that we're both women."

Looking frustrated, Eleanor stood up and started for the door, then turned back for a moment. "One of us is kind of a bitch sometimes," she said.

Devon just grinned. "Yes. That would be me."

CHAPTER EIGHT

I opened my office door and almost collided with Eleanor Ivory who appeared to be leaving in something of a huff.

"Well," I said, "it's the invaluable Miss Ivory. Is there a problem?"

"No, I'm fine," she said with just the slightest hint of snippy. Out of the corner of my eye I saw her stick her tongue out at Malone as I went to hang my jacket on the hall tree. My partner was sitting on her side of the partners desk, leaning back with a grin that seemed to grow ever broader.

"Are you sure there's not a problem?" I asked them both as I went to my side of the desk and stashed my Smith and Wesson in the upper right-hand drawer. The two of them had never gotten along very well, primarily because Malone stubbornly refused to acknowledge Eleanor's value to the agency, but they'd not sunk to elementary school level before.

"Eleanor just wanted to show me a magazine," Malone replied, still grinning.

"What magazine?" I asked.

"Never mind," said Eleanor, holding it down at her side away from me. "I need to get back to work."

"You got time to do some work for me?" I asked.

Pause, chin up, carefully not looking at my partner. "Sure."

"I want you to find out everything you can about a local community organization called the Lifestream Foundation, especially its finances and its board of directors."

She frowned thoughtfully. "Never heard of it...hmm...the finances part will take some time...."

"Will your other clients allow you to get some of it done by tomorrow morning?"

She nodded. "It's not the end of tax season crunch yet and nobody's currently being audited. There's a corporate restructure going on, but then there's always a corporate restructure going on. I may have something for you later today."

With that, she left.

I cocked an eye at Malone. "And what, exactly, was that all about?"

Shrug. "Just girl stuff."

"Right."

No response.

"You, of all people, do not do girl stuff. So what was going on between you two?"

Another shrug. "I was just giving her a hard time. I should probably stop doing that."

"Yeah, you wouldn't want anyone to think that you're feeling competitive with an accountant."

For that, I got a long, considering look from the woman across the desk. "Sometimes," she said, "I worry that you're getting to know me too well."

"Is that honestly a worry of yours? That someone would get to know you too well? What's wrong with being understood by someone who cares about you?"

And just like that it was back to her monitor. "What was your friend Veronica's problem?" she asked without taking her eyes from the screen. Apparently I'd have to check with Eleanor if I wanted to know anything more about what had happened between them. And I'd have to chalk up another failed attempt to generate some intimacy with this impossible partner of mine.

"One of her girls is having problems with her ex-pimp and Veronica's worried the guy might cause trouble. She just wanted me to have a chat with him."

Malone checked the little clock in the corner of her screen. "A chat?"

"I haven't done it yet. He sounds like he might be a real nasty one and I'm waiting to see if she can come up with a little more background before I go see him."

28

"I gather she's not planning to pay for your time and whatever risk you assume."

"She's a friend. It will just be a quick chat. How are your cases going?"

She reached over and patted the manila envelope in her outbox. "Final report and invoice for Mrs. Wyman here. Husband guilty as charged. Two of the skip traces are just about pinned down but I'm having trouble with the third. That's probably what I'll be doing today. You?"

"I'm sure I know which employee is the hardware store thief and I have some ideas about how to prove it. I'll try to wrap that up while I'm waiting to hear from Eleanor about the foundation and Veronica about the pimp."

"Sounds good," said Malone.

And we moved on.

CHAPTER NINE

Malone wasn't in yet when I hit the office the next morning. I turned up the thermostat, shed my jacket and hung it on the hall tree, transferring the cell phone to my pants pocket at the same time. Then I stowed my gun, retrieved a plastic container of ground coffee from the shelf beneath the counter, and loaded the coffee pot filter. Finally I trooped down the hall to the common restroom for some water, noting on the way that Eleanor Ivory's office was still dark.

Back at my desk, water poured and the coffeemaker beginning its susurration, I took a moment to look out at Stark Street glistening through the rain-streaked window. I like our office. It *does* feel like a private eye's office, by golly.

Yesterday had been a rousing success on my side of the partners desk. With only a shred of evidence, buttressed by a strong gut feeling and a few threats, I broke that store clerk like a twig. He was bawling and promising to pay it all back when I left with my check. I don't know if the owner called the cops or not. I don't need to know.

On the negative side of the ledger, I called the potential client with the potentially cheating wife and he decided we were too expensive. Still, the day was an overall big plus.

I turned to my desk and picked up the notes from yesterday's interview with George Heatherly. The time passed quickly and by nine I had the Heatherly case organized on my hard drive with a good idea of how I was going to proceed. Malone had appeared in the meantime, grumpy that she still had not resolved her third skip trace. At least she could send out invoices for the first two. Give it another couple weeks of the media coverage fading away and we'd be doing all right again, I thought.

So I was feeling pretty upbeat when I answered my phone at ten thirty. The caller ID said it was the Pen and Pastry. Good.

31

Maybe Veronica had some more info about Guth.

She did, but not the kind I'd wanted. "Guth got to LeAnn" were her first words after I said hello.

Shit. "What happened? Is she all right?" Malone stopped typing and started listening.

"He found her new apartment and was waiting for her outside last night when she got off work. It wasn't as bad as it could have been. She has some bruises and she's scared, but she just finally got here about a half-hour ago. Clint, she still won't tell me anything beyond the bare facts of what happened. Apparently the apartment manager saw the confrontation and threatened to call the cops. Otherwise Guth would have probably beaten the shit out of her and forced her to stay with him. She wouldn't be waiting tables at the Pen and Pastry this morning."

"Okay," I said as calmly as I could, meanwhile kicking myself for putting off my talk with Malcolm Guth. I was retrieving my Smith and Wesson from the drawer as I asked, "You have any idea where this asshole might be?"

"As a matter of fact, I thought you might want to know that. I rousted Reuben out of bed and he said that Guth usually starts his day at a back table in The Gentlemen's Lounge on Burnside. It's where he collects from his girls for the night before. The place opens at eleven. Reuben wasn't happy that I woke him up," Veronica went on, "and he wanted me to tell you that you owe him another one."

"I'll bet."

Reuben Keys was Veronica's last pimp, the one who got her off drugs and gave her a chance to escape the life. It's Reuben's most prominent eccentricity, that he's a major drug dealer, fence, and pimp who insists his whores have to be clean of drugs. That one little quirk does not, of course, make him a good guy by any stretch of the imagination. He helps me out now and then, but you couldn't say we were buddies. Malone more or less loathes him.

Veronica and I ended the call with mutual assurances that we would be careful. I looked at the clock. Twenty to eleven. If the bar was Guth's "office," he would probably be there when it opened and stay through the lunch hour; he'd want his girls to be paid up and back out on the street by mid-afternoon. He'd only be collecting money from the early morning tricks anyway; he'd have been on the street himself until one or two, collecting as the girls finished each job. I wanted to catch him early today, while he was still waking up.

"Who's hurt?" Malone asked as soon as I hung up. I noticed she had gotten her own gun out as well.

"It's that girl of Veronica's. The pimp attacked her last night and gave her a beating. I should have been on it already."

"She hurt bad?"

"No, he got interrupted before he could do much damage. She's at the Pen and Pastry right now. Guth should be over at The Gentlemen's Lounge when it opens. I'm planning to have a little talk before he does any more damage."

Malone had already holstered her Glock and hooked it to her belt. She stood up. "Well," she said. "That sounds like fun."

CHAPTER TEN

We scampered across the street through a heavy downpour to get my Subaru Outback from its assigned space in the parking lot.

It would have been a nice half-hour stroll in good weather, six blocks to the bridge, the equivalent of another three for the bridge itself, and then four more to the bar. Not today. It was March. In Portland.

Imagining the walk, however, reminded me that the Lifestream House, as the Foundation's new shelter was called, took up most of a block just this side of the bridge. Wouldn't hurt to have Malone along when I checked them out, so I decided to kick-start both cases with one drive and stop by there on the way back, just for a look-see. Malone wouldn't mind. Actually, she wouldn't have a choice.

There is something about establishments where women display themselves to men, an aura of unrequited lust. It's different in a real bordello, where everybody's getting off. In the bars where women only dance naked, you can smell the stale, throttled desire.

The Gentlemen's Lounge, as I knew it would be, was such a place.

We stopped for a moment just inside the front door to give our eyes a chance to adjust to the dimly lit interior. The layout was an L-shape, two ancient pool tables to our left, a restroom entrance directly ahead, and the cash register end of the bar to our right. The bar turned a sharp corner and followed the long stroke of the "L" out of sight to where recorded music was already blaring. That's where the stage would be. Also, I was sure, Mal Guth's table would be there—back in the shadows, as far from the entrance as possible.

I could see a couple of older guys sitting at the bar just beyond where it cornered. They sat facing the entrance but did not look at us, nor to their left toward whatever was happening on stage. They seemed already lost in the beers that glistened before them.

The bartender was a woman in her twenties, shoulder-length blond hair, wearing jeans and a long-sleeved work shirt with the cuffs rolled up. She'd glanced at us as we came in, registered that we appeared to be a couple, but now ignored us. She would be used to men stopping just inside the front door, deciding this wasn't how they dared to spend their time, and leaving again without a word. She probably wondered a bit about Malone, but wouldn't pay attention until we declared ourselves actual customers by sitting down somewhere.

I wasn't planning to do either, of course—leave right away or sit down anywhere. I headed around the corner, Malone keeping pace, and toward the stage.

There was no one else sitting at the bar and only two other people immediately in sight, one sitting with his back to me at the edge of the small, brightly lit stage. The stage itself displayed a single floor-to-ceiling metal pole in the center and a slightly chunky—and happily not naked yet—young woman bumping up against it. She leered over the man's head at us as we approached. There was already a dollar bill shoved partially down the flimsy panties that she wore. She would be naked soon...and all the more pitiable for it. Her audience of one was not the guy I was looking for.

The room widened out beyond this end of the bar to provide more tables around the stage, and one of those tables, the one in the corner farthest from the bright light, was occupied.

I could see well enough as we approached that the man was a white guy, probably in his thirties, wiry and hard-looking, his face thin with a beak nose and sharp cheekbones. Cold eyes appraised us from beneath combed-tight, greasy, pale blond hair. He reminded me of a knife.

A cup of coffee sat squarely in the center of the small round table.

We stopped a couple of feet away and looked down at him. I spoke loudly to be heard over the din of music.

"Malcolm Guth?"

He raised the coffee cup almost to his mouth and glared at us. "Who the fuck are you?" Then he drank.

"My name's Clint McCall and this is Devon Malone. You are Malcolm Guth?"

He put the cup down hard, sloshing hot black liquid on the table. "I'm Guth. I never heard of you or your bitch. What do you want?"

Oh my goodness, that was a mistake. Malone doesn't like pimps, or assholes in general, or very many men as far as I can tell...but somebody who's all three and calls her a bitch in that tone of voice? I didn't even see her draw but one very big step took her to Guth's side of his little table and suddenly her Glock was sticking out of his ear.

"You want to call me a bitch again, motherfucker?"

Guth could have been carved of stone at that point; he was not twitching a muscle although his eyes, glaring up at me, were speaking volumes. After a very long four or five seconds, his mouth barely moved. "No."

"Good," she said, and holstered the gun as she stepped back to my side.

He transferred his glare to her but still hadn't moved otherwise. I figured he had a gun of his own somewhere within reach and was considering his options. I pulled my jacket open and rested my hand on my Smith and Wesson. I guess he decided his options were limited.

"What do you want?" he grated.

"You've heard of a young woman named Jewel?" I asked politely.

His eyes widened and he sat back looking up at me for a long moment. "What about her? What you got to do with her?"

"We're private investigators working for a party who wants you to leave her alone. There are plenty more where she came from. Let this one go."

His eyes widened even more and his body tensed as he leaned

37

forward over the table. "You're private cops? Fuck you and your party! Get the fuck out of here!" Just like that the man was freaking out, his arms waving wildly as he shouted the final words, apparently no longer caring that we were both armed and one of our guns had recently been in his ear.

Definitely something here besides simply wanting to keep a whore in his stable, but I didn't know what it was and Malcolm Guth was unlikely to tell me.

I glanced over at Malone to see what she was thinking. She caught my eye and then deadpanned Guth. "You've been warned," she told him. She had also decided it was time to go.

I stepped back and half-turned to leave. "We'll talk again," I said to Guth, and then we headed back the way we'd come.

"Fuck you!" Guth howled at our backs. He really needed to work on his vocabulary.

Leaning now against this end of the bar was a young black woman who had obviously been watching us, probably one of Guth's girls waiting for the chance to pay up and go get some sleep. She gave me a little smile. "That went well," she whispered dryly as we passed.

Everybody's got to be a comedian.

CHAPTER ELEVEN

I took a page from my partner's habitual gestures and punched her lightly in the shoulder as we walked back to my Subaru. "I cannot believe you stuck a gun in that creep's ear," I said.

She grunted. "Nobody calls me as a bitch in that tone of voice and gets away with it."

"You know," I offered as we opened our respective doors and climbed into the car, "if they ever decide to remake the Dirty Harry movies, they should recast them as Dirty Harriet with you in the starring role."

She grunted again.

"You mind if we stop by the Lifestream Foundation on the way back?"

"No problem."

Yep. I had the female version of Harry Callahan right here in my car. Good luck with the whole relationship thing.

I tried to put that speculation out of my mind as I drove back across the Burnside Bridge and looked for a place to park near the Lifestream House.

Remarkably, I found an empty two-hour spot near the corner of Second and Davis and paralleled the Outback right into it—truly remarkable since mid-day parking spaces in Portland's Old Town are as rare as courteous pimps.

Old Town is a felicitous mix of multi-cultural art galleries, jazz bars, and ethnic restaurants--with a less happy assortment of panhandlers, drunks, and dives for spice. The centerpiece is the Classical Chinese Garden, a full city block of Zen serenity in the middle of the metropolis.

It was well into the lunch hour when we got to the Lifestream House and they had a good turnout for what looked (through the window) like some kind of stew and a variety of fruit. The building was low and unobtrusive, constructed of wood with shingled siding. A series of large picture windows faced Burnside, the first two exposing the cafeteria-style space and probably forty diners. The third window revealed a lounge area with a couple of couches, a few over-stuffed chairs, and a TV. One old man, either a fast eater or heavy sleeper, dozed in the corner of the nearest couch. No hiding the clientele or their activities for these folks.

On the other hand, only a small metal plaque next to the entrance identified the building as housing the Lifestream Foundation. There was no other signage of any sort.

Just inside the entrance was a small, brightly lit lobby area. The floor was covered with cheery orange carpeting that was probably donated because it didn't go with the yellow tinge of the off-white walls. An archway to our left opened into the lounge and beyond to the cafeteria. There was a closed, unmarked door directly in front of us.

A young woman, no more than eighteen or so, dressed in jeans and sweater, sat at an old wooden desk to our right. She was turned away from the lobby, toward another closed door behind her desk. That door carried a "Lifestream Foundation" plaque identical to the one outside. From the way she was hunched forward, phone to ear, I guessed it was one of those intense personal conversations young people are prone to.

We ambled together over to the desk and I cleared my throat.

"Eep!" said the girl and nearly dropped the phone as she jerked around to look up at her two unexpected visitors.

"Call you back," she muttered out of the corner of her mouth into the phone, perhaps hoping we wouldn't notice it was there, and hung up.

She settled herself for a moment, undoubtedly would have shifted some papers around on the desktop had there been any, gave her short blond hair a shake, put on a big welcoming smile, and asked, "What can we do for you folks?"

"We just have a few questions about the Foundation," I said. "Is there someone here we can talk to?"

She grabbed the phone again. "Oh sure. I think Tanya's here." Punched a couple of numbers. "Tanya? There are some people out here who want to know about the Foundation. Yeah. Okay." Hung up. "She'll be out in a minute."

It was more like thirty seconds when the door opened and a short, broad woman with thick, shoulder-length dark hair burst into the lobby. She braked next to the desk, gave us both a quick head-to-toe once-over, and then stuck out her hand to me. "I'm Tanya Petosky," she announced in a well-modulated but powerful contralto voice with a slight Russian accent.

I shook the hand, which turned out to have a dry, firm grip. My bet was that the woman had been very beautiful in her youth, but since then her peasant ancestry had achieved ascendancy. I put her in her mid- to late fifties. Most of her was as thick as her hair--body, mouth, nose, eyebrows. The impression was of great earthiness, an almost massive presence even though she was no more than five-six. She wore an expensive business suit, obviously custom-fitted, with a *lot* of gold accessories.

"Clint McCall," I said.

"And I'm Devon Malone," my partner announced as she also shook hands with the woman.

"You have some questions about the Foundation?"

"A few," I said.

"Come on back then." She led us down a short hallway to a large room, the centerpiece of which was a huge, battered conference table that probably seated fourteen or so—obviously the veteran of many years of meetings, its once glossy surface marred by coffee cup rings and pockmarked with scratches.

One door off this room stood open to reveal a small bathroom. Another was closed. Tanya Petosky escorted us through the third into a small office with plain metal desk and file cabinet, wooden coat rack, and two minimally padded visitors' chairs.

The Spartan surroundings made our office look like a corporate suite. The Lifestream House itself might be new, but the ac-

41

couterments certainly were not. There were two unusual touches off in the corner vibrating and staring at us with protruding eyes. Chihuahuas. I would have bet on the woman before us owning a couple of bulldogs rather than these delicate creatures, but what do I know? I'm a cat person.

Petosky plunked herself on the swivel chair behind the desk and waved us to the two visitor chairs. She glanced over at the two creatures who looked like they would have seizures and collapse at any moment. "It's okay, boys," she said soothingly. "Nothing to worry about." They did not appear to be reassured.

"What are their names?" I asked, just to break some ice.

"Wilbur and Orville."

"Brothers?" I inquired over a snort from Malone.

"Of course. But, luckily for us all, they don't fly." Her grin took years off her age momentarily. Then she sobered. "But back to business. What is your interest in the Foundation?"

Malone jumped in to take the lead on that one. "We're private investigators here on behalf of a client," she said.

Petosky's eyebrows jumped. "Really? Is there a problem?"

"That is the question."

Time for me to speak up again. I had no real plan, other than to poke around a bit, so I decided to start with something simple. "You don't exactly fit my image of a homeless shelter director," I said.

She chuckled, just a little, but still looked concerned. Not that I blamed her. Most people never find themselves confronted by private detectives in real life.

"That's because I'm not," she said. "I'm a member of the Foundation board."

Well, this would be interesting. We didn't have any of the information yet that I'd asked Eleanor to dig up on the board members, so I was going to be winging it. Which was fine with me at this point. Sounded more genuine to be totally ignorant, anyway.

"That makes more sense," I said. "You do look like a Foundation board member. I guess we were lucky to catch you here."

She waved that aside. "Not really. There's usually a board member here. We try to be hands on. No director, really, just a small professional staff of counselors. A nurse. A dietitian."

"I see."

"Then we have Crystal out in the lobby, our receptionist and clerical help. She's the daughter of one of the other board members, Barbara Schilling. Crystal Schilling. I always want to say 'crystal chandelier.' I'm not sure why."

Tanya Petosky didn't so much talk as do a routine—patter with the cadence and timing of a stand-up comic. I wondered if she'd grown up with kids making fun of the accent and had adopted this mask as a defense.

"Were you born here?" Malone asked. Mindreading, as usual.

The other woman paused at the question. "Here? Oh, the 'Rooshin' accent." She laughed. "Yes, I was born right here in Oregon, but my parents were part of the Russian community in Woodburn. They were Old Believers. I turned out to be a new believer and left home pretty young."

Woodburn is a little town twenty miles or so south of Portland. I knew there were a lot of Russian émigrés there and I could hear the capital letters, but wasn't sure what she was talking about. "Old Believers?" I asked.

"Russia's version of the Puritans," she grinned. "They broke off from the Russian Orthodox Church in the 17th century and fled to the United States to escape persecution."

"Interesting." That was Malone again. We had pretty good routine of our own going.

"Difficult would be a better word. To this day my family insists on the old, old traditions: no meat on Wednesdays and Fridays, no TV, movies, pop music, no fun, you know, just like the Puritans. Peasant-style dresses, with a belt. Got to have that damned belt.... You can't even eat off a dish that's ever been used by a non-believer. Ever. Which puts all restaurants off limits." She laughed gently.

43

"That's really why I left. I love to eat out."

The laugh faded into a rather sly grin; apparently she'd put her concern aside. "But enough about me. What do you want to know about the Foundation?"

I noted that she hadn't asked us why yet. "Just generally curious," I offered unhelpfully. "The Foundation hasn't been around very long, has it?"

"Three years, a little more. Social services were really hurting back then, as they still are for that matter, and we formed the Foundation to raise money for the House." Her gesture took in the building around us.

"You were one of the original board members?"

"We're all still the original board members. Me, Barbara, Max Overton, Norm Albright, Stan Nakagawa, and Jesse Carter. The six of us started it."

I recognized Albright as George Heatherly's uncle-in-law. Some of the other names rang vague bells. Probably all prominent families whose names I'd seen in the paper--with the apparent exception of the ex-Old Believer sitting before me. I would be interested to see what Eleanor had on her.

Malone spoke up again. "You offer just about every service here, don't you?"

"Yes. Unfortunately not to everyone who needs them. It's a big place, but you'd need a dozen of these to take care of all the homeless in Portland." She opened the center drawer of the desk and pulled out a large, glossy brochure.

"Here." She handed it to Malone. "This looks like it should be for a resort in the South Seas, but it's our 'fundraising instrument,' as they say. Describes the House and all the services we offer. You could give it to your client if you think it would help." She looked expectantly from Malone to me, obviously wanting some further explanation. Which we were not going to provide.

"Both the client and what he or she is interested in are confidential," I said. "You understand."

"Well," she responded with a small resigned shrug, "I do hope you'll let me know if there is a problem. That's what the Board is for, to deal with problems."

"You can count on it," replied Malone in her best female Terminator voice. I stifled a grin.

We exchanged handshakes and I thanked Tanya Petosky for her time, then we showed ourselves to the lobby. I'm not sure that Crystal Schilling, again hunched over the phone, even noticed our passage.

CHAPTER TWELVE

It began raining hard as I drove downtown the next morning. Really hard. One of those Pacific Northwest gully washers that comes in walls of water rather than sheets. Half the streets were near flood level within minutes and the Outback felt as if it were punching through sheetrock to get from one intersection to the next. That's late winter/early spring in Portland, Oregon: wet, followed by wetter.

Malone and I had spent the remainder of yesterday afternoon in the office, dealing with the occasional inquiry and paying bills. She finally had some success with that last skip trace and I finalized my notes on the Petosky interview. I almost went back to the Pen and Pastry at one point, when Veronica called to report that Guth had driven by again, but he was already gone as far as she knew and there was nothing I could do about it. Right then.

Later in the evening, at my dojang, I did do something about it. By the way, if you've ever seen a martial arts movie you've probably heard of a "dojo," the space where the students train and spar. It's a Japanese term, actually—and a "dojang" is the same thing, only Korean. My martial art is the Korean taekwondo, which translates loosely as the way of punching and kicking.

I did both for several hours with the five other black belts who had shown up for the evening. In between sparring matches, I also arranging for a couple of them to cover both LeAnn Hannaford and the Pen and Pastry itself in case Guth decided to make more trouble.

Portland Homicide Detective Lieutenant Mike Whitehall was one of those present. He and I were senior, with fourth degree belts. The four third-degree black belts were corporate lawyer Bobby Brewster, who was also Mike's live-in partner, independently wealthy Daisy Mansfield, retired Army Colonel Roger Arbuckle, and veterinarian Carmen Gonzales. The only person missing was second-degree black belt Eleanor Ivory, a member of our little private group by special dispensation because she'd been a student of mine from the beginning of her training.

The seven of us had gone together to rent the space when our old teacher retired. His school continued under some other senior black belts but we all needed more flexible schedules than teaching permits so we set up this dojang just for us. There had rarely been an evening that there weren't at least two of us in attendance. Which is all you need for sparring.

Needless to say, I could not recruit my old friend Mike to bodyguard duty but it had already become something of a tradition among the others to play amateur detective and backup when I had something they could handle. For more serious backup jobs, I relied on a couple of old retired detectives named Johnny Crew and Hap Harbaugh.

Among my friends here in the dojang, Roger and Daisy were particularly good for this kind of job because their days were entirely their own, so I asked Daisy to watch LeAnn Hannaford and Roger to cover the café. They readily agreed, also agreeing as always that if there were any question of serious danger or illegality they'd call me or the cops immediately.

They enjoyed playing detective and it was nice that I didn't have to pay them, but they understood that any real threat called for real law enforcement.

Getting LeAnn and Veronica covered had gone a long way toward my getting a good night's sleep—a good thing, since the Wednesday morning downtown traffic was clogged and cranky, drivers feeling their way from street to street in the downpour. I finally pulled into my parking space in the lot next to the Home Run Sports Bar a few minutes before nine, then sat for a couple more minutes wishing the rain would ease up or that I had an umbrella in the car. It didn't and I didn't, so I finally took a deep breath, opened the door, and plunged into the deluge.

There was no use bolting for the shelter of my stairway; I was drenched the moment I stepped out of the Subaru. Couldn't have gotten any wetter if I'd just stood there watching the few pedestrians in sight hunch hurriedly along the sidewalk. So I slogged across Third at a leisurely pace, resigned to enjoying the wild, cold rain.

Our mailbox is one of four at the bottom of the narrow wooden stairwell that opens onto Stark Street just west of its intersection with Third. I took my time as I unlocked and opened the box, wanting to drip-dry as much as possible before reaching my office. The box was empty, as I'd expected. I'd seen Malone's Jeep was already in her spot so she would have picked up the mail.

I found her settled in on her side of the partners desk, reading what looked like a brochure of some kind. She'd pulled her hair back into a ponytail, which was unusual for her. Maybe because it had gotten wet, but she looked a lot drier than I was. The office was warm and cozy, the coffee already made, and my mail was stacked neatly in the center of my half of the desk. It is good to have a partner.

She glanced up as I hung my wet jacket on the hall tree and came over to my chair. "Good morning. Do you think we should get fancier business cards?" She held up the colorful brochure. "Says right here that it might triple our business."

We both had a supply of simple agency cards that provided name, address, and phone numbers. That plus our private investigators licenses had always been enough. I know I frowned a little as I looked first at the ad and then at her. A little twitch at the corner of her mouth gave it away. "You're joking, right?"

"Yep," she said as she crumpled the brochure and tossed it. "Not that it would hurt to triple our business."

I noted that my message light was blinking and that not all my snail mail appeared to be junk. "Let me see what I can do about that," I said and picked up the phone, punching in the voicemail connection.

There were two hang-ups with no message, a young guy inquiring how much it would cost for us to follow his girlfriend around

49

(more than he'd be willing to pay, was my bet), Johnny Crew just calling to say hello (really to find out if we had any work for him and Hap), and an old client asking for my recommendation of a new security firm for his stores (I'd have to ask him what was wrong with the current one; it's always good to know who *not* to recommend).

The one piece of legitimate mail that wasn't a bill turned out to be a letter from a woman in the tiny community of Biggs Junction, located about a hundred miles to the east on Interstate 84 where it intersected with north-south Highway 97. She wondered if I could help her get the money owed by her ex-husband. I put that one aside. Malone and I had headed into Eastern Oregon on a case once before; I'd give the woman a call later and see what the job sounded like.

Finally I checked my e-mail, which was one hundred percent spam.

I looked over at Malone and gestured at the one envelope I'd retained. "Possible job in Biggs Junction."

She snorted. "You really want to head out into the desert again?"

"You never know," I said. "I'll check it out later. See what they have to say."

"Anything overnight on Guth or Heatherly?"

"I spent most of the evening at the dojang. Daisy is going to be keeping LeAnn company today and Roger will stake out the Pen and Pastry in case Guth shows up."

"Okay," was all she said. Malone still doesn't quite understand my utilization of amateur talent, though I'll bet she appreciates the money saved.

"As for Heatherly," I went on, "let me see if Eleanor has any-thing yet." I picked up the phone again.

CHAPTER THIRTEEN

I dialed Eleanor's number. She did indeed have some information on the Lifestream Foundation board members and a half-hour before her next client was due, so she'd be right down.

She was dressed for the chilly wet weather, wearing a long-sleeved tan sweater, and dark brown pants, blond hair styled in what I think is called a chignon. I was glad she finally seemed to be just about recovered from the injuries she'd sustained at the hands of the psychopath that I later killed.

She said hello to both of us and got a muttered reply from Malone, then sat down with a grin that had been blossoming as she crossed the room from my door. "You look like you were just rescued from the river," she said.

"Thanks," I replied. "And you both look like you're smart enough to keep an umbrella in your car."

She exchanged a glance with Malone, who was just as dry and put together as my accountant—and who, to my amazement, almost smiled before she focused back on her monitor.

"Of course," Eleanor said a little smugly.

"Okay, tell me about the Lifestream board—and start with Tanya Petosky."

"Petosky, Petosky," she said as she flipped to a different page of her notes. "She is the most mysterious one, now that you mention it. Left a strict religious home early on and acquired a series of 'mentors.' That's what she calls them in the news stories I could find. She seems to have served as 'executive assistant' to a number of powerful men and it's not exactly clear how that resulted in her present wealth—which is sizable—or social position. There's a rumor that she's related to the tsars."

"Really?"

"It's mentioned in a couple of stories and I haven't seen anywhere she denies it."

51

"That doesn't surprise me."

Eleanor looked up from her notes. "You know her?"

"We stopped by the Lifestream House yesterday and she was there." I noticed that Malone had given up any pretense of working at her monitor. "That's all you have on her?" I asked Eleanor.

"That's it."

"Okay. What about the others?"

Back to the first page of the notes. "The chair is Norman Albright. Family is big in the timber industry. He's an older guy, late fifties, gay."

"Gay?"

"Very open about it, apparently."

"Interesting." A little fact about his uncle-in-law that George Heatherly hadn't gotten around to. And he'd thought the caller might be gay as well, simply because of his "delivery." Sounded like our client might have some conflicted feelings about his relative.

"There's nothing improper I could find about Albright's finances. Nothing out of line about any of the Board members, for that matter, and the Foundation itself seems to be legit."

"Okay."

"Let's see. Barbara Schilling is the very wealthy widow of a guy who manufactured plumbing fixtures. Mid-forties, has a daughter Crystal who works for the Foundation. Does good works and gets her hair done."

That drew an amused sound from Malone but she continued to just listen otherwise.

"Stanley Nakagawa is a younger guy, late thirties. Vice president and chief loan officer of the downtown Oregon First Bank. Very influential in the Japanese community.

"Jesse Carter is even younger, twenty-eight, black guy, one of those genius software developers. As far as I can tell, he's already retired. I should have gone into software."

"You do all right as the best accountant in town."

"Thanks, but I don't see retirement looming any time soon."

Back to the notes. "Last we have Max Overton, who is apparently the token straight white guy. Fortyish. Family owns a couple of very successful local jewelry stores. He's manager of the one right downtown here. Otherwise plays golf and sits on a lot of volunteer boards."

Malone finally joined in. "Other than their sound finances, anything interesting about the Foundation?"

More page-turning. "Not really. Created three years ago by the six current board members. All the initial planning of the Lifestream House was funded out of their own pockets, it looks like, and then they began a number of fundraising activities to actually build and maintain it. The Foundation seems to be well supported by the city's best families." She looked up as she laid the notes in her lap. "The fundraisers are champagne brunches and evenings at the opera rather than bake sales. And that's all I've got."

"Nothing fishy?" Malone followed up.

"Not that I can see. Even with our specialized search engines I can't get detailed financial records. Lifestream is a registered charity, but still a private organization. I was able to look at the public material they file with the state. No obvious problems, there."

"Who's the treasurer?" I asked.

"Overton. And the Foundation's money is in Nakagawa's bank, of course."

"Good enough. Thanks for all your work. Great job."

With that, she bounced up and headed for her office. In Assistant Detective mode, Eleanor is usually all business.

CHAPTER FOURTEEN

Eleanor hadn't been gone more than two minutes and Malone and I hadn't gotten beyond comparing notes on the sodden weather outside when the door opened and a major problem appeared.

As if it had been choreographed, we both swiveled our chairs a little toward the doorway, maximizing access to the desk drawers containing our weapons.

"Well," I said to the dark dripping figure who was closing the door behind him, "this is a surprise. What can we do for you, Mr. Guth?"

Surprise was hardly the word for it.

He was dressed in black, mid-length leather jacket over open-neck shirt and dress slacks. The thick, slicked-down hair sat on his head like a pale blond helmet. He kept his right hand in the jacket pocket as he crossed the room; if he didn't have a gun there, he wanted us to think he did.

He stopped at the edge of our desk, glared at Malone, and leaned down at me. There was enough liquor on his breath to make *me* tipsy if he got any closer. Out of the corner of my eye, I could see Malone easing her top drawer open. By this time Guth was literally in my face and I'd begun to think that maybe he would keep on leaning until he was in my lap.

He did manage to catch himself before reaching that point. "There's somethin' you can do for yourself, McCall," he rasped, "and that's stay the fuck out of my business."

I didn't move a muscle, didn't even blink as I met his fierce gaze. "We're going to have a problem if you don't back off, Guth. From us and from LeAnn. Leave her alone; that's all you have to do. I told you before: There are plenty more where she came from."

He was still in my face, dripping on my desktop, and practically choking me with liquor fumes. I could see his hand tightening up in that pocket.

"You don't know shit," he said, his face knife-sharp with intensity and his eyes beginning to bulge oddly, his voice slurring a little. "I do my thing and your fucking ass is dead if you get in the way. You hear me, old man? Fucking dead! You and the cunt here, both!"

It struck me that this was very weird. There was surely *something* I hadn't paid enough attention to. Guth's driving by the Pen and Pastry, hassling his ex-whore, blowing us off on his own turf...that all fit. But walking into my office the next day to threaten our lives? It made no sense. It was *way* over the top.

But I couldn't take any more time to think about it right now. Malone had that drawer all the way open and with one smooth motion she brought her Glock out, stood up, leaned over the desk a bit, and stuck it right back in Malcolm Guth's same ear. One of these days he was going to learn not to call the woman disparaging names—and to keep his eye on her.

"I want you to bring that hand straight up out of your pocket," she said in a cold voice. "Slowly—and it had better come out empty."

Looking grim and maybe a little embarrassed, he pulled the hand free and then spread them both wide. "I got no gun. Not this time."

"Okay," I said, "Now why don't you get the hell out of here?"

Guth took a deep breath and gave me a good glare. He dropped his arms slowly to his side and leaned slightly into me even as Malone's Glock moved with him. "You sure you understand me, McCall? I'm gonna get the cunt back."

I couldn't believe he was just plowing right ahead with his crazy control routine while he had a large gun stuck in his ear. He was either very drunk or very nuts. Maybe both.

"Not today," I said finally. "Out. Now."

Malone pulled the gun away and Guth straightened up. He waited another beat on principle and then turned to go. He took a step, then looked back at Malone. He just couldn't let it go. "You could make a lot of money for me, bitch," he said low and hard, "if you was a little younger. Too bad."

She flushed and I would bet came within a millimeter of pulling the trigger, but said not a word. Admirable control, I thought. Guth had no idea how lucky he was.

CHAPTER FIFTEEN

Guth closed the door behind him and Malone closed the desk drawer on her Glock. "We are taking that son of a bitch *down*," she announced as she sat back in her chair. "I don't want him running around on my planet."

"I understand," I said, and quickly added that I agreed as she began to glower at me. "Given his anger management and control issues, I have no doubt he'll give us a good excuse to do exactly that before this is over." I paused, looking for the next words. "But I am glad you didn't just shoot him."

Her look softened. She knew I was again picturing Daniel Habash's brains splattered on the motel room wall. And probably she knew I was wishing I hadn't felt the need to do exactly that with Habash. One of these days we were going to get past it. If and when I did.

"We'll find a way," she said firmly. "A good way. Don't worry about it."

I took a breath and relaxed a bit. "I'll tell you what does worry me: that I've got two amateurs covering LeAnn Hannaford and the Pen and Pastry. I didn't realize just how out of control and dangerous Guth might be. I think it's already time for some reassignments."

I picked up the phone and dialed Johnny Crew's number. Johnny answered the phone himself, a possibility for which I'd prepared myself by holding the phone away from my ear. "This is Johnny," he boomed. Had Guth still been standing in our office doorway, he could have heard the announcement clearly. Johnny Crew was a small, dapper man whose voice should have belonged to his huge, schlumpy partner Hap Harbaugh. On top of that, he cusses a lot.

"Hey Clint!" he roared after I identified myself. "How the fuck are you?"

"Other than the imploding eardrum, I'm fine. How are you?"

"What? Oh. Fuck. Sorry. I just got that kinda voice, you know?" he said as he lowered it to merely loud.

"Yes, I know."

"I got a great one for you today," he enthused. Johnny spent a lot of time trawling the news for weird stories that he insisted on sharing with all his friends. "There was this idiot college kid in Tennessee who decided it would be fun to slide down what he thought was the campus library's laundry chute, which was really a two-story drop into a trash compactor. They could have buried him in a shoebox. Do you believe that shit?"

"Guess he needed a little more education."

"You can say that again. Anyway, what can I do for you?"

"You and Hap got some time over the next couple of days?"

"Sure. What do you need?"

His response was exactly what I'd expected. Johnny and Hap had been detectives together on the Portland PD, then after retirement had their own private agency together, which was where I had apprenticed for my own license. Now that they had retired from the agency their only excitement was providing occasional backup for my business—somewhat to the dismay of Johnny's wife Gerry. Hap's new wife Wilma was happy when he even moved off the couch.

"Veronica's got a new waitress who's getting hassled by her old pimp." I told him, "and I want you and Hap to keep an eye on the Pen and Pastry until I figure out how to handle him. He might show up there to make trouble. He was just here at the office with exactly that in mind. Right now I've got one of my black belts on the waitress and another one watching the café, but I'm going to team them up as bodyguards for her while you two watch Veronica's place. If that's okay with you guys."

"No problem. Good coffee, great pastry...sounds like our kind of job. I'll give Hap a call. Probably we can start this afternoon. When does this girl work?"

"I think she works the breakfast and lunch shifts. The kid's name is LeAnn Hannaford. This plan will put you two *and* the black belts on the premises when she is. Can't do any better than that. Check with Veronica to confirm the work schedule before you head out. She can give you the kid's background, too."

"Will do."

"Normal rates?"

"Maybe even a discount considering the goodies we'll get."

"All right. Call me right away if there is any trouble."

"Sure."

We hung up and I dialed the Pen and Pastry's number. I gave Veronica a heads up about Guth's latest threats and the impending arrival of the two old detectives, then she handed the phone over to Roger and I told him to team up with Daisy after Johnny and Hap were on scene.

Malone was sitting, just looking out the window when I ended the call. She turned her attention to me. "We need to talk to LeAnn again, do some checking around on the street, find something we can use on Guth before he kills somebody. Besides, I think something else must be going on. Something more. He is just *too* pissed off."

"You could be right," I said. "Why don't you take that to start with? I really need to do something on the case we've been paid for —finish interviewing the Foundation board, at least. LeAnn might open up if it's just her and another woman."

She thought it over for a second. "Done. We can check back in with each other later today."

CHAPTER SIXTEEN

Malone headed out almost right away, but it was another half-hour before I'd dealt with my morning's messages. Didn't want to leave any potential clients hanging. Nothing new developed, unfortunately. Mostly more media craziness that I did my best to ignore.

I called our possible client in Biggs Junction and Mrs. Ratched explained that we'd have to find her husband somewhere in Eastern Oregon before we could collect the money he owed. Way too much travel involved, plus she wanted us to work for a percentage. I had to decline. I resisted the impulse to ask if she was a nurse or ever flew over a cuckoo's nest.

My old client's problem with his current security firm was that his fast food stores had been robbed three times in the past five weeks, which was not a minor glitch. Apparently "Security Now!" should have called themselves "Security Some Other Time!" I added them to my list of companies I wouldn't recommend and passed along the name of a more reliable firm.

The kid with the problem girlfriend? He was reduced to stuttering incoherence by my daily fee and hung up without saying goodbye. That took care of my callbacks for the morning.

I finished a little more paperwork and took my time over an early lunch at the Home Run. I wanted to talk first to the banker, Stanley Nakagawa, and we all know what their hours are like.

The downtown Oregon First Bank is across the street from Pioneer Courthouse Square, just an eight-block walk. The rain had stopped, so I hoofed it in the shimmery clean air and arrived in the bank lobby at one-thirty. Mr. Nakagawa had just now returned from lunch, his attractive blond executive assistant informed me, and could give me only a few minutes before an important two p.m. meeting.

I said that would be fine and was briskly escorted into an office just slightly smaller than the entire second floor of my building.

Stanley Nakagawa himself was not nearly as pretentious as his surroundings. A smiling, open-faced young man immaculately suited and coifed, he came around the desk to shake hands and offer me a seat on the seven-foot leather couch that stretched along the west wall. He settled a few feet north of me, looking genuinely pleased that I'd come to visit.

"I've never met a private detective before," he explained with a big grin. "What are you investigating and how can I help?" The grin faltered. "You're not just here fundraising for your association or something, are you?"

I smiled in return. "No, I'm not looking for money," I assured him. "I'm asking questions about the Lifestream Foundation. You sit on the board, right?"

His eyes widened in surprise and his lips lost their curve. "You're investigating the Foundation? For whom, if I may ask?"

"Just someone who's curious about how it works."

The beginning of a frown now. "How it works?"

"I'm investigating money rather than soliciting money."

"Ah." He shifted an inch or so further north. "Well, I am the Foundation's banker but not the treasurer. That's Max Overton. Neither one of us, however, can tell you any more than what is already public record. Lifestream is a private foundation, as I'm sure you know."

"Yes, I knew that," I said. "You're not aware of any problems with the Foundation's finances?"

He stood abruptly and looked at his watch. A Rolex. "No, of course not," he said with the anger starting to show. "I'm sorry to cut this short, but I have a meeting to get ready for. You'd better talk to Max. He's just a couple of blocks from here."

I stood up myself, surprised that he'd volunteered even that much. "You mean right now?"

Slight grimace. "I guess so. He left me a voicemail while I was at lunch. Asked me to call him back at the store downtown here." Hostile glance. "I haven't had a chance to do it yet."

As soon as he'd given me the store's name and location, I departed with a brief handshake and the certainty that he'd find time to make that call before his important meeting.

CHAPTER SEVENTEEN

Devon Malone stopped just inside the entrance of the Pen and Pastry, shaking her hair loose after pulling the elastic free. She surveyed the room. She'd been here a number of times, with Clint or his daughter Colleen, but never on business before. Good food, interesting atmosphere. She recognized Roger Arbuckle, the retired Army colonel who was one of Clint's black belt friends, sitting off to one side. They exchanged a nod. No sign of the two old detectives or the other black belt, Daisy Mansfield.

Then she saw the owner, Veronica Fortune, just coming out of the kitchen. Veronica saw Devon at the same time and offered her a tentative smile as she came around the counter to greet her. "Is Clint with you?" the taller red-haired woman asked as she shook Devon's hand and looked past her at the entrance.

"No, he had another case that took priority. But we believe that there's more to be learned from LeAnn and thought she might be more forthcoming if she were talking to another woman."

The hesitation was almost too brief to catch, but Malone caught it. "Oh, okay." Veronica glanced around and focused on a far corner of the café. "Let's get you a table out of the way and I'll send LeAnn over when you're settled."

She doesn't know me any more than I know her, Malone thought as they traversed the space together. *And maybe she wonders about me, just like I wonder about her.*

There was no clarifying those issues today, or probably any other day. Malone sat down and told Veronica she'd be happy to have a cup of coffee and croissant. As the older woman walked away, Malone saw Daisy Mansfield joining Roger at his table. She must have been in the restroom. When Johnny and Hap arrived, probably soon, they would certainly have enough coverage for now.

It was only about two minutes later that LeAnn Hannaford delivered both coffee and croissant, then sat down across from Malone with a coffee of her own. She didn't appear to be happy about having to do it.

"What do you want?" she asked, more in a resigned than hostile tone. Apparently Veronica had already explained who Malone was.

"The rest of it," Malone responded simply.

The younger woman took a slow sip of her coffee and set it down. "The rest of what?"

Malone gave her a hard stare. "Look. Malcolm Guth may be a nasty, obsessive, asshole pimp but I have to believe there's more to the story than him wanting you back as his girlfriend. He can have any of his girls any time. Are you really that special?" She watched LeAnn's hand tremble against the coffee cup in response.

"Yes. No. I don't know. I must be, to him."

"Bullshit. Yes? No? You don't know? What's really going on? Why is he after you? What does he want?"

LeAnn was literally jerking in her seat with each question as if it were a blow. "Nothing!" she shouted, drawing the attention of everyone in the room and especially, Malone noticed, that of Roger and Daisy. She held up a hand to stave them off.

"He came to my apartment last night," the younger woman suddenly announced.

That brought Malone's attention back to her. "What do you mean? He got into your apartment? What did he want? What did he do?"

"He didn't get in. It was after Daisy had left, after I'd gone to bed. All of a sudden he was out in the hall banging on my door. It was locked. It's a good door. He didn't get in." The girl seemed to have calmed down and Malone wondered if it was because she'd managed to change the subject.

"That's it? He banged on the door?"

LeAnn didn't respond for a moment, as if she were deciding what she could say and what she couldn't. "Oh, he was just acting crazy. He wouldn't leave. Kept saying he needed to talk to me. But that's all. He finally went away when the guy in the apartment across the hall yelled that he was calling the cops."

"Huh," said Malone. "You've got this very dangerous man all over your ass, stalking you, threatening you, showing up at your apartment...and you won't tell me what's really going on, what he really wants."

And that set the younger woman off again. "He doesn't want anything!" A beat. "I can't say!" Another beat. "Leave me alone!" And with that, LeAnn Hannaford was up and hurrying back toward the kitchen area.

Well, Malone thought to herself, *there was a big fucking waste of my time—except that I'm even more sure now the kid is in danger and is holding back the reason. So what now?*

She sipped her coffee, finished her croissant, exchanged one last look with the two black belts across the room, and headed for the front door. Maybe she'd have better luck going at it from the other end, learning more about Malcolm Guth and his possible motives.

She exited the Pen and Pastry and went looking for Merritt the Ferret.

CHAPTER EIGHTEEN

City Jewelers was, as promised, two blocks away on Morrison across from Nordstrom. The location may have been prime but the red and gold marquee sign was slightly tacky.

For some reason, that irritated me and confirmed what I'd been thinking during my short walk: it was time to go into provocation mode. The word was out that a P.I. was investigating. No further point in being subtle (to the extent I ever am). Maybe if I stirred the pot more vigorously something more interesting would rise to the surface.

I spotted Max Overton as I entered the store. Eleanor had given me neither a physical description nor an age for the guy, but the middle-aged shrimp staring bug-eyed at me from an office doorway in the back had to be him. Nakagawa had called, all right, and Overton clearly hadn't taken it as good news. I gave him a jaunty wave and he flinched. This, I decided, might even be fun.

He forced his face into a smile and came out of the doorway with hand extended to meet me at the nearest showcase. I made him as being in his late forties. Slight build, balding, wire-rim glasses, pasty complexion, watery protruding eyes, facial features that had somehow begun to blur with time. He was wearing casual but spendy pants and knit shirt, collar open to reveal a thick gold chain. The hand that furtively shook mine sported a couple of heavy gold rings. There was another Rolex, even bigger than the banker's. This guy was a mugging waiting to happen. He didn't look like he could defend himself against a sneeze.

His voice matched the rest, soft with an underlying hint of whine. "You're Mr. McCall?"

"That's me," I said, giving his soft, clammy hand a good firm shake that made him flinch again. "I gather Stanley Nakagawa returned your call."

Eyebrows up, eyeballs front and center. "What? What? Oh, yes.

He must have told you. Yes, he called to say you were coming. He called just now. Yes." Back a step, firming up the shoulders a little. "What...what can I do for you?"

I just stared at him for a moment, getting a firm grip on the bat before swinging. "I'm looking into some possible financial irregularities at the Lifestream Foundation," I said in my best Joe Friday monotone.

A good line drive, that was.

"What?" he squeaked as he took another step back. Several of the clerks and customers looked our way and his face turned a nice light pink. He scuttled to the end of the display case to unlatch a gate for me. "We should go to the office," he babbled. "Talk there. This is terrible, terrible. Too public. Can't talk out here. Come in, come in."

I was thinking, as I followed his fleeing figure back to the office, that this had to be the most insecure rich guy I'd ever met in my life. I hoped I wouldn't have to interview his parents.

It was a small office, standard retail: metal desk, swivel chair, file cabinets, stack files, invoices and other papers covering almost every available surface. Overton indicated the one visitor's chair that was free and scurried to put the desk between us.

"Sorry for the mess," he prattled on. "Office isn't mine. My assistant manager had some kind of medical emergency, something. I'm filling in for the day." Apparently he didn't view his own position as manager to be vital. Maybe it wasn't. He looked around helplessly, as if he didn't know where to seat himself. "A mess in here. I don't have an office of my own but if I did it would be much neater than this. Family business, you know. Nobody else to fill in today. It's a mess."

"Aren't you the manager?" I asked, just for fun. This whole concept of the manager filling in for the assistant manager fascinated me.

Bug-eyed hesitation. "What? What? Oh, yes, of course. Family business, as I said."

"Okay," I said as if that explained anything. It had quickly become obvious that my task with Max Overton was not to provoke him into talking, but rather to keep him calm enough that his words might make some sense.

"Please understand," I said carefully. "There is no evidence of any criminal activity, just some questions that my client has about how the finances of the Foundation really operate. I've been asked to look into it."

He more or less collapsed onto the swivel chair, which squeaked loudly on his behalf. "But you said, you said irregularities. You were asking about irregularities. There aren't any...."

"That was mentioned as a possibility, but maybe only because the finances of the Foundation aren't fully understood. That's why I'm here. I'd like to understand them better."

Between the eyebrows and the eyes, he managed to look perplexed and panic-stricken at the same time. "But I don't...I can't.... It's all very simple. All of the money comes from the six board members, either our own funds or money we've raised from events we sponsor, from our friends and other contacts.... It's all properly reported and accounted for. There's no problem, nothing to understand."

Well, then, why not go for it? "I'd like to see your books, if I may, just to confirm that."

He looked at me as if I'd just offered to castrate him. "The books? Our private financial records? No, no, you can't see those. They're private. We make filings with the state, everything required; that's public record. Go look at that."

"I have. It doesn't tell me much."

He pressed his lips together so hard that they made a pout. "It's all you're going to see," he said after a moment, his voice hardening with a kind of desperate stubbornness, eyes bulging even more.

"It would be easier if...."

"*Who* wants to know all this about us?" he interrupted. "You must have important clients. Tanya said...." He stopped dead.

"Tanya Petosky called you about me?"

"She sure.... Surely she called everyone, on the board I mean. It's not good if someone thinks we're criminals or something, being investigated, it's not good at all you know. Tell me who it is."

"I can't do that."

His body suddenly relaxed a little and the corners of his mouth twitched with what might have been the beginnings of a smile. "Well then," he said with unexpected firmness. "If I can't tell you and you can't tell me, you might as well leave."

Apparently he was feeling more secure now that we'd reached a stalemate. And he was right, of course. So, after we eyed each other for another moment or two, I stood, inflicted another handshake, and headed back to pick up my car.

CHAPTER NINETEEN

Merritt the Ferret was a dealer in illegal goods, both buying and selling, and there were probably very few criminals in Portland with whom he had not done business. He had been one of Devon Malone's informants when she was with the Portland Police and she saw no reason he couldn't continue to serve in that capacity.

He had his own little storefront a block or so north of Sandy on 28th, almost under the Banfield Freeway. He lived in some back rooms of the shop, which appeared to be an unusually junky junk store—the point being to have nothing worth buying on display. In the Ferret's line of retail, the last thing you want are legitimate customers. It was next door to a "barbershop" in which all the barbers were female and nobody ever got a haircut.

Otherwise the Ferret's neighborhood was basically a light industrial area with little foot traffic and no distractions for those intent on buying or selling illicit goods and services.

Malone parked her Jeep at the curb right in front of the Ferret's shop and just sat there for a moment, taking a deep breath and remembering the last time she'd been at this spot. A deranged ex-spy, one of Eleanor Ivory's ex-boyfriends, had tried to kill Devon and the Ferret himself had been shot when he inadvertently distracted her attacker.

The memory was not very cheering, nor was her failure to get any more useful information from LeAnn Hannaford, so Malone was not in a particularly good mood when she stepped into the poorly lit, chaotic, and generally smelly interior of Merritt the Ferret's premises. She stopped just inside, as was her wont, and surveyed the place. It really did look like a miniature junkyard with tables. She could vaguely discern the proprietor in the back of the room, behind what might have passed for a counter if it weren't piled just as high with dirty kitchen ware, rusty gardening tools, and other such attractive items as any of the tables or the floor itself.

He came out from behind his semi-concealment and met her halfway. He was a pale little man who could have been any age between forty and sixty, with sharp features, slightly protruding teeth, and a head of soft brown hair that was indeed almost fur-like. All that plus his habitual quick, nervous movements made his nickname almost inevitable. He was wearing brown slacks and a gray-white dress shirt open at the collar with well-scuffed dress shoes and, of all things, a green cravat.

"Malone," he said.

"Ferret."

He shook a bony finger at her. "I've told you before not to call me that. Only my mother calls me that."

"Sorry...Merritt. I forgot. How are you doing?"

He shrugged and winced simultaneously. "Still hurts now and then. You come to thank me again?"

She grinned. "That, and looking for some help."

"Ah ha. You owe me, but I'm the one who pays. Ain't it always the way?"

"I paid your hospital bill and you were barely hit in the first place. Let's call it even and get down to some business, okay?"

His shifty eyes lit up. "Business? Money for info? I might be able to do that. What do you need?"

"Anything you can tell me about a pimp named Malcolm Guth."

The little man's face soured noticeably and he moved back behind the counter before answering. "He's a nasty motherfucker, I can tell you that. You wouldn't want to be one of his girls."

"Nasty how? Mean? Violent? Controlling?"

"All of the above and then some."

"How about obsessive? Any chance he'd get obsessed with one of his girls and not be willing to let her go?"

Merritt the Ferret snuffled, rather in the way Malone imagined his namesake might. A tiny, high-pitched snuffle. "You mean, like he's in love? Romantically obsessed? Not a fucking chance. The

76

cocksucker don't got a loving bone in his skinny-ass body, guaranteed."

"Well, how about he's a controlling son of a bitch who doesn't ever let anyone leave on principle?"

The Ferret had to think on that one for a moment. "I know girls who've left. He doesn't like it, but I didn't hear that he came after any of them. It's a business, you know. You give your employees too much trouble and you got no employees after a while."

"There's one that he's coming after and doesn't want to let go."

Another shrug and wince. "It ain't because he's in love with the bitch. She's got something he wants—or has something on him, is all I can think."

"Any other ideas why? Something more specific?"

He spread his little hands. "That's all I got."

Malone could see that she'd tapped all she could from the Ferret. She thanked him and laid three twenties on the counter. "There's more if you find out anything else," she said as she turned to leave.

"Malone!" he called and she stopped to look back.

"Guth's a hard guy. I'll let you know what I hear but I ain't gonna get in the way again if he tries to shoot you."

Malone laughed. "Fair enough," she said, and exited the shop.

CHAPTER TWENTY

Norman Albright was next on my list and he lived in Portland's Mount Tabor neighborhood, a good fifteen minutes' drive from downtown in weekday traffic. Just as with Nakagawa and Overton, I was not going to call ahead—but I'd be curious to see if anyone else had.

On my way, I kept going over the three interviews I'd done so far. Despite Overton's opinion that Tanya Petosky would have called all the others, it was obvious to me that she'd called him and not Nakagawa; the latter wasn't that good an actor. So why would that be? Maybe she liked the jeweler and not the banker. Maybe Petosky was Overton's parental figure on the board; he probably needed one. Maybe Nakagawa was the only board member she didn't call. Maybe, maybe, maybe.

And what was with Max Overton, anyway? Petosky might be a character but Overton was a basket case. The man's nervousness, at least until right at the end, had been so far over the top I couldn't tell if he was guilt-ridden, unable to cope...or something else. That last reaction of his, that little twitch of a smile, bothered me; it didn't fit with the rest. Right now I was voting for something else.

Albright's home sat ensconced behind a wrought-iron fence with the gate standing open. Plenty of room to park on the curved driveway. I pulled over near the late-nineties black Corvette that was already there.

Mount Tabor rises six hundred feet among the surrounding houses and businesses of Southeast Portland, its gentle green bulge a familiar landmark to city residents. The mound has lent its name to the surrounding park and neighborhood, an area of large old homes and expensive newer dwellings. Albright's house was one of the former, very near the park boundary. It looked like the upper floor would have a great view of the city.

The first *clank* of the over-sized ornate door knocker brought an answering rattle of the interior doorknob. He must have been waiting for me. Big surprise.

The man who opened the door was an impressive specimen, especially if he was the guy in his late fifties Eleanor had told me about. A good three or four inches taller than me, broad shoulders, a full head of dark brown, well-oiled hair brushed straight up from the forehead pompadour-style. Relatively unlined face except around the eyes. Flawless white teeth. He had that look of being very, very well cared for.

"Mr. Albright?" I asked.

"Yes—and you must be Mr. McCall."

"I gather," I said as we shook hands, "that the board does not have a communication problem."

He laughed. "Not really. Come in, come in. Stanley called me. He said you were making inquiries and would probably be dropping by."

He escorted me through a large vestibule into the library. Yes, a library, just like in the old British movies. Floor to ceiling bookshelves, all loaded with real books as far as I could tell. Big old-fashioned desk sitting before a bay window looking out onto a spacious, well-manicured grounds. Nearly everything in the house constructed of highly polished wood. More money in sight than I'd make in a lifetime.

Albright motioned me to a comfortable-looking overstuffed chair, glanced at the grandfather clock on one side of the room, and headed for the glass-fronted liquor cabinet opposite. "I see it's after three," he said. "Would you care to join me in a drink?"

"Gin and tonic would be good," I replied. "Fairly dry."

"Coming up."

He prepared my drink and poured himself a good shot of Bacardi rum. Then downed it and poured another before bringing the drinks over to me and taking an adjoining chair.

"So what can I do for you, Mr. McCall?"

"You've been chairman of the Foundation board from the beginning?"

"Yes."

"Isn't it normal for boards to rotate officers—and get new members occasionally, for that matter?"

"Yes, I suppose that is more 'normal' as you say, but the Lifestream Foundation is our little project. The six of us had the idea and provided the initial funding and still provide more than half of it. If someone else had equal interest and wanted to contribute equally, they'd certainly be welcome...but there has been no such person." He tossed back his second shot. "As for the officers, when we first incorporated Barbara Schilling volunteered to be secretary, Max Overton to be treasurer, and I to be chair. It's simply the case that no one has since volunteered to replace any of us. The other three have their roles to play."

"What is Tanya Petosky's role?"

Albright laughed as he got up and went over to the rum bottle again. "Ah, the lovely and dramatic Tanya. You've spoken with her already?"

"I ran into her down at the Foundation office."

"And thus," he said as he returned with renewed rum glass, "you have already seen her role. We all take turns downtown, but she is the primary public face of the Foundation. She's the one you will usually run into at the office."

"Do you happen to know if she's really related to the tsars?"

He nearly choked on his rum and was laughing again as he wiped a little excess from his lips. "As a gentlemen, I certainly do not question the word of my dear friend." Another sip. "I will say that she enjoys being colorful."

"And is not above adding a little color?"

He smiled. "I didn't say that."

"Do you know where her money comes from?"

He waved that aside. "These are questions for the lady herself, don't you think, Mr. McCall?"

"Probably, but it never hurts to hear what others know...if

81

they're willing to share. I am focusing on money here, after all, and she's the one board member whose fortune seems a little mysterious."

Albright chuckled. "Not surprising. I believe Tanya may love mystery even more than she does drama."

"So you can't tell me anything about her so-called 'mentors.'"

He raised his nearly empty glass in salute. "That is correct."

"You understand that I am looking into possible improprieties in the Foundation's finances."

He leaned toward me. "I can assure you, Mr. McCall, that there is nothing amiss with the Foundation funds."

"My client has received information to the contrary."

Again that wave of dismissal as he sat back again. "Well, you know, reporters hear things all the time. Can't take them all seriously."

I could feel my face flush at the same time my spine felt like it was getting drenched with cold water—and it pissed me off. I was getting tired of these people giving me adrenaline rushes. "Reporters?"

He offered me a slow, big grin. "Oops."

I was had again, no question, but I was not going to concede the point. "Why do you think my client might be a reporter?"

"Let's just say a little bird told me."

Shit. Time to make another less-than-graceful exit. This was *really* beginning to piss me off.

CHAPTER TWENTY-ONE

Luckily for him, George Heatherly wasn't answering the phone the rest of the day. Repeated calls got me only his voicemail, both at his office and his home.

I puttered and muttered around our office an hour or so before Malone returned. We compared notes, me telling her about my encounters with the three board members and her relating her conversations with LeAnn Hannaford and Merritt the Ferret.

We agreed that Guth wasn't acting like LeAnn had something of his, neither money nor anything else of value. On the other hand, if she had something on him why didn't he just kill her? He didn't strike either of us as a guy with moral qualms.

He did strike Malone as a coward, however, and she speculated that he didn't want the grief of being the obvious prime suspect if his former employee turned up dead. That was as good an explanation as any until we had more information.

Malone headed home a little before five and I finally left voicemail messages for Heatherly at both his home and work around five-thirty, saying I needed to talk to him and his wife tomorrow.

It almost had to be one of them, Heatherly or his wife, who'd given the game away to Albright. If it wasn't either one, then I was really lost. I don't like being lost. I *really* don't like clients who aren't straight with me. It was probably good that I'd be sleeping on it before meeting with the Heatherlys. Plus, I wanted to sleep on the question of why Albright had given the game away to me. That had been no slip; he wanted me to know that he knew.

So tomorrow I was looking at meeting with George and Shanna Heatherly as well as the two board members I hadn't talked to yet, Barbara Schilling and Jesse Carter. Meanwhile Malone was going to continue tapping her street resources to see if she could get anything more helpful about Guth or LeAnn.

Right at the moment, I just wanted to sleep. I was grumpy and tired and tomorrow was going to be a big day. I turned out the lights, locked up the office, and took myself home. No stopping by the dojang this evening.

I was well into that sleep I needed when the phone's jangle cut through the night.

Blearily I read the clock to say two-twenty a.m. as I fumbled with the receiver. If it wasn't a wrong number, it couldn't be good. It was never good at two in the morning.

"Mr. McCall?" It was a young woman's voice, scared and weepy, familiar but unidentifiable in my grogginess.

"Yes. Who is this?"

"It's LeAnn. "I'm at Providence Medical Center. Could you come down here?"

I sat up. "What's happened? Are you all right?"

"I'm okay. It's your detective friend, Johnny. Mal hurt him pretty bad, I think. The doctors are working on him now and they won't tell me anything. Can you come down?"

"On my way," I said and hung up the phone as I threw back the covers. There would be no more sleep tonight.

CHAPTER TWENTY-TWO

I called Malone as I pulled out of my driveway and she arrived at the hospital just a couple of minutes behind me. When she rushed in I was standing with Johnny's wife Gerry, his partner Hap, and LeAnn. Everybody said a quick hello and we got back to sorting out what happened.

The short version I'd gotten so far was that Johnny had told Roger and Daisy to take off because there was no need for four of them covering the café, especially given that two of them were unpaid volunteers, and then he had escorted LeAnn home alone because Hap had an errand to run for his wife. That turned out to be not such a great idea, since Guth had been waiting outside her apartment.

Apparently Johnny distracted Guth long enough for LeAnn to get into the apartment and lock the door; then he was down and she called the police as Guth tried to break in.

"How is he?" Malone asked.

"We don't know," LeAnn replied. "They said they'd come and tell us." She looked around woefully. "But nobody's said anything."

"It's all my fault," Hap moaned as he stood with his arm around Gerry. Hap Harbaugh is a big man, bald, always dressed in clothes looking as if he'd slept in them. He's a year older and probably a third taller and heavier than his 68-year-old long-time partner and he practically had to lean over to embrace the short and round gray-haired woman. "I should have had his back."

Gerry reached up and patted him on the shoulder, but said nothing. Her usually florid complexion was dead pale and she looked like she might be in shock.

I went over to the information desk but could get nothing beyond the same assurance that someone would come and talk to us soon. Meanwhile Hap had eased Gerry down into one of the waiting room chairs and LeAnn had seated herself on a kind of padded bench next to it. Hap stayed on his feet, pacing heavily back and forth. Probably none of the chairs would have held his bulk anyway. Malone was leaning against a wall near the desk.

I sat down beside LeAnn on the bench and laid a hand on her arm. "Tell me what happened," I said to her as gently as I could. "Everything this time." I felt her body shudder. Malone stepped over closer to us, no doubt also wanting to hear the details.

"Johnny took me home after we closed up and Mal was waiting outside my apartment, just down the hall. He came running up when we got to the door. He was crazy. He wouldn't leave. Kept saying he had to talk to me. Johnny did everything he could to back him off, but nothing worked. I got the door open and told Johnny to come in with me, but he didn't have a chance. Mal tried to follow me in and that's when he hit Johnny."

"With his fist? Guth didn't have a weapon?" I'm pretty sure my voice trembled a little with the rage I was feeling.

"I don't think so," she said miserably. "I got the door closed and locked and called 9-1-1. I knew Johnny must be hurt because Mal was banging on the door, trying to break in. I guess then he heard the cops coming, the sirens. He was gone when they got there."

"Did you see how badly Johnny was hurt?"

"Noooo," she moaned. "They were already working on him when the cops took me down to their car and I couldn't see. There was blood. I saw some blood."

I stood up and exchanged a glance with Malone. "Great," I said. Anxiety slid in there with the anger.

Malone reached down, put her finger under the young woman's chin and tilted her face up, inspecting what I now noticed was a bloody lip. I hadn't even seen it. "Did Guth hit you, too?" she asked.

LeAnn shook her head. "No. I think I bit my lip while everything was going on."

"Okay." Malone straightened up and focused past me. I

glanced over my shoulder to see a young dark-skinned man in a white coat approaching us.

"Are any of you here for Johnny Crew?" he asked.

Everyone was on their feet by the time he finished the question and Gerry stepped forward. "I'm his wife and these are his friends. Is he okay?"

To my great relief, he grinned. "I'm Dr. Labatti and your husband is fine. I'm sorry it's taken so long but we wanted to do a very thorough examination given his age. He has a bloody nose and a possible mild concussion; that's all. Nevertheless, we'd like to keep him overnight—again because of his advanced years."

At which Gerry smiled a little. She knew as well as I did that Johnny Crew would not be thrilled to hear some young whippersnapper referring to his "advanced years." He was a tough old son of a bitch and proud of it.

CHAPTER TWENTY-THREE

It was nine-fifteen when Malone and I sat down with Hap at the Pen and Pastry—still half-filled with people who apparently had nowhere to go but deeper into their morning paper and coffee cup.

She and I had finally left the hospital and temporarily gone our separate ways around four a.m. Gerry and Hap both stayed, even though we'd all visited with Johnny and had seen for ourselves that he was coming along nicely. LeAnn turned down the offer of Malone's couch and also stayed. She clearly felt almost as guilty as Hap did. If only.... The two most useless words in the English language.

I didn't know about my partner but I'd gotten maybe a whole hour of good sleep before it was the cats' breakfast time. And now here we were together again. Hap looked terrible, something like a mountain subject to severe erosion. He told us that Gerry and LeAnn were still at the hospital waiting for Johnny's release but that he was out and about because he wanted to do something. Very likely kill Malcolm Guth.

"It's not your fault, Hap," I said for what must have been the tenth time. "If it's anybody's fault, it's mine. I knew that Guth had gone to her apartment and banged on the door before."

"Wilma really wanted them laxatives, Clint. She was really hurting and I had to...."

Malone stopped him with a peremptory palm held out. "We don't need the details. You were there for your wife. That's good. And Clint's right. Johnny getting popped by Guth was not your fault. It wasn't Roger or Daisy's fault; they were told to take off. I don't think it's Clint's fault, either. Who would have thought that Guth would try the same stupid shit again? Plus, Johnny's okay. No harm, no foul."

Hap took a moment as his face went from guilty to grim. "Johnny's got a busted nose and it could have been a lot worse. I say we go after this Guth guy right now."

I held up my own hand at that one. "And my guess is that Guth is laying low, really low if he's heard on the street that it was a retired cop he attacked. Word is getting around the force already, I'm sure, and everybody will be on the lookout for this asshole—but until he's caught we still need to keep an eye on LeAnn. Can you do that?"

"You bet. I already told Wilma I ain't running to the store for nothing else until this is settled."

At that moment the front door opened and the young woman in question stepped inside, pausing to look around until she saw us.

LeAnn started across the room toward our table and Malone tapped Hap on the arm. "First thing," she observed dryly, "is to tell her, again, not to travel around town on her own." Didn't even glance my way when she said it.

CHAPTER TWENTY-FOUR

The kid arrived at our table looking at least as tired as I felt. Her shoulders slumped, making her tall, thin frame appear even more frail than usual. Her mousy brown hair hung lank, swaying only slightly as she advanced toward us. Her face was pale and drawn.

"Johnny's okay?" Hap asked LeAnn.

"Gerry was getting ready to take him home when I left." She was rubbing her eyes as she spoke. "He's doing fine." She dropped her hands to her lap and flushed slightly. "I snuck out." Glanced around and made eye contact with Veronica who was just coming out of the kitchen. "I'm supposed to work the morning shift."

"How'd you get here from the hospital?" asked Malone.

"Bus."

"Do you think that was smart?" Apparently Malone wasn't going to wait for Hap to take her suggestion. "Just last night Guth was trying to break down your door and now you're out and about with no protection. Have you decided you want to be with him?"

"No! I just...." She looked an appeal at her boss, who had just joined us. "I have to work this morning."

"I'll stay here and keep an eye out," rumbled Hap. "I hope Guth shows up. I really do."

"And I'll see that she works a good long shift," Veronica added. "With plenty of pastry and coffee for Hap here."

I made eye contact with Malone. "Then it sounds like we should get back to our paying customer," I said as I stood up. "We're right in the middle of a case that has lots of players and we haven't even talked to them all yet, much less done any detecting." Malone offered me a slight frown, but also stood.

LeAnn half rose from her own chair and looked at me appealingly. "Can I talk to you? Just for a minute? Alone?"

"Sure," I said. I glanced around. "Let's just step over there." I gestured to an unoccupied table in the corner.

My hopes were doing a little dance as we strolled over to it. I knew there had to be more to the young woman's situation than she'd shared with us so far. Guth had a reason he wanted her back. Maybe she'd decided it was time to tell me what it was.

We stopped beside the table but didn't sit down.

"I know you're really busy," she began. I swear she was literally wringing her hands. "And you're already using all these people to help me out. I don't know how I'll ever be able to thank you."

Oh crap, I'm thinking to myself. The kid's not going to offer to take it out in trade, is she? Why did I leave Malone back there with the others?

"You don't have to thank me," I said as sincerely as I've ever said anything. "It's a favor for Veronica, really."

"Okay...."

Jesus. Now she was wringing her hands and gnawing on her lower lip. It was beginning to bleed again.

"If you have something to tell me," I said, "I'd like to hear it."

Finally: "My friend Kristi needs help."

"What?"

"She's trying to get away from Mal, too, and she's afraid he's going to hurt her. I told her about you and she said she knew you."

"She knows me? Wait a minute. What are you talking about?"

"Kristi is another one of Mal's girls. We're friends. I called her from the hospital this morning. I needed somebody to talk to and figured she wouldn't be asleep yet. She said she saw you talking to Mal, down at the Lounge."

I had to think about that for a second. There had been that one young woman standing at the bar when I left, the one who made the joke.... "Is your friend Kristi black?"

"Yeah."

"Okay, I probably know who you mean. If she wants out, tell her to come down and talk to Veronica like you did. We can keep an eye on two of you just as easily as one, I guess. We've got to deal with Guth anyway."

92

"That's not what she wants to do. She wants...a better situation, you know, get off the street."

I think my eyes must have actually bulged like Max Overton's as I looked at her incredulously. I could see in my peripheral vision (perhaps improved by the bulging) that Veronica was still at the table with Malone and Hap, watching our conversation curiously. She'd love this one. Only a kid who'd been on the streets for a *long* time could imagine that this was a sane request.

"So you want me to help your friend move up in the world to a call girl service?" I asked as calmly as I could.

LeAnn smiled with relief at my slow but dawning comprehension. "Yes, exactly."

I took a deep breath and put my hand firmly on her shoulder. "Look, LeAnn, I don't think you understand what you're asking. I don't want to see your friend hurt, but I'm not going to spend resources to make her a better prostitute, okay? Either the police or I will be taking care of Mal Guth, whichever one of us gets to him first, and that should take some pressure off your friend—but that's the best I can do."

Her face was collapsing as I spoke. She grabbed my extended arm with both hands. "Please!" She whispered fiercely. "Please talk to her at least. She's my best friend. Please. He could kill her if he finds out she wants to work for somebody else. I know it! I know *him!*"

Now everybody in the place was watching. I gently pulled my arm out of her grasp. "Okay, okay. You have an address for...Kristi, is it?"

She did, an apartment house on Burnside not that far from the Gentlemen's Lounge. I committed it to memory, if not my to-do list, and signaled Malone that it was time to go.

CHAPTER TWENTY-FIVE

Malone's Jeep was parked right in front of the café and we stopped beside it for a quick consultation. "You really want me along on this Heatherly thing today?" she asked, "Or was that just a line to get us out of there?"

"There are going to be plenty of people looking for information about Guth and for the man himself before the day's over."

She thought about it for a moment. "You're probably right. So what's first on the agenda?"

"Talking to George Heatherly again if he's home."

"Okay. You want me to drive?"

"Your Jeep's right here and there's no point in us driving separately."

"What was that last little chat with LeAnn about?" she asked as soon as we'd both gotten into her vehicle.

"She wants us to help another friend of hers get away from Guth."

Malone grunted and turned the ignition. "What are we? The prostitute underground railroad now? What did you tell her?"

"That I'd talk to the girl. I didn't say when."

I got out my cell phone and called George Heatherly's house as the Jeep pulled away from the curb. A woman answered, identified herself as Shanna Heatherly, and handed the receiver over to George at my request. He said he was working from home this morning and it would be fine for us to come by. I said we'd see him in twenty minutes and hit the "end" button on the cell phone.

The Heatherlys lived on southwest Terwilliger Boulevard near Duniway Park with a view of Mt. Hood to the northeast. The mountain this morning was mostly obscured by gray March clouds.

No circular driveway, definitely not a mansion, but a much nicer split-level home than the average ad-rag journalist and young librarian would be able to afford. It looked to be an older home than most on the block, but also one of the larger ones. Nothing like having your youth *and* a rich wife. I could see why George wanted to be very careful about pissing off the in-laws without good cause.

As we came up the weathered wooden steps, the front door was opened by what I thought for a moment was a girl maybe twelve years old. Then I saw it was a small woman—early twenties, four-ten, thin but fit, dark hair cropped short; the only thing about her that was big was her smile.

"Mr. McCall? Miss Malone?"

"Yes," I said as I hit the small porch and held out my hand. "Mrs. Heatherly?"

"Shanna, please," she said as she turned to Malone and took her hand. "Come on in."

Just inside the entrance was a cozy foyer; down was to the left and up to the right. We went down to what looked like the family room.

George Heatherly was standing by the couch when we appeared. He was wearing tan chinos and a green University of Oregon sweatshirt. There was a laptop on the coffee table. The couch faced a pair of picture windows looking out at the cloud-shrouded mountain. Not a bad place to work.

We both shook hands with him and he gestured toward a couple of nearby overstuffed chairs. His wife inquired if anyone wanted coffee or tea. We all opted for coffee. She left to get it as the rest of us sat down.

"How are things going?" He addressed the question to me. "Any progress yet?" His own dark hair was about the same length as his wife's and a good deal less combed. Eyes wide behind the wire-rimmed spectacles. Body posture all pins and needles. This was not a guy who was certain he wanted to hear the news.

"Not yet," I said, and he managed to frown in disappointment and slump with relief at the same time.

I glanced up at the foyer. "Can we talk in front of your wife?"

"No problem," he answered with a wry smile. "Shanna's a very curious person—I guess librarians are a little like detectives in that way—and she knew something was going on. She kept at me until I gave in. It is her family, after all. Maybe. Maybe her family is involved. When do you think you'll have some answers?" This time he seemed to include both of us in the question, but Malone sat back to let me answer it.

I was relieved to hear that I wasn't going to have to participate in a deception of Shanna Heatherly. There appeared to be way too much of that going on already. Did his wife tell her uncle what was going on? Probably, but I needed to confirm it. Why did Max Overton react the way he did? Was it true that Tanya Petosky hadn't called Albright? If not, why not? Was anything at all going on besides a bunch of rich folks playing mind games with yours truly?

All I could say right now in answer to our client's perfectly good question was, "I don't know." I'm sure Malone couldn't have done any better.

The return of Shanna Heatherly with the coffee interrupted our exchange. She set the tray nearby, passed out the cups and then joined her husband on the couch. As I was taking my first sip of coffee, Malone apparently decided to jump in. With both feet.

"Mr. Heatherly, did you ask your wife not to tell her uncle about our investigation?"

That produced an interesting and abrupt contrast of expressions: surprise on Heatherly's part and serious discomfort on his wife's. As far as I was concerned, that confirmed my suspicion, which Malone must have shared.

"Of course," he said.

I sat back and let Malone continue. "So. Shanna. Why did you tell your uncle anyway?"

Her lips crimped in exasperation, she threw up her hands. "Oh...all right, you got me." Turning to her husband, whose surprise appeared to be edging toward dismay: "I'm sorry, honey, but I knew Uncle Norman wasn't doing anything wrong and I thought

97

he could help." Back to Malone: "He wasn't supposed to *tell*, though!"

I took over again. "He didn't rat you out," I assured her. "but he did indicate that he knew and there weren't that many people who could have told him."

George Heatherly found his voice at this point. "I asked you not to tell him, Shanna! What were you doing? That's why I hired these people, for Christ's sake, so Norman wouldn't know it was me behind the investigation!" He was literally bouncing up and down on the couch. "I might as well have saved the money and done it myself! Damn! This is terrible!"

His wife put her hand firmly on his arm as if to hold him down. "I'm *sorry*, George. I guess I didn't think it through, but I knew Uncle Norman...."

He pulled away and jumped up, swinging around to look down at her. "If we could really *know*, we wouldn't need to investigate at all! You *think* your uncle's a good guy. You want to *believe* your uncle's a good guy. The investigation might have *proved* your uncle's a good guy, damn it. That's different!"

"That's enough!" Malone pointed at the empty spot on the couch. "Sit down, Mr. Heatherly. You two can deal with the power balance in your marriage as soon as we're gone." She glared him back to his seat, then focused on his wife. "Are you going to report this meeting to your uncle as well?"

Shanna Heatherly was looking pretty miserable by this point. "No," she said. "I won't say anything to anybody about any of it." She sent a glare of her own in her husband's direction. "Will that make you happy?"

Malone stood, pointing a finger at George. "Don't answer that. Not until we're out the door, anyway."

Which sounded like a plan to me, so I stood as well and we both moved as quickly as we decently could to and through the front entrance. I'm not sure the Heatherlys even noticed.

Outside, we were just starting down the walk when one of the steps behind me exploded wood chips and I heard a distinctive *crack* in the distance off to my right.

CHAPTER TWENTY-SIX

I dived left onto a conveniently located small lawn and had the Smith and Wesson out before I scrambled forward to crouch behind Malone's Jeep. She had gone to the right into some bushes and crab-walked up to join me, cursing with Glock in hand.

"You hit?" she asked as we both cautiously surveyed the area, me over the hood and she past the trunk.

"No. You?"

"I'm fine. There!" She was pointing at a figure running into the park a block-and-a-half down the street to our left. Maybe it was my imagination, but I thought he or she was carrying a rifle.

"What's happening?" came George's cry from behind us. I glanced back over my shoulder to see him standing on the porch looking at us like we were crazy.

"Somebody's shooting at us!" I shouted. "Get the hell back in the house!"

He scampered back through the doorway and we took off toward the park, running low, zigzagging, using cars for as much cover as possible.

My mind was racing even faster than my body. Was it Mal Guth out there in the park with a rifle? How would he know we were here? Why would he try to kill us anyway? But who else could it be? The Heatherly case? It was their house that took the bullet. *What the hell was going on?*

We got to the last car, across the street from where I'd seen the figure enter the park, and dashed across the street, then dived for cover behind a bush. I heard a passing car slow down behind us and then rev the engine. I glanced back. A new Beetle with a middle-aged woman driver I didn't recognize looking back as she sped away. Probably not the shooter. She had a great story to tell somebody when she got home, though, about the man and woman playing cops and robbers outside Duniway Park.

If nothing else, it made me realize how dumb we looked. I listened. Nothing. I glanced over at Malone, who also seemed to be perceiving no current threat. I stood up slowly. Nothing. I scanned the park slowly and carefully. Nothing. Malone stood beside me in the silence. The shooter apparently wasn't interested in taking another shot and was probably long gone.

I felt a light punch hit my right arm as I holstered my weapon. I looked over at my partner, who was frowning very slightly back at me.

"You think it was Guth?"

"No idea," I replied. "Could be."

"The fun never ends," she said.

I couldn't read her tone any better than her expression. Finally I turned to fully face her. "Is there a problem? Other than somebody taking a shot at us, I mean?"

"I thought sure you were hit. I don't know why. You weren't hit?"

I took a moment to make sure there was no significant athletic insensibility at play in my body. "No, I told you already I wasn't hit. You okay?"

Now she was beginning to look angry, I thought. I, of course, was getting progressively more bewildered.

"I'm fine," she snapped. "It just.... It pisses me off, that's all. It pisses me off."

So, I thought to myself as she stomped off in the direction of the Heatherlys' house, *at least I was reading her right there at the end.* Not understanding, mind you, just reading.

I glanced once more around the park, then followed behind her.

CHAPTER TWENTY-SEVEN

Sensible young people that they were, George and Shanna Heatherly had called 9-1-1 while we were gallivanting down the street after the shooter. Several police cars had pulled up by the time we had walked back to their house. The television news crews weren't far behind.

Among the latter, to my dismay but not surprise, was Alison Roberts. Twenty-seven years old, five-nine with shoulder-length black hair and a face made for TV, she specialized in old-time ambush journalism and was my own personal nemesis. In just a few years she had gone from second string on-air reporter to co-host of a local afternoon talk show to her own late evening mix of soft features and breaking stories called "Inside the News," all on Channel 11, the city's one independent (i.e., least viewed) channel.

She was tenacious, talented, and apparently convinced that I was her ticket to the big time. Her expression when she saw us on the scene at the Heatherly's house was that of a lioness who comes upon a pair of crippled gazelles: Oh boy! Munchies!

She practically leaped through the police officers and other camera crews that were milling about, faithful cameraman Murray Kravitz close behind her. Kravitz was a big, beefy guy with a goatee and long gray hair pulled into a ponytail. He looked like a refugee from Berkeley in the sixties and he was already taping as Roberts landed in front of us, microphone extended.

"Here's our famous local private eye Clint McCall," she said intensely, "already on the scene along with his faithful partner Devon Malone. Was a client of yours involved in the shooting, Mr. McCall? Or was somebody shooting at you? What exactly happened here?"

My immediate response was to take a quick step between Malone and Roberts. The last time, which wasn't the first time, our young journalist friend had referred to Devon in that "Clint's faithful companion" tone she'd come very close to having her clock cleaned and reset on hospital time.

I really didn't want to see my partner featured on the evening news decking a reporter, so I held my position even as I felt her tensing up behind me. I looked straight into the camera. "No comment," I said with as much finality as I could muster.

The microphone thrust closer to my face. "Come on, McCall. You didn't just happen to be here. Who's shooting at you this time?"

"No. Comment." Then, mainly because I still feared that Malone was going to duck around me and make on-air mayhem, I pushed the mike aside and leaned over to whisper in Roberts' ear, "Shut down the damned camera and I'll tell you what I know."

She pulled back with a sour look, hesitated, and then waved back over her shoulder at Kravitz. "Cut it, Murray." She stood looking at me expectantly, focused entirely on me in fact and ignoring Malone. Which had to stop.

"One ground rule first," I said.

"Which is?"

I stepped back to my original spot and pointed at my partner. "This is Devon Malone, co-owner of the agency and my partner. You will give her the same respect and irritating bullshit questions that you give me or you get nothing but no-comments from now on."

I swear that everybody froze for a second, long enough for me to wonder if I'd just made a very bad move, but then Malone's mouth twitched and she seemed to relax. "Nothing but no-comments and a fucking concussion," she said to Roberts whose mouth was hanging a little open. Kravitz, standing a little back from our group, was now grinning with what looked like genuine delight.

Roberts closed her mouth, looked from one of us to the other. "Fine," she said to me. "My apologies, Miss Malone. Now. Would either one of you like to tell me what happened here? Maybe even on-camera?"

"As far as I know," I said in my sincerest tone, "it was a random drive-by shooting. We just happened to be in the vicinity. You'll have to talk to the police spokesman to get any other information."

Roberts flushed crimson and stared wide-eyed at me. "That's it? You lecture me about respect, I apologize, and that's what I get? You just happened to be in the vicinity? Talk about bullshit!"

I stuck to my story in the face of her outrage and there was no one to contradict me. Malone certainly wasn't going to. The Heatherlys didn't know about Guth. And Mike Whitehall, who arrived soon after the news crews, wasn't inclined to share any speculations with the press.

On the other hand, Mike privately expressed to me that the Bureau would now be taking even more interest in Malcolm Guth, just in case he was taking potshots at local private investigators and, more importantly, the homes of respectable citizens. I did not discourage this plan. Whether it was Guth I'd seen running into the park or not, I wanted him off the street.

CHAPTER TWENTY-EIGHT

We found the Heatherlys huddled together on the couch down in the family room, apparently just about stupefied by the time all the law enforcement and media had left the scene. They looked up at me as if they couldn't quite remember who I was.

I dropped into the same overstuffed chair I'd occupied before. Malone stayed on her feet beside me. "You guys okay?" I asked the young couple. "Anything we can do for you?"

"No," George responded after a moment. My guess was that he was answering both questions. Then he looked hard at me. "You don't think that had anything to do with us, do you?"

I sat forward, intent to reassure them as much as possible. "All I can say is that it's more likely another case we're working on— and, if it is, I'm very sorry you ended up with such a terrible fright —not to mention the damaged front step."

He waved that aside. "It's okay." He and Shanna looked at one another and then he turned back to me. "But what if it does have to do with the Foundation?"

"I don't know. There's nothing to indicate any of the people we've talked to have done anything wrong, much less have a reason to shoot at us. They're a pretty eccentric bunch, and a little mysterious, but I'd have to see a lot more to believe one of them is behind this."

They glanced at each other again. "Then keep looking," George said firmly. "We're certainly not going to rest easy until we know for sure that we're safe."

Shanna mumbled something that I didn't hear and George squeezed her even more tightly. "It's okay, honey. It isn't your fault."

Shortly after that we said our goodbyes again and left.

We were both scanning for threats as we walked to the Jeep. "You were quiet in there," I said to Malone.

"You didn't need to defend me."

It took a moment. From the Heatherlys? From the shooter? No. From Alison Roberts. I had wondered when that shoe would drop. "I know I didn't need to. I wanted to. You're my partner."

"Hmm."

I got nothing else until we were settled in the Jeep. Malone reached for the ignition and then paused to look at me. "Do you think about death a lot? I mean, besides when somebody is trying to kill you."

Wow. I'd never gotten a question like that from her before. "What's our next step?" or "What do you want for lunch?" would be more typical. This was new territory. I was going to have to answer honestly.

"Every damned day," I said.

She dropped her hand from the ignition key and turned a little more toward me in her seat. "Really? You're that worried about it?"

"Not worried. It's just something I've learned to do. Martial arts training has taught me that in any serious combat between equally skilled fighters the person most willing to die will win. My meditation tradition teaches me that contemplating death gives you a better perspective on life." I grinned. "And then there are the people who in fact try to kill me. One way or the other, I think about it every day."

She seemed to unfocus for a moment, processing maybe. "That's interesting." Pause. Breath. "You want to have dinner some evening soon and talk about it more?"

My grin suddenly got a lot bigger. "You mean, like, a date? Our very first real date?"

That drew a frown in response. "I mean, like, dinner. To talk. Get to know each other better since we're partners now." She grabbed the ignition key again. "But if you want to make a fucking big deal out of it...."

"No! No," I broke in, "no big deal at all. I would be pleased to have dinner with you and talk. No big deal. Little deal. Very little."

All of which finally brought a smile to her lips. "Good

enough," she said as she started up the Jeep. "We can pin down those details later. So what's our next step?"

And we were back.

CHAPTER TWENTY-NINE

I'd suggested to Malone that we again go our separate ways for the afternoon and then compare notes in the morning. Neither of us mentioned going to dinner right away.

In fact it was around one o'clock the next morning before I finally got home, fed the very hungry cats, and fell into bed.

I didn't know yet what my partner had done with her time, but I had first made some changes in LeAnn's protection and then spent the rest of the day and part of the night looking for Guth. I'm not sure why I wanted to be on my own. I suppose I needed some space to process our newest personal development.

I confirmed that Johnny was on his feet, then called off my amateur black belt friends and assigned him and Hap full-time to LeAnn. At my strong suggestion, she cut her work-shift short and they escorted her home. My plan was to keep her there under guard until Guth was under control. Now that bullets were flying, I had to act on the possibility that the young lady's former pimp, for whatever reason, was pissed off enough to kill somebody. No time for amateurs.

No luck for professionals, either. Reuben Keys had nothing on where Guth might be. I even checked with his fellow pimp and not such good buddy of mine Big Avenue, but the huge Samoan also claimed to know nothin' and nothin'. What kept me up so late was trolling the streets to talk to as many ladies of the night as I could, but even the ones reputed to be with Guth swore that they hadn't seen him. I, in turn, did not see LeAnn's friend Kristi among the night's prowlers. I had hoped to get that off my list but no success there, either.

So here I was, up again at six, groggy in the early Friday March darkness but already beginning to pump adrenaline as I remembered that step exploding just behind me—and that I hadn't been able to find Mal Guth yet. I assumed Malone had had no better luck since I hadn't heard from her.

I always begin my day, after feeding the cats of course, with a half-hour of that meditation I'd just mentioned to Malone, called zazen in the Zen Buddhist tradition. Sitting on a cushion on the floor, resting my weight on my knees and lower legs, Samurai-style, I try—quite often in vain—to empty my mind.

Definitely in vain this morning. I finished dressing and headed in to the office.

Malone was getting out of her Jeep as I pulled into my parking space. Her hair was hanging loose and she was wearing her standard uniform of jeans, gray t-shirt, leather jacket, and battered boots. I suppose I was wearing mine as well: khaki pants, open collar shirt with a vest for the chilly weather, casual shoes, and sports coat. We greeted one another a little awkwardly and walked across the street, around the corner, and up the stairs to the office without exchanging another word.

There was no mail in the box yet and nothing on our voicemail beyond more messages from the media to ignore. We settled down on opposite sides of the partners desk with our first cups of coffee and compared notes without any reference to personal matters.

It turned out the notes were practically identical. She had also concluded that since Malcolm Guth might have been the shooter it was worth spending the day looking for him. She'd tracked down a couple more of her old informants and had even stopped by the office of Portland crime boss Carl Gunther, Sr., but had no more success than I had. And, unlike me, she'd apparently knocked off around five and headed home. She did look better rested than I felt.

There came a moment when I realized we were just sitting there looking at each other across the desk. I thought about suggesting dinner this evening. It seemed too soon. I imagined her discomfort. Or maybe I was imagining my own. I moved on.

"I can't think of anything else to do about Guth, can you?" I inquired.

She sighed. "Not a thing. It sounds like we both exhausted all our resources yesterday. The boys and girls in blue are still out there looking for him. They're not going to forget the attack on Johnny Crew, nor the possibility that he was the shooter yesterday. So back to the Heatherly mess?"

"I'd say so—and that's a good word for it. A complicated mess. Stanley Nakagawa called Max Overton to warn him I was coming. Shanna Heatherly gave Norman Albright a heads up. Tanya Petosky apparently called just about everybody. There seems to be a lot of ass-covering going on for an innocent charitable operation."

"I agree. On the other hand, they're all very rich and very upper class. Not used to being questioned."

"We haven't even talked to Jesse Carter and Barbara Schilling yet."

Malone sat up straight and opened the desk drawer to retrieve her weapon. "Sounds like that's our next move."

CHAPTER THIRTY

Before we went dashing out the door, I thought I'd check to see if either of our targets was available. Jesse Carter's line was busy, so I dialed Barbara Schilling's number. She answered on the first ring, an efficient-sounding slightly raspy "hello." I introduced myself and was not surprised to learn that she was not surprised. She readily agreed to see us that morning and gave me detailed directions to her house in Lake Oswego, an upper-class suburb just south of the city.

We took my Subaru this time. It was a pleasant drive down Macadam Avenue along the Willamette River, then southwest on Taylors Ferry Road over to Terwilliger Boulevard well south of the Heatherlys' neighborhood. The Schilling home—and this one was a mansion—was up one of the narrow curving streets on the north edge of Lake Oswego near Tryon Creek State Park. Unlike nearly everyone else I was visiting lately, she did not actually have a view of her nearby park.

I half-expected a maid or butler to open the ornate, oversized front door. Instead, it was the lady of the house herself. She had the same short blond hair, slender nose, and widely spaced green eyes as the receptionist at the Lifestream Foundation. On this woman, however, every strand of the hair was in place, the nose was pinched, and the eyes were hard. Her smile accorded with the rest of her face only in that it was tight.

"You must be Mr. McCall and Miss Malone. Come in."

The big living room was over-furnished with a plush couch and huge coffee table, antique sideboard, numerous well-padded chairs —each with its own side table—and all the available wall space covered by paintings and tapestries. Everything in sight--almost everything--just so. It looked like a parody of a *Masterpiece Theater* set.

The one jarring note was Crystal Schilling, sometime Foundation receptionist, who sprawled awkwardly at the far end of the massive couch swigging a soft drink and looking like she was every bit as uncomfortable with the room as it was with her. She was wearing what appeared to be the same jeans and sweater she'd had on when we saw her at the Foundation office. The phony welcoming smile was replaced by a glum and rebellious expression as she lowered the can and looked me over.

"You guys were at the Foundation the other day," she said.

"This is Mr. McCall and Miss Malone, Crystal," Barbara Schilling replied briskly before either of us had a chance to speak. "They are private investigators looking into possible financial irregularities at the Foundation."

"Whatever." Another long swig.

Well, at least we didn't have to explain what we were doing here.

"Anything to drink, Mr. McCall? Miss Malone? Coffee? Tea? Water?"

I glanced at Malone, who shook her head. "No, we're fine thank you."

"Please, sit down." She gestured Malone to a nearby armchair and offered me the other end of the couch from Crystal. I accepted and found myself sinking deeply into the unusually soft cushions. It was like being caught in a velvet trap. I prefer to be in a position from which I can respond quickly if there's an unexpected attack, even when an attack is highly unlikely. It's just part of the training. Currently, getting up was going to be like pulling myself out of a pit. I'd have to rely on Malone, who was shifting about as if her chair were too firm.

Mrs. Schilling was dressed tastefully in a blue short-sleeved, knee-length dress. Like the other board members, she wore a Rolex. She seemed to be aware of—and amused by—our discomfort. Her smile had turned smug as she settled carefully on the front edge of a chair across from me. Apparently a very comfortable chair. The woman knew how to establish leverage.

"I asked Crystal to be here because, after all, she is an employee

116

of the Foundation. I assumed you would wish to speak to her as well."

Disingenuous, too. No doubt a lot of big money passed over the reception desk. Interesting that she would offer up her daughter as another suspect. It was a first, for me anyway. Intended as a distraction? Simply evidence of yet another seriously dysfunctional family? As Crystal would have said: Whatever.

I was already expecting by this point to learn nothing much from these two. Under our questioning Barbara Schilling admitted that she was the board secretary, which in her case apparently meant that she took notes at the infrequent formal board meetings —and that was all. She knew nothing about the finances except that Max Overton always gave a short report indicating there was plenty of money. None of the other board members questioned him, so she assumed his reports were fine. Not much else worth noting would occur at these meetings; they were pro forma, required by law, and quickly adjourned for the serious drinking and gossip to follow. No notes were available on those latter activities. She claimed to know nothing of interest about relationships among her colleagues.

Daughter Crystal contributed little beyond the occasional smirk or sniff during her mother's interview. She was trying hard to convey that she knew lots of good gossip herself, but I doubted that much went on in the Foundation lobby we needed to know about. Since each smirk and sniff was met by a glare from mom, I wasn't going to find out this morning anyway. I did ask the younger Schilling if she knew anything about the Foundation's finances and of course she said no. That, I believed.

I got no hint that either of them knew we were working for a relative of one of the board members, so maybe Norman Albright was more discreet than I'd feared. Maybe.

I tried Jesse Carter's number again as soon as we were back in the car and got another busy signal. This was the software genius, so I couldn't believe he was using his regular phone line for Internet access. Must be a very talkative fellow, then, which was promising. I hoped he didn't mind our interrupting a chat. We headed back into Portland proper.

CHAPTER THIRTY-ONE

Jesse Carter had chosen a more middle-class, but still very nice, neighborhood for his large rustic home. He was, of course, near a park—Laurelhurst Park, in his case, a few blocks south of Glisan Street in northeast Portland.

I pulled into the driveway behind a brand new gold-colored Toyota SUV. Just out of habit, I glanced inside and then touched the hood on my way to the front porch. The dashboard bristled with every electronic toy including a GPS screen and ominously blinking security system. The engine was cold.

We mounted the porch. I rang the bell and waited, rang it again, then knocked. No answer. I punched his number into the cell phone again, feeling a little odd about calling a man from his own front porch, and got another busy signal. Even more odd. Had we finally found someone who didn't want to answer questions? How exciting.

Malone meanwhile was shading her eyes as she looked in one of the front windows from the porch. I joined her. We could see a spacious, rather starkly furnished living room with a huge home entertainment center. No sign of life there. There was something about how empty of life it looked.

"His phone is still busy?" Malone asked.

"Yes."

"I've got a bad feeling about this."

"Me, too. Let's look around."

We left the porch and moved around the side of the house, careful to avoid the multi-hued flowers planted along the foundation. Another view of the living room and then a large high-ceilinged kitchen centered on a butcher block table that looked like it alone could seat six.

At the back of the house were some sliding glass doors, curtains wide open....

"Oh crap," my partner muttered.

There was a young black man lying on the floor next to the doors, his face turned toward the neatly trimmed grass. Arrayed behind him were computers, printers, scanners, other electronic gear —and a phone that was clearly off the hook. The staring eyes and significant pool of blood told me we didn't need to hurry.

He was barefoot, wearing a sweat suit. It looked like he had settled in for a morning of playing with the high tech toys when death arrived. His left arm was flung up against the glass, the loose sweatshirt sleeve falling halfway down to his elbow. At least Jesse Carter had dared to be different. He was wearing an Accutron.

CHAPTER THIRTY-TWO

"We have *got* to stop meeting like this," Mike Whitehall said as he came up to where Malone and I were standing next to my Subaru in Jesse Carter's driveway. "Your karma is not looking good lately. For either of you."

"Yeah," I replied with a grim smile of greeting, "and our biorhythms probably aren't so hot, either."

"Speak for yourself," chimed in Malone. "Is that Jesse Carter in there?" she asked Mike.

"Yep. So what's the story? Is he a client of yours?"

"No," I said, "just somebody we wanted to talk to. Which isn't happening now. What was the cause of death?"

"Looks like a blow to the back of the head but, you know, we have to wait for the official word. What can you tell me? This isn't the same business that put Johnny Crew in the hospital, is it?"

"I doubt it."

"How about the shooting yesterday? Anything to do with that?"

I exchanged a glance with Malone and shrugged. "Maybe, but I'm damned if I know how it relates. We're just looking into the finances of a local charity. Carter was on the board. I suppose it could be a coincidence that someone killed him at this particular time."

Mike looked justifiably dubious, as did Malone and I for that matter. "Could be," he said. "Well, write down the name of the organization and whatever you can say about your investigation. We'll check it out."

"There's not much. We won't give you our client."

"I understand."

Uncle Norman might give George up if you talk to him, I thought to myself, but I'm not going to.

I scribbled some brief notes for Whitehall and we managed to leave before any news crews showed up. I knew Mike would see to it the Police Bureau's public information officer didn't mention our names, so I had some medium-high hopes I could actually get through twenty-four hours of this investigation without appearing again on Alison Roberts' news segment.

CHAPTER THIRTY-THREE

I parked the car in its usual spot across from the office and we sat for a minute considering our options. Early afternoon now. Should we go on over to the Home Run Sports Bar and have lunch or stop by the office first to check messages? Malone, of course, voted for an immediate lunch but I convinced her that we should at least check in on our business first.

Besides, dead bodies do not enhance my appetite. I don't think the Apocalypse itself would affect Malone's.

I noted as we crossed Third that the gray clouds were clearing; there was even a hint of sunshine. There weren't many pedestrians. Our edge of downtown Portland caught only a relative few of the throng that would be bustling around Pioneer Courthouse Square on a Friday afternoon, but everyone seemed to be enjoying the crisp March air as far as I could tell and the energy was good. Maybe our day was on the upswing.

Then again, maybe not.

As we got to the stairs that would lead us safely up to the office, I saw a vaguely familiar young black woman hurrying toward us down Stark from the east. Where had I seen her before? Oh yeah. At the Gentlemen's Lounge. It had to be LeAnn's friend Kristi.

"You Clint McCall, right?" she said as she stopped neatly between us and the doorway. Her eyes jumped over to Malone. "And...Devon something?"

"And you must be Kristi," I said, putting a hand on Malone's slightly vibrating left arm.

"Yeah. LeAnn said you guys would help me out. We gotta talk."

She was medium-height and a little chunky with short ebony hair done in cornrows. She wore a shiny blue short-sleeved summer dress, entirely inappropriate for the weather, and dirty tennis shoes. Every finger sported a ring and both wrists carried heavy bangles.

Early to mid-twenties was my guess, though she could have been a well-used seventeen. She was practically jumping up and down with urgency.

"You gotta help me! Mal knows I called New Faith and he's lookin' to kill me. I know he is!"

I was attempting to process what she'd just said when Malone jumped in. "You called who?"

"New Faith. Really a great place to work. Best girls in town and money to go with it. Very, very discreet, you know? Nobody gonna be beatin' you up on a call there."

Malone frowned. "An escort service? Okay. The name sure wouldn't give it away. Never heard of it."

Kristi responded with a fleeting expression of disdain. "You wouldn't," she said to my partner. Then looked at me expectantly.

"Me neither," I said. "Look, I already told LeAnn: I don't see why we should help you move up to a high-class call girl outfit."

"I don't need help movin'. I need help stayin' alive!"

"I find it hard to believe," I allowed, "that Guth tries to kill every girl who wants to leave his stable."

"He doesn't! Sure, he spouts shit like that, makes threats, but the truth is he throws girls out himself, all the time, if they're gettin' old and skanky. But LeAnn and me are still good money and, besides, he's got something else goin' on that I...."

She paused as my eyes focused past her and widened. Over her shoulder, I saw a familiar figure stalking up the street toward us. It looked to me like Mal Guth did indeed have murder on his mind. His face was flushed, sharply etched with rage and hate.

I spoke low and fast to Kristi. "I want you to head for the corner behind me and keep going. Now."

She glanced back over her shoulder. "Holy shit!" she squealed and catapulted between us, as suggested.

Guth's eyes followed her for only a moment and then came back to me. He stopped four feet away. I could see pedestrians behind him crossing hurriedly to the other side of Stark. There was

124

no mistaking that this guy was trouble. His feet were planted shoulder-width, arms ramrod straight down from his shoulders with fists clenched, muscles bulging in his thin neck. Definitely out for blood--and mine seemed to be nominated.

He was *still* ignoring Malone. I was beginning to think he really liked having a Glock in his ear. Well, we'd see how it went this time.

Before Guth even had come to a stop, Malone and I had taken advantage of Kristi moving between us to separate even a little more. I'd shifted my left foot back so that I could drop instantly into a fighting stance if I needed to and knew that my partner was also getting set. I willed my body to be completely relaxed and kept my expression neutral.

After he and I had looked at each other for a few seconds, I spoke softly: "What can we do for you, Guth?"

His jaw worked as if he couldn't find the words or couldn't get them past his lips. Finally, a low rasp: "You're in my way, old man."

"It's a wide sidewalk, kid. Go around."

"I want you out of my fuckin' way."

It was too much for Malone but at least she didn't draw her weapon on the Portland sidewalk. She did take a step forward, as if he'd been addressing her.

"Tell you what," she said. "We'll go on up to our office"—she gestured up the stairwell—"and you keep going wherever you're going. We're just doing a favor for a friend of Clint's, you know? No big deal. All you have to do is leave LeAnn alone and we've got no problem. She can't be that important."

He squinted a bit and his eyes moved slowly, painfully, from me to Malone. It looked like it took every bit of strength he had just to turn his head slightly. I thought to myself, *This asshole really doesn't like women. He may be in the wrong profession.*

"I can't...I ain't lettin' her go," he grated through clenched teeth. At least he wasn't taking such a belligerent tone with my partner. Maybe he had had enough of large guns in the ear after all. "And now she's got Kristi all hot to be somewhere else. She knows what

125

will happen if she doesn't come back. You tell her. You tell her I said she *knows* what will happen."

He was sounding slightly whiny to me, but he took a step closer to us, eyes hard as marbles as he focused exclusively on me again. "You know what will happen to you, too. I'll pound your ass and spit you out."

I stared him right back in the eye. "Careful, Guth. Bad enough you go around threatening bodily harm. I draw the line at mixed figures of speech."

We were beginning to attract a lot of attention. I could see one pedestrian on his cell phone across the street. From the way he was looking at us as he talked, I had a feeling trouble was being reported—officially, I hoped. Ideally, I wanted to keep Guth occupied until the police arrived without—tempted though I was—actually getting into a fight.

My latest verbal sally apparently had provoked some confusion. His face scrunched with concentration as he tried to decide if I'd just insulted him or what. Finally he resorted to his usual witty repartee:

"Fuck you."

He even finally decided to include Malone: "And you."

Meanwhile I was trying to sort out what was going on with him.

He hadn't moved closer and his body wasn't telegraphing an attack. He was furious, hostile, tense...but not poised. Then he twitched ever so slightly and glared down the street behind us. I glanced back to see a blue and white three blocks down coming in our direction.

Guth's eyes met mine when I came back to him. They were gleaming, whether with hatred or even tears I couldn't tell. "I got to have LeAnn back," he said with grim finality and then headed across the street at a near-trot. The pedestrian with the phone scampered away ahead of him, though I doubt Guth even noticed.

Malone and I stood there for a moment. Then she punched me

lightly in the arm. "What the hell was that?" she asked.

I had no answer.

CHAPTER THIRTY-FOUR

We went on up to the office and left the cruiser to cruise by with nothing to see.

Malone dropped into the chair on her side of the partners desk but didn't bother to stash her weapon in the drawer, a clear message that heading back out to lunch was still a high priority. She hadn't said a word since I'd failed to answer her last question.

I'd retrieved the mail from the box at the bottom of the stairs on the way up and now tossed over her share. It looked like neither of us had anything but bills and junk. The message lights on the main number and my direct line were both blinking.

Mine was a voicemail from Colleen who had somehow already heard about the shooting at the Heatherly's, inquiring somewhat urgently if I was okay. She said she was worried because she'd tried my cellphone and I didn't answer. I pulled the cellphone out of my pocket and saw that the battery had gone dead. I plugged it into the charger and called my daughter back, only to get her voicemail box. I assured her I was okay and that my cellphone would soon be functional again.

Malone hung up from listening to the main voicemail box. "One wrong number, three reporters, one possibly legitimate inquiry that will probably amount to shit, and a voicemail from your daughter who is concerned for your well-being. Why aren't you answering your cellphone?"

"It was her in my voicemail as well," I said. "I just left her a message back. I pointed to the charger. "The cellphone was dead."

"Dead seems to be going around lately." She stood up. "Let's head for lunch before I have to worry about my own death by starvation." She noted that I glanced at the charger again. "Leave it. I'm not going to wait for your damned phone to recharge. It will be all well again by the time we're done eating."

I conceded the point and we hoofed it down the stairs, across

129

the street, and into the Home Run. No one accosted us on the way, which was probably a great relief to my partner.

It was mid-afternoon by this time and we had our choice of many empty booths and tables. We picked a booth toward the back with a good view of the entrance. We also had a view of three over-sized TV screens set high on the walls, each turned to a different sports channel, but every seat in the house could see at least that many. It wasn't called a sports bar for nothing.

After the waitress had taken our identical orders for large burger, fries, and coffee, Malone put both hands flat on the table top and gave me a look. "This is our dinner date," she announced.

"What?" I didn't know whether to be bewildered or outraged. I opted for both. "What do you mean, this is our dinner date? This is lunch in the middle of our workday, just like every other lunch in the middle of our workday. The others weren't dates. Or dinner. Why is this our dinner date? And what does that even mean?"

"Calm down. You're repeating yourself. You're close to gibbering, actually."

I took a deep breath. "I am not gibbering," I said as slowly and calmly as I possibly could.

"What I mean is that we're going to talk about our relationship, such as it is..." She held up a finger to stave off anything I might say. "...but first we're going to talk some business—just as we would if this were an evening and we were having dinner at some nice restaurant. Maybe that will help you calm down."

Irritation was already doing the trick quite nicely. "I am fucking calm."

She actually grinned at me, which was even more irritating. "Great," she said.

The waitress arrived with our coffees, which gave me a chance to do a little more smoothing out. I had no idea what was coming after we talked business but the anticipation was kind of exciting now that I thought about it.

Malone took a sip of her coffee as the waitress walked away

and then set her cup down carefully. "So, what do we think of Malcolm Guth now?"

Which was a good question, all things considered.

"He wasn't the shooter at the Heatherly's house," I said.

Her eyebrows went up a little. "Because?"

"We just had our third face-to-face confrontation with the asshole and so far he's all words, no action where we're concerned. Crazy, yes. Dangerous, no doubt. We know he exploits women for a living and can put an old retired detective in the hospital, but trying to assassinate one or both of us in broad daylight in a residential area with a rifle? I don't see it."

She nodded. "I agree with that, for now, though I think he's got the potential to escalate. Which means it was either a random shooting or it probably has to do with the Lifestream Foundation —where we've already got one dead guy. Any bets on which?"

I took a good swig of my own brew. "I have to bet on the latter, but that would mean there's a lot more at stake than we've identified so far."

"Which would be about zero, so far."

"About that."

She shrugged and took another swallow of her own. "Well, that gives us plenty more billable hours, anyway."

"Good attitude," I said.

She set her cup down again, even more carefully this time, and surveyed the room. I picked up my own cup and started to drink, thinking to myself that this might be the moment of truth, or of further confusion, or something.

"So you want to be my boyfriend now?"

I think I dribbled a little down my chin. Hastily grabbing a napkin, I tried to come up with a clever but thoughtful answer. My initial effort was something like, "Errrh...."

"From gibbering to growling. I'm not sure that's progress. Maybe we should stick with talking business."

I dabbed my chin, gritted my teeth, and took the plunge. "Yes,"

I said, and found that I really was calm now. "I thought I'd been making that pretty clear for a while. You're a great partner and I don't want to lose that, but I also think you're a fascinating, attractive, tough, and really smart woman that I'd like to have a personal relationship with. Much more personal than we've been so far."

"You want to get me in bed."

"No question. But I also want to get into your head. I want to know who you are, where you came from, what you think about all kinds of things besides the next move we should make in the case we're working on or how hungry you are. It's not just sex I'm interested in. I'm interested in you."

She'd been very subtly leaning further and further back as I spoke, which did not lead me to think that this was going well. She didn't break eye contact, though. "I'll tell you something personal," she finally said.

"Okay."

"I'm scared."

I'm quite sure that if she'd given me several days to guess what she was going to say, that would not have been on my list. But I went with it.

"I'm sorry. Am I scaring you, or is it something else?"

"You, me, what would happen if you really did get in my head.... It all scares me. And pisses me off."

Which gave me some space to breathe. "Ah," I said, "that sounds more like the Devon Malone I already know." The one who is usually feeling pissed about something or another. She was still leaning back, still looking me in the eye, and I kept going for it. "How about this? Do you feel anything else? Like any of the things I feel for you?"

She was the one who took the deep breath this time, and the exhale brought her forward. "Yes. I feel them. A lot of them. I don't know if I feel them the same or as much as you do. That's something we'll have to find out. And hope we survive it. But...slowly, okay? You want to know where I come from? Where

132

the fear comes from? That will take a while. Okay? I don't want to lose you as a partner, either."

And now I was breathing easy. Now I felt like I was breathing pure oxygen. I reached over and simply rested my hand on hers. "We can take all the time you want."

Whatever has hurt you, I didn't say, *we will deal with it.*

With exquisite timing, the waitress delivered our food right then and essentially ended our first official relationship talk. We went back to speculating about the Lifestream Foundation and Malcolm Guth as we ate our burgers and fries, then companionably crossed Second back to the office when we were done.

CHAPTER THIRTY-FIVE

The message light on the main line was blinking away as we settled down on our respective sides of the partners desk. I punched both the speakerphone and voicemail buttons.

The first message was a male voice I didn't recognize, very soft but tight with tension:

"Mr. McCall, Miss Malone. I wanted to tell you that I'm very sorry. I just wanted...." I heard what might have been a very dry chuckle. "Love is a bitch, you know? I thought if he had some trouble, if he knew what it was like...." Long pause. "They were just parties. Not that important...." Another long pause, then the voice came back a little stronger. "I think this is all my fault." Deep breath. "I was wondering if you could...." This time the silence stretched for thirty seconds or more and I was afraid my voicemail would cut him off before he said anything else. I didn't know if there was a limit on the time for messages or not.

Then I heard a very soft, "Oh fuck it," followed by the sound of a receiver being placed gently in its cradle.

Malone and I looked at each other across the desk.

"Good fucking grief," she finally said. "Do you have any idea what that was about?"

I shook my head. "Not a clue. Did you recognize the voice?"

"No. You think it was a crank call?"

Again I shook my head. "I'm afraid not."

She sighed. "Me neither." She gestured at the still-blinking light. "Maybe he called back."

There were three more voicemails, so maybe he had. I punched up the next one. But no, it was from Max Overton. And he was definitely not speaking softly.

"This is all your fault!" he wailed right after identifying himself. "We were all fine before you started nosing around and now Jesse's dead and the police are coming after the rest of us and...!" He couldn't even voice whatever dreaded events might go beyond those. "Just leave us alone!" he shouted after a pause. "Leave me alone!" and hung up with a bang.

The next message was from the Foundation banker, Stanley Nakagawa, a more moderate version of what we'd just heard. He ended by saying, "I know some of the board members are very concerned that you're bringing this trouble with you. *I'm* very concerned about it. This is clearly a police matter now and we would all appreciate it if you terminated whatever business you're involved in and left us in peace. Thank you."

The last was a message from Norman Albright, his resonant voice and careful diction unchanged by the circumstances. "The police were just here," he informed me. "They say that Jesse is dead. Terribly murdered. Please call me. I'm hoping this has nothing to do with your investigation for George. I'd like to be reassured of that at your earliest convenience. I told the detectives nothing about it, of course. Call me. Thank you."

I swiveled my chair around and contemplated the chill March late afternoon beyond the office window, then looked over at Malone who was also checking out the weather. She cocked an eye over at me.

"At least we didn't hear from Petosky or Schilling," she said.

"Maybe Mike hasn't gotten to them yet."

She reached over to her phone set and punched a couple of buttons. "Let's listen to the weird one again."

The soft male voice filled our office again: "Mr. McCall, Miss Malone. I wanted to tell you that I'm very sorry. I just wanted.... Love is a bitch, you know? I thought if he had some trouble, if he knew what it was like.... They were just parties. Not that important.... I think this is all my fault. I was wondering if you could.... Oh fuck it."

She punched it up a third time, I guess just in case it would start to make sense with repetition. Then she sat back and stared out the window again. "Okay," she said, "we have an unidentified male

136

who is sorry about something. Given the timing, most likely Jesse Carter's death. He wanted something, apparently having to do with love—for another man? Carter? He intended to cause this man some trouble to make him 'know what it was like'? He hoped for some result from whatever he intended. That they'd get back together? Maybe. And what the hell about parties? What the fuck does that mean? Maybe whatever he had planned was supposed to be relatively minor, innocent, and it turned out otherwise? Like with a dead guy?" She swiveled her chair back and forth a few times. "Parties.... Parties...." She swiveled around to glare at me. "Beats the hell out of me. Does this idiot message have anything to do with anything?"

I held up my hands. "*If* it does, it's almost certainly about the Lifestream Foundation Board. And," I lowered one hand to point at her, "I can think of one person who may know things about the board we haven't heard yet. All we have to do is catch her away from her mother."

CHAPTER THIRTY-SIX

It took a number of phone calls to track down Crystal Schilling and then she was reluctant to talk with us. However, she finally agreed to a lunch-time meeting the next day, Saturday.

Which was how we found ourselves at the Pizza Panoply, a hole-in-the-wall place near Powell's Books that featured pizza by the slice and a clientele primarily of punks and street kids who could afford no more than that. Dressed as she was in dark purple top, distressed black leather jacket, and faded denim skirt over black tights, Crystal fit right in.

Malone and I, not so much.

My partner was wearing her classic leather jacket and jeans, hair pulled back in a ponytail again, and I my sports coat and chinos, hair thinning as usual, both of us with guns clipped to our belts and the demeanor of someone willing to use them.... It was all going to scream "Cop!" at these kids. Not that many of them would let on that they cared.

One did, I noticed, a young customer who departed hurriedly, pizza slice in hand, as soon as we arrived. Probably grabbing a snack right after a crime. The rest were cool, pretending not to watch us as we picked out our slices—two multi-meat for Malone, a pepperoni with cheese for me, two vegetarian for Crystal—and found a table in the corner.

She took a bite and looked us over appraisingly. "You want to know everything about everybody because Jesse Carter was killed."

"Your guess is pretty good," I answered. "We want to know everything about everybody."

"I ain't telling you anything about my mother."

"Okay. Fair enough. What about the others?"

"I don't give a shit about them." She wiped her mouth with a brown recycled-paper napkin. "What kind of stuff do you want to know?"

"You know any reason somebody would want to kill Carter?" asked Malone.

Crystal's eyes went wide. "Fuck no! He was a nice guy. A little weird, maybe—almost embarrassed, seemed like, to be running around with other people who had lots of money. He was the brainy one, kept real quiet. He's the last person anybody would want to kill."

"Actually it looks like he was first on somebody's list," my partner pointed out.

The younger woman paused, shrugged, and took another bite of pizza.

"I guess."

"How about the others?" I asked.

"Not much to say about Stan or Max. I mean, how exciting can you be if you're a banker or a jeweler? I see 'em come and go but I've never heard anything about either one. Max seems to be pretty tight with Tanya, like they're good buddies, and I don't know what that's about. He's not exactly her type. Maybe she mothers him."

"So tell us about Tanya."

"Now we get to the good stuff. She and Norm Albright are the showboats."

"Showboats?"

"You know: interesting, complicated; there's something to *say* about them."

"Okay. What?"

Pause. Chewing. "You know Norm is gay."

"Yeah, we knew that."

"Well, he's not just swishy. I mean, he's a *flamer*. He's got more guys than, like, a celebrity."

"Really?"

"Sure. He's good looking, stacked with money, and into guys. Why not? It's all expensive restaurants and trips to high-class resorts, you know, nothing creepy. I wish I had some of the guys he's got."

140

I pictured the tall, immaculately groomed gentleman I had visited on Wednesday. It made sense.

"Anything about Jesse Carter being gay?"

"Nah." She popped the last bite of pizza into her mouth and chewed thoughtfully. "Could be, I guess. I never heard about a girlfriend. He and Norm weren't a thing, if that's what you mean."

"Just asking."

Malone jumped in again. "You still haven't told us about Tanya Petosky."

Crystal sat back and grinned. "Tanya," she announced, "is a kick."

"In what way?"

"Oh, she's just very funny—and really friendly, you know? She's much nicer to me than any of the other board members..." Slight grimace. "...including my mom. I'll bet she really liked to party when she was younger. Maybe she still does, for all I know. She's popular; I'll say that."

"Popular how?" my partner inquired around a big bite of pizza, while I thought to myself that the word "party" rang a big bell.

"Lots of people call her up at the Foundation. Seems like I'm transferring a call to her every few minutes when she's there—and she's there a lot."

"Isn't that her job," I asked, "to be the 'public voice' of the Foundation?"

"Yeah, yeah, that's true—but, you know, I don't think that many people are *interested* in the Foundation. Tanya gets a lot more calls than we get contributions; that's for sure."

"Well, who's calling then?"

She shrugged. "Fuck if I know. They don't say."

"You don't ask who's calling?"

She looked surprised. "No, it's not my business."

I thought of suggesting she sign up for receptionist school, but decided it wouldn't help that much. "Are they mostly men?"

That brought a grin. "About half and half." Bigger grin.

141

"Maybe *she* is, too."

All our pizza slices were gone and so, apparently, was Crystal's reservoir of information. I offered her a ride to wherever she was going but she said she would be happy to stay put for a while. We thanked her for her time and took our leave.

"I think we need to talk to Tanya Petosky again," I said as we headed back to my Subaru. "It sounds like she might know a great deal more than she let on."

"Agreed," Malone said as we got settled in the car. "It's Saturday. I'll call the Foundation office and see if she's there. You know where she lives if she isn't?"

"Got it right here," I said and extracted my cheat sheet with the addresses and phone numbers of all the Lifestream Foundation board members from my sports coat side pocket while she made the call.

Malone was listening to her cell but saying nothing, so I assumed she'd hit a recorded message. No surprise, since the Foundation's receptionist was behind us in the pizza place.

She disconnected. "Nobody answering. Which doesn't mean nobody's there, but that's the best bet. You have Petosky's address on that piece of paper?"

"I've got the whole Board on this piece of paper. Petosky lives just off Holgate out near Gresham."

I was about to pull away from the curb when my cell phone buzzed. It was from the Pen and Pastry. I punched it on. "McCall."

I heard what sounded like an indrawn breath from a sob. My adrenaline shot up.

"Clint?" It was Veronica and she did sound very upset. "Something's happened."

"What?"

"LeAnn's friend. The girl named Kristi she told you about? She's been murdered."

CHAPTER THIRTY-SEVEN

I swear my body went numb as though drenched by a tide of ice water. I could feel Malone next to me go on the alert. I must have looked like I'd been shot.

My brain couldn't seem to process what I'd just heard. I looked over at Malone and superimposed on her face was the image of Mal Guth crossing the street in front of my office yesterday, walking away from me, going free.

I struggled to find my voice. "Was it...? What happened?"

"I don't know exactly," Veronica answered. "LeAnn just called. One of Kristi's friends found her dead in her apartment about an hour ago. LeAnn didn't give me many details. She could barely talk. It sounded like Kristi was beaten to death."

"LeAnn's all right?"

"Yes. She said Johnny and Hap were there with her."

"I'd better check in with them," I said. I wanted to get the hell off the phone. "And see what else I can find out."

"Okay. You take care."

"You too."

I disconnected and sat staring out the front windshield. After a moment I realized Malone's hand was gripping my forearm. I looked over at her again.

"What?" she inquired urgently.

"Kristi is dead."

"LeAnn's friend? The one who confronted us on the sidewalk yesterday? Was it Guth?"

"Yes, it's her. I don't know who did it. Veronica thinks she was beaten to death, but she's not sure. LeAnn called her with the news but didn't have any details. She wasn't the one who found the body."

Her grip on my arm tightened. "But she's okay? LeAnn?"

"Johnny and Hap are on the job."

143

Now she was the one staring out the windshield. "We let him walk away."

"I let him walk away."

She turned back to me with a frown. "We were both there. You can't blame yourself. And I don't blame me, either. Much. We didn't have any reason to stop him right then."

I pulled away from her a little bit. "Yeah, we did. There was a patrol car coming down the street, for Christ's sake, and he's wanted for attacking Johnny...." I had to stop for a second to control the surge of regret that was choking me. "I was playing games I didn't need to play. The girl said he was out to kill her. She'd just told us that a minute before! There was every reason in the world...but I let him go."

Now Malone punched with the fist that wasn't gripping my arm. "Stop that. We let him go—and it seemed like a good idea at the time. You know very well that if we'd held him for the patrol car, he'd have been out on the street again in a couple of hours at most." She took a breath. "We didn't know what this girl's story really was. We still don't. Shit, there are all sorts of people who think they're in danger. You can't jump every time somebody asks for protection. We don't even know it was Mal Guth who killed her."

"It's a damned good bet."

"Let it the fuck go. The guilt, I mean. Not the girl's death. We'll get somebody for that. Count on it." One final squeeze and she lifted her hand from my arm.

Meanwhile my emotional paralysis had eased and my brain was working again. "Okay," I said. "Okay. We've got two, maybe three, things. One is to conclude the investigation for George Heatherly. Call me crazy, but I still think our first obligation is to our paying client—especially since we can't be sure he isn't in danger as well."

"Agreed."

"The second is to get Mal Guth off the street."

"Agreed, in spades."

"The third depends on whether the Portland Police Bureau can

144

track down Kristi's real name and her next of kin. If not, we're going to do it. I owe her at least that much."

"We can do that," she said quietly.

I made two more calls while we were still sitting there in the car near the pizza place.

One was to Mike Whitehall. It turned out he wasn't assigned to Kristi's murder but he was of course keenly interested to learn that she'd told me she thought Mal Guth was going to kill her. He promised to pass it on to the detectives who did have the case. If we were all lucky, that right there would take care of our second chore.

He also promised to put in an encouraging word about tracking down her identity and relatives, but wasn't much more optimistic about it happening than I was. If she'd been arrested before, maybe she had some genuine ID on her at the time. Maybe her fingerprints were in the national database. Maybe she had no one who gave a damn.

The second was to Tanya Petosky's home, where I got voicemail just as Malone had at the Foundation office. At which point I drove us back to the office. Even though it was a Saturday, we both decided to go back up there for at least a little while in case anything else developed.

And, it turned out, something had.

CHAPTER THIRTY-EIGHT

The message light on our main line was blinking again and it was George Heatherly urgently requesting that I call him back. We had last talked to him after the shooting at his house...just yesterday morning? It seemed much longer. He'd probably heard by now about Jesse Carter's death and was feeling even more frightened as a result.

Actually it seemed odd to me that almost all the Board members had called before George did. Maybe they had better sources of information. Or even more reason to be worried.

I punched up the speakerphone for Malone's benefit and then the Heatherlys' number.

"McCall! Thank God. We've been dying to hear from you. Why didn't you call before now?" His words were measured but his voice was practically squeaking with tension.

"Take it easy, George. There hasn't been anything new to report...."

"Nothing new? Nothing *new*? One day somebody's shooting at our house and the next day one of the board members is murdered. That sounds like news to me—not very good news, either. Shanna and I are trapped here in the house afraid to go grocery shopping, much less to work. Our lives are at a complete stop! We're even getting crazy crank calls.... Everything's going to shit! Do you think it's the same person? Surely it is. It would be too much coincidence...."

"Calm *down*, George. Take a deep breath and calm down. In the first place, I'm pretty sure whoever took a shot at your house was aiming at us, not you. There are a lot of people, unfortunately, who might want to take a shot at Malone or me...so it's quite possible that shooting isn't related at all to Carter's death. It's also possible Carter's death has nothing to do with this investigation, although...." I exchanged a look with Malone across our partners desk. "Tell us about these crank calls. Devon is here and you're on speaker. What kind of calls?"

"Oh, it was just one call really—this morning. I *guess* it was a crank call. It was very strange. We...."

"What time did you get the call?"

"Mid-morning. Around ten, maybe a little after. Why?"

"Tell me about it."

"All I heard was dead air at first. I said hello a couple of times and was about to hang up when there was this voice, very soft. Just a couple of words, maybe something about parties or...I don't know. I didn't have a chance to ask who it was before they hung up. It could have been kids playing around. I don't know."

"It sounded like a child?"

"I don't *know*. The voice was so soft, I couldn't even tell if it was a male or a female. There were just a couple of words."

"But one of them was 'parties'?"

"Maybe. We're hoping it was a prank. Do you think it means something?"

"I'm not sure. Is there any possibility the caller was your source, the man who has been calling you about your uncle?"

That brought a sharp intake of breath, followed by a long pause.

"Crap! Well, I guess it's possible. He was kind of soft-spoken anyway. It never occurred.... Why would...?"

"I don't know. Not yet. But it gives us some more things to check out."

"So you think...."

"I don't think anything at this moment. Just let us do our job. In the meantime, order in some wine and cheese and enjoy another day off with your wife. Tomorrow's Sunday, anyway."

"I.... Okay, so we'll stay put." There was a note of resignation in his voice, but at least it no longer sounded like it was going to break at any second. "We've already got wine and cheese. We can have some other stuff delivered. What the hell. Why not, right?"

148

We said our goodbyes and I hung up.

Malone was sitting back, contemplating me. "Another mysterious call about parties."

"Yeah," I said. "It has to be the same person. But what the hell does it mean?"

She smiled, a little tightly. "No clue—but that's par for the course in this investigation so far."

I thought about it. "If he's home tomorrow, I say we go see Norman Albright before we visit Tanya again. See if maybe he got any strange calls. Or has any idea who could be calling."

Malone nodded. "Sounds fine to me. I'll be interested to meet him, anyway."

CHAPTER THIRTY-NINE

I spent the evening in the dojang sparring with Carmen and Roger, got up early for a particularly deep meditation, and by seven was scouring the kitchen for appropriate edibles as Maxine and Stella demanded breakfast. I needed to get to the grocery store. Meanwhile we all had to settle for dry cereal (kibble for them, toasted oats for me). I didn't mind, but they were grumpy about it.

While the girls yowled their dissatisfaction in the kitchen, I called Norman Albright from the living room. It was just after eight a.m. on a Sunday, but what the hell. I had places to go and promises to keep; others would have to cope.

Albright, in fact, sounded wide awake and ready to talk. "When can you be here?" he asked as soon as I inquired about another interview.

"How about nine?"

"Or even earlier would be appreciated. I'll be here," he replied and hung up. Very business-like.

I called Malone, who said she'd come by my house, and then finished dressing. She was knocking on my front door by the time I was put together.

Sunday morning is not a busy time for Portland traffic and it took me less than ten minutes driving straight east on Hawthorne to hit the Mt. Tabor neighborhood. Albright wanted earlier? Eight-forty-five should make him happy.

Again the gate in the wrought-iron fence was open and again the black Corvette was parked in the curved driveway. In fact, it was parked precisely as it had been when I was here on Thursday—same spot, same angle. Either Albright had not driven it or he was obsessive about where he put his car.

"Fancy place," Malone commented as we approached the front door, which opened upon her words.

Dressed in blue, well-pressed pants and maroon smoking jacket, every hair of his dark brown pompadour in place, Norman Al-bright looked like he had spent the night preparing for our visit. He looked inquiringly at Malone who stuck out her hand.

"Devon Malone," she said. "Clint's partner in anti-crime."

He smiled slightly at that little sally as he shook her hand. "I'm pleased to meet you," he said.

"I had expected to hear from you before now," he said to me as he showed us in. "You didn't get my message?"

"Yes," I said as we continued into the library. "I got it. I got messages from most of the Board after they heard about Mr. Carter." I settled into the same overstuffed chair I'd occupied on my first visit. Malone took the one next to it.

"Then why didn't you call me?" He remained on his feet in the middle of the room, obviously a man used to people returning his calls posthaste.

"I did call you, just a few minutes ago," I replied coolly and then plunged ahead before he could express further indignation. "Had any other interesting calls lately?"

His irritation faded into puzzlement as he considered my question. "What do you mean? I have many callers...."

"This would be a male," explained Malone, "speaking very softly, saying something was his fault, possibly saying something about parties, hanging up without identifying himself."

Albright's expression was carefully neutral as he lowered himself onto the sofa opposite me. He seemed to be thinking hard—and, given the attention to controlling his face, my guess was that he was working on a really first-class lie.

"Well," he finally said slowly. "That would indeed be memorable...but I'm afraid I've received no such call."

"You're sure," I said.

"Yes, of course. Why?"

"Because we got one at the office—and your nephew George got one."

He exhaled like a balloon deflating, his face and shoulders falling as if they were the balloon itself. "So you do think Jesse's death is related to what you're doing for George."

For the first time he looked to me like a man nearly sixty years old.

"It's a distinct possibility," I said. "What can you tell me about it?"

He raised his hand palm toward me and waved it slowly, lips pursed and head down. "Nothing," he said quietly. "There's nothing I can tell you about it."

"You're sure," Malone said, echoing me.

The hand came down and the head up. I could see he'd made some decision and the energy was coming back, but this was all like watching a film with the sound off. I couldn't tell what the story was.

"Absolutely sure," he said firmly and rose from the couch. "Would either of you care for a drink?" He headed for the liquor cabinet.

I glanced at my watch. Ten after nine. "A little early for me," I allowed.

"Me too," agreed my partner.

"I hope you don't mind if I do," he said as he was pouring a double slug of bourbon.

Malone and I watched him down it, exchanged a shrug, and reached an unspoken agreement that the interview was over. Albright had poured a second shot by the time we reached the library door. He did not offer to show us out.

CHAPTER FORTY

As we left his porch and walked together down the sidewalk toward the car, I momentarily put my hand on Malone's back, just testing out casual touching. The test did not go well.

She stopped abruptly, shook off my hand, directed a glare my way. "Whoa! The whole guy escorting girl with hand on back thing isn't going to cut it. We may end up fucking like bunnies but I'm still me and I'm not going to put up with condescending shit like that."

I just looked at her for a moment, having to work my way past the fucking bunnies before I could even respond. "What? A relationship with no touching?"

She snorted. "Think about it, Clint. Touching is one thing. Acting like I need guidance walking down the sidewalk is another."

"I didn't intend to imply that. I was just...touching. Pardon me all to hell. Has anybody ever mentioned that you're kind of oversensitive in these matters?"

"It's been mentioned. I considered it. Rejected it. Live with it. Now, let's move on."

"Independently."

"You got it."

It occurred to me, not for the first time, that this might turn out to be something like getting intimate with a porcupine.

On the other hand, I now had that whole bunny scenario to contemplate....

Once we were both settled, a little stiffly, in the Subaru I tried Tanya Petosky again.

"Still no answer," I said to Malone as I stashed the cell phone in my jacket pocket.

"We'll track her down. Albright was lying, you know."

"Yeah, he was. He sure as hell knows something about the mysterious caller. Or thinks he does. He shut down tight to try to

155

conceal it but that only made it more obvious."

"Well, now that the tree is shaking maybe something will fall out of it."

"Let's hope so." Deep breath. "I hate to say this, but I think it's time we go talk to LeAnn. Just like Albright, she knows more than she's saying. Maybe we can learn something useful about that situation while we're waiting for Tanya to show up—and I have to face her sometime, extend my regrets about her friend's murder."

"Not your fault."

"I know. I know. Still...."

"It's something that needs doing. Let's go."

CHAPTER FORTY-ONE

LeAnn Hannaford lived in a small complex called Garden Terraces. There are several definitions of "terrace," none of which fit any part of the multi-story beige boxes that bordered the small, trash-littered parking lot just off Killingsworth. No gardens anywhere in sight, either.

LeAnn's apartment was on the third floor of the eastern-most building. Johnny Crew opened the door with Hap Harbaugh looming a few feet behind and off to his right. They both looked ready to pull a gun at any second. I raised my hands. "Just us, guys. Didn't you check through the peephole?"

Johnny stepped forward to glance both ways down the corridor and then made way for me and Malone. "I learned a long time ago not to trust what I could see through them fuckin' things," he rasped. "Too much weird shit goin' on."

"You're right about that," Malone said to him as she surveyed the room.

There was no one else in the small, sparsely furnished living room. There was a small archway leading to a narrow hall and a couple of windows that must have had a fine view of the parking lot. The kitchen, bedroom, bathroom, whatever else, had to be down the hall. Basically a shotgun apartment.

"Where's LeAnn?" I inquired as Johnny bolted the door behind us.

"She's just gettin' dressed I think," replied Hap, indicating the archway.

"Okay," I said. "How are you guys doing?" Johnny seemed steady on his feet but his nose was still showing plenty of discoloration from the encounter with Guth.

"We're fine. It's an easy gig so far," he said in what he probably considered a whisper--only slightly louder than normal speech. "She's a sweet kid."

157

"You bet," agreed his much larger and more unkempt partner. Hap was dressed, if you want to call it that, in his usual worn canvas trousers and baggy short-sleeve shirt, all broadly held together by an ancient set of suspenders.

Johnny, in typical contrast, was wearing a sport coat and tie and looking as if he'd recently arrived from the Justice Center to do interviews.

Just then I heard a familiar—and completely unexpected—laugh from down the hallway. "Colleen's here?" *What the hell was my daughter doing here?*

"Yeah," answered Johnny. "I guess she made friends with LeAnn at the Pen and Pastry. She showed up a couple of hours ago. Said she just wanted to do something to help."

"Huh," I said.

"Hey, Colleen!" Johnny roared, "Your dad's here!" The volume erupting from his small, dapper form was unbelievable. If anyone else in the apartment complex was named Colleen, she was probably be looking around for her father right then.

Moments later my own daughter abruptly appeared in the archway. She repositioned the glasses that had slipped down her nose, surveyed the room, and glared at the smaller of my two old mentors. "My God, Johnny, you scared the shit out of me."

"Sorry," Johnny muttered. Even his mutter was loud.

My daughter is twenty-four years old, a drama major (in more ways than one) at Portland State University. She was currently wearing her usual granny glasses and well-worn sweatshirt with faded jeans, punk-cut blond hair capping her head.

"What the hell are you doing here?" I inquired.

She transferred her always intense gaze from Johnny to me. "Dad. How are you today?"

"I'm fine. What the hell are you doing here?"

"I'm visiting a friend."

"Johnny? Hap?"

"No. LeAnn."

158

"Since when is LeAnn a friend of yours?"

"Since we got to know each other at the Pen and Pastry. She works there, you know. I hang out there. We've become friends and I came over to see if I could help out."

"Help out how?"

Before she had a chance to respond I felt a familiar punch on my arm.

"How about we postpone this father-daughter interrogation to another time?" Malone asked dryly. "We came to talk to LeAnn. She is here somewhere, right?" That last was directed at Colleen.

At which point the young woman in question appeared just behind my daughter and I didn't feel so fine anymore. Without saying a word, LeAnn Hannaford pushed past Colleen and took one step toward me, focused as if there were no one in the room but the two of us.

Her drab brown hair was still wet from the shower, plastered in tangled strings to the sides of her pallid face. There were dark circles under her hazel eyes and her wide mouth was grimly downturned. She hadn't even finished dressing. She did have on a skirt, but it was skewed sideways, the side zipper on the front of her left hip. Otherwise she was barefoot and holding together a flimsy dressing gown that veiled her small breasts no more than it did that zipper.

She stood there for a moment, taking me in like I was some giant, repulsive bug. Her voice, when she finally spoke, was fiercely accusing:

"You said you'd help her."

CHAPTER FORTY-TWO

Colleen reached forward as if to take LeAnn's arm, but then held back.

"I'm sorry that you lost your friend," I said.

LeAnn pulled herself up absolutely straight. "Fuck your sorry," she replied scornfully.

At that my daughter uncoiled around her to the left, turning as she moved to face my accuser. "My father would never...."

"Colleen!" I interrupted.

She looked back at me, mouth set in grim defense even as a tear trailed down from behind her glasses. I never loved her so much as at that moment.

"Let it be," I said quietly. "LeAnn is entitled to whatever she feels."

The young woman looked from me to Colleen and back again, then turned her face down onto Colleen's shoulder. "Fuck," she sobbed, "oh fuck it all."

My daughter wrapped her other arm around her friend and held her tight as the rest of us formed a tableau around them.

The silence was punctuated only by LeAnn's sobs until Hap spoke up with forced joviality. I have to hand it to him: even in the midst of emotional duress, the big man maintained his agenda. "Maybe we could all go out to breakfast," he offered.

It was just silly enough to draw a few smiles. The tension went out of the room with an almost audible whoosh. Even LeAnn raised her head to look at him, eyebrows up in astonishment if not amusement.

Colleen took off her glasses and used the sleeve of her sweatshirt to clean them. "We were just talking about putting something together, Hap," she said as she put them back on. "Bacon and eggs sound good to you?"

"Great," he answered sincerely.

She gave him a little smile. "Scrambled?"

"Don't care."

She donned the glasses, eyed LeAnn and nodded her head decisively. "I'll go get it started," she announced, and disappeared down the hallway.

LeAnn watched her go and then turned back to us. "I need to finish getting dressed," she said softly. She followed after Colleen.

"She's a nice kid," Johnny said.

A nice kid who is withholding information and probably hates my guts, I thought to myself.

"I'm going to see how Colleen's doing," I said out loud.

I followed the sound and smell of sizzling bacon to the end of the hall where I found a small but cozy kitchen. Colleen was not so much scrambling the eggs as making sure they were dead, the large bowl clutched against her stomach and the whisk churning madly.

"Hey," I said as I paused in the doorway.

She eased up on the whisk and took a deep breath. "Hey, Pops."

"You okay?"

"Yeah, I'm fine." She set the bowl on the laminate counter top. "You staying for breakfast?"

"No, I've got to go talk to some people."

She motioned for me to come closer. "Before you go," she said softly but urgently, "I want to tell you something."

We huddled next to the counter, her eyes darting to the open doorway over my shoulder.

"What's up?" I asked.

"I've been here a couple of hours," she said. "I woke up this morning feeling like I ought to do something, you know? She's having a tough time."

"That's true."

"Anyway, I just came over to visit, see if I could help out—at least say hello to Johnny and Hap. I figured they must be going stir crazy."

162

"Uh huh."

She leaned in even closer to me. "LeAnn started to share something with me but didn't quite get it out."

"What?"

"It sounded like this Guth guy has something on her."

"Did she say what?"

"No, all she said was that she's not afraid Guth will kill her. What she's afraid of is that he'll get her put in prison if she doesn't go back to him."

We both glanced back at the doorway while I processed that one. "You sure? He just killed her friend—pretty certain he did anyway—and she's not worried he'll kill her?"

"I'm sure. She's worried about going to prison."

"That's very odd. Also interesting."

"I promised her I wouldn't tell you." She took a long look at the doorway this time. "I hope she'll forgive me. And that it wasn't too bad." She looked at me, her face carefully neutral. "Whatever she did."

I gave my daughter a quick hug. "Whatever she thinks Guth has, if he's the only one to testify against her it might not make much difference. No court would believe him. Let me find out what's going on and then we'll see."

"Okay."

I left her to rescue the bacon and finish the eggs. We weren't staying for breakfast, lunch, whatever it was, even though Malone would probably be disappointed.

The door to the bedroom was still closed and I could hear sobs from within as I passed it. I'd try to talk to LeAnn again later, when she was less upset and it wouldn't be so obvious where the new information had come from. Maybe I'd ask Malone to do it, in fact. Right now I was going to give Tanya Petosky another try.

I rejoined the other three in the living room and punched in Tanya's number again. This time she answered, sounding harried.

I identified myself and immediately announced that we needed

163

to come over and talk with her. I wanted to get the demand in ahead of her saying she was too busy or stressed out or whatever was going on. I needn't have worried.

"McCall!" she gasped with an undertone of amusement in her strong contralto voice. "Your timing couldn't be better! By all means, come on over and join the party. I've already got cops here and paramedics have been called."

"What's happened?" I asked in surprise. "Are you okay?"

"I'm fine," she replied. "It's Max. Max Overton. Our treasurer? He showed up at my door fifteen minutes ago, bleeding and in a panic. He's been shot—not bad, just a nick on his left arm, but he's in a state I'll tell you. Maybe you and your partner can help us settle him down."

"We're on our way."

CHAPTER FORTY-THREE

The quickest route was to hop onto Interstate 5 heading south and then take I-84 east to the 122nd exit. It was nearly noon and traffic was heavy with weekenders headed out to whatever adventures they had planned. Off the freeway, I went south on 122nd to Holgate and turned left.

Tanya Petosky's ranch-style house, while substantial, was a more modest abode than that of most of her fellow board members. On the other hand, even if there hadn't been several police and emergency vehicles in front, it would have stood out from the other upper-middle-class homes on the cul-de-sac at the end of Holgate. It was painted a ripe pink with glossy white trim, looking like a child's birthday cake.

In addition to two patrol cars and the paramedics van, I recognized Mike Whitehall's unmarked car. We had to stop meeting like this.

A patrolman in a freshly pressed uniform waved us through the door after we identified ourselves. Apparently Mike had learned we were on the way and left word that we could come in. The earnest young fellow informed us that Detective Whitehall was in the back bedroom with the victim and pointed down a corridor leading from the spacious living room.

I could hear which room it was long before we got there. Max Overton's voice dominated, very loud and whiny rather than soft and whiny as it had been in his jewelry store. He was interrupted occasionally by the professionally calming voices of—I supposed—the paramedics. They seemed to be having no success at the calming part.

I almost laughed when I got to the open doorway. There were four men in what had to be the most girly bedroom I'd ever seen: pink and white just like the exterior of the house, with satin bedding lavishly trimmed with lace, ditto the lampshades and curtains, a large collection of colorful dolls on shelves against one wall. Just a moment behind me, Malone did laugh out loud.

Max Overton was perched in a nest of pink towels on the shiny bed looking about as out of place as a man could. There was a bloody dress shirt on the floor, arranged carefully so that it wouldn't stain the plush carpet. I guessed that was Tanya's doing rather than the paramedics.

Overton had on a thin white undershirt that highlighted the heavy gold chain around his scrawny neck. He was holding his wire-rimmed glasses in his right hand, left upper arm bandaged, eyes even more protruding and watery than usual, face flushed. Confronted as he was by three much larger men, he looked down-right diminutive, his bald head shining like another pink bedroom decoration.

The two paramedics, one black and the other Hispanic, were standing in almost identical postures of frustration, feet apart and arms akimbo, looking down at the little jeweler. Whitehall was off to the side, observing it all with a half-smile. He saw me and nod-ded a hello.

"I tell you I won't go!" Overton was huffing. "You can't make me go!"

The paramedics looked at each other and then, together, over at Whitehall. "You going to back us up on this, Mike?" inquired the Hispanic guy. "All shootings are supposed to be transported."

Whitehall shook his head. "I'm not going to make him go un-less his life's in danger. It looks to me like a superficial wound. If that's true, it's his choice."

The black guy let out a big sigh and they turned to finish putting away their equipment. "Okay, okay," he muttered as he closed his box of gear. "It is superficial, so we're done here. Means a hell of a lot more paperwork when we get back, though."

"Hospitals," Overton announced to no one in particular, "are death traps. You go in with a 'superficial wound' and come out with a fatal infection. No way am I going to one of those places."

166

No one bothered to reply and a moment later the paramedics brushed past me with grim expressions.

Whitehall moved over to where Malone and I were standing. "I heard you'd be dropping by," he said.

Overton apparently registered our presence just inside the doorway for the first time. He focused on me, of course, with no way to know who Malone was. "You! This is all your fault!" He turned to Whitehall while pointing his glasses in my direction. "I want this man arrested for inciting someone to shoot me!"

CHAPTER FORTY-FOUR

Having already lost the smile now that he had the floor again, Mike heroically kept a straight face at this request. He ran a hand over his short brown hair as he considered. "Ookay," he said slowly. "Why don't you stay put while I ask him a few questions? After I have him in custody—or whatever—I've got some more questions for you."

"Don't let him get away," cautioned Overton as Mike motioned for me and Malone to step back into the hallway and followed right behind us.

We found Tanya Petosky standing just outside the room with a large drinking glass in her hand. She was relatively dressed down for her Sunday morning at home, with simple but expensive brown pants and cream-colored blouse set off by a heavy gold chain and bangle earrings. Her thick, dark hair was loosely held back with a gilded barrette.

"Ms. Petosky," Malone said, "I wondered where you were."

"I was getting a drink for Max," Tanya said to her, "but I didn't want to bring it in until the paramedics were gone." She shifted to a mock whisper: "They might not approve." She gently swished the light amber liquid in the full glass. Looked like brandy to me. A lot of brandy.

"You have to forgive him for making such a scene about the hospital," she went on, focusing on Mike this time. "He hates hospitals, just hates them—and, of course, he's incredibly upset. You understand." Apparently he didn't need to be forgiven for trying to get me arrested.

"Of course," Mike said.

She swept into the bedroom bearing brandy and solace for her wounded friend.

Whitehall, Malone, and I moved a little further down the hall to ensure we wouldn't be overheard.

"You going to arrest me, too?" inquired Malone as we came to a stop.

"No, but I'm wondering," Mike smiled a little grimly as he leaned back against a wall, "if maybe the guy doesn't have a point. So far you two don't seem to be having a positive impact on the Lifestream Foundation board."

"I'm not willing to concede that," I said. "All we're doing is asking a few questions—and not getting any good answers. We don't have a clue what's going on...do we?" I directed that last question at Malone in case she'd had some inspiration since we last spoke.

She shook her head. "I'm not even sure it's related to our investigation. We could be innocent bystanders. We certainly haven't learned about anything that would warrant people getting shot."

"That we know of," I added.

The smile faded as Whitehall closely examined our faces. "Unrelated to your investigation? Maybe. Stranger things have happened," he said finally. "But I wouldn't bet on it and I don't think you would, either. You will let me know if you get onto anything, right?"

"Absolutely," I said.

He nodded. "Now, what's the story on this Overton character? Seems like a real nutcase."

"*That* I can agree with," I said. "He owns a jewelry store downtown and serves as the treasurer of the Foundation board. My guess is that he's neurotic about a lot of things besides hospitals. He's pissed at me, obviously. There's not much more I can tell you."

Mike looked at Malone, who shrugged. "Just met him for the first time," she said. "I've got nothing."

"Well, somebody has it in for this board all of a sudden. I'll see what I can get out of him." Mike's mouth curved back into a slight smile. "At least I have a good lever. If he won't talk, I'll make him go to the hospital after all."

"That should do it," I agreed.

"I'd better get in there before he's downed all that booze. See

170

you later."

I put a hand against the opposite corridor wall to block his path. "Anything on Guth?"

"Not yet."

I dropped the hand. "Okay. Later."

He joined Tanya Petosky in the bedroom and, within moments, she'd been banished back into the hallway. Always interrogate your subjects one at a time

CHAPTER FORTY-FIVE

She bustled between Malone and me and took both our arms, barely pausing as she led us toward the living room. Suddenly it wasn't clear which of us was planning to interview the other.

Worse yet, Orville and Wilbur, the Chihuahua brothers, already had the room. They were yipping and seizing around our legs the moment we crossed the threshold, eyes bulging and tongues protruding. I had no idea until now how irritating I found the breed.

Petosky shooed them across the room with a high-pitched admonition to behave themselves and, remarkably, they settled into a pair of dog beds on the far side. Well, not exactly settled. Vibrated in the same spot, more like.

"Sorry about that. Let's make ourselves comfortable," she said as she returned to us. "Do either of you want anything to drink? Coffee?"

We both declined, so we all proceeded straight to the largest of three couches stationed around the big front room. The décor in here was much less frilly, tending toward leather and earth colors. Besides the couches, there were two loveseats and a set of four comfortable-looking chairs. The walls were hung tastefully with reproductions (I assumed) of Picasso, Dali, and others I couldn't identify. One end of the room was dominated by an entertainment center that did not include a television. There were speakers mounted on all four walls. It was a space longing to be filled by witty conversationalists and music lovers.

Alas, our hostess had only me, Devon Malone, the dogs, and the smartly groomed young cop still manning the front door.

I sat down at one end of the couch and watched Tanya Petosky arrange herself carefully near the other end. Malone scooted the nearest chair a little closer and sat down across and at a slight angle from us.

Tanya settled herself just so, hands in lap, legs crossed with no wrinkles in the slacks. Maybe the beauty was going with age, but she seemed determined that the elegance would not.

"These are interesting times," she said to me.

"In what way?" I asked.

She smiled grimly. "The old Chinese curse, you know: 'May you live in interesting times.' And here we are. Jesse is dead. Someone tried to kill Max. We're all being investigated by the police and at least two private detectives. And someone's shooting at you, too. Suddenly the Lifestream Foundation is in the middle of very interesting times."

"Did Mr. Overton tell you what happened?" asked Malone. "Where did the shooting occur?"

"He wasn't making much sense when he got here. Wherever he was, he didn't see where the bullet came from; that much was clear. I guess he ran for his car and came straight over here. I called the police for him."

"You two must be pretty good friends."

The smile she directed at Malone was warmer this time, with a hint of irony at the corners. "Max is...not socially adept. I don't mind it, don't judge him the way some people do. He values that and usually comes to me when he's upset or in trouble."

"Which is not quite the same thing as being good friends."

The slightest of shrugs. "No."

I chimed in. "How about you? Anybody threatened you lately? Mysterious phone calls? Anything like that?"

She shook her head. "No, nothing. Is that why you called? You expect them to come after me, too?"

"Them?"

"Whoever."

"We don't know, Ms. Petosky...."

"Call me Tanya, please." She gestured graciously to Malone. "Both of you, of course."

"Okay, Tanya," I went on, "I don't know whether you're in any danger or not, but I think it would be reasonable to take some pre-

174

cautions until we find the attacker."

"Crystal Schilling says you're quite the partier," Malone announced.

That brought a long, boisterous laugh, with Tanya's head thrown back, the Russian peasant stock exploding through the elegant veneer.

"Crystal," she gasped through ongoing chuckles, "Crystal can tell you about partying all right. If her mother only knew!"

Malone pressed on. "Norman Albright ever come to your parties?"

Petosky rolled right with it, a woman not easily caught off guard. She took a moment to catch her breath, the chuckles easing into a wide grin, her eyes examining Malone's face closely. It seemed to me that the eyes were not amused. It also occurred to me that, given the recent weird phone calls, it was interesting that we were talking about parties. I felt pretty sure that wasn't lost on my partner, either.

"Certainly," our hostess responded. "I usually invite all the board members to my parties. They don't all come. Barbara never does. Norman, though, he's always here."

"Does he bring a date?"

"Sometimes."

"Do you know of any trouble he's had with any of his dates?"

I could see her relaxing again. Obviously we weren't going where she thought we might be. I wished I knew where that was.

She shook her head, emphatically this time. "No. Norm's a charming man and he always brings other charming men. Don't tell me you're thinking one of his lovers is out to get the rest of us."

"Just poking around."

That brought another hoot. "Believe me, that is something Norman does *not* do. He's very selective and discreet."

We got no further. It was like interviewing an extremely pleasant and gracious padded wall, all the impacts absorbed with little bouncing back. At least I can say she probably found us about as

175

helpful.

Whitehall and Overton were still in the back bedroom when I ran out of questions and patience. This was obviously not the time to try to talk to the jeweler, so we wished Tanya Petosky and the watchful young patrol officer a good day.

CHAPTER FORTY-SIX

The day, which earlier had been chilly and clear, was now turning colder and wet. A light rain was falling and the trees seemed to shiver in the wind.

"You know," offered Malone after we'd settled in the car and I'd turned the heat up, "for your above-average charitably inclined citizens, these board members are awfully good at lying and evasion."

"Speaking of lying and evasion, I haven't had a chance to tell you what I learned from Colleen at LeAnn's apartment."

"Hah. I thought you had that look when you came back into the living room. Spill."

"According to Colleen, Guth has something on LeAnn. She isn't afraid he'll kill her. She's afraid he can send her to prison."

"And she knows this...."

"Because LeAnn shared it with her, confidentially of course. Colleen wasn't supposed to pass it on."

"Hmm. If Guth killed LeAnn's friend Kristi, why wouldn't he kill LeAnn? You think she was telling Colleen the truth?"

"I don't know. I'd sure like to discuss it with Guth."

"I'd like to discuss it with LeAnn."

I watched the rain running down the windshield for a moment. "Can you think of anything else we can do right this minute on the Heatherly case?"

"Other than continuing to stir the pot? No."

"Then I'm going to call Reuben again. Maybe he's got a lead on Guth's whereabouts by now."

Malone grunted. "That's the great thing about having two cases that are going nowhere: there's always another dead end to pursue."

I punched in his number and he answered with a growled "yeah."

"Reuben? This is Clint McCall."

"McCall?" His voice was up half-an-octave, still raspy. "I'm sorry, but I can't help you, man."

"You don't have anything new on Guth?" I asked, wondering why he sounded a little distressed.

"Nothin'. I got nothin'. I don't want to be in the middle of stuff like this."

Now it sounded like he was holding the phone away from his mouth as if to avoid contamination. This was getting very strange even for Reuben. I exchanged a glance with Malone. "What's going on with you, Reuben? What stuff?"

"Contract stuff. You know. A hit. Word on the street is, you dead."

I sometimes have trouble with Reuben's tenses. "Already dead or just dead pretty soon?" I asked by way of clarification.

"Right up against it, my man, from what I hear."

"Interesting. And do we know to whom I owe my impending demise?"

"What the fuck?"

"Who's supposed to kill me, Reuben?"

"Oh. Whoever takes the contract. Like usual, you know."

I was beginning to lose patience. "And who is paying the goddamned contract?"

"Mal Guth."

Surprise, surprise.

"You ain't even heard about all this?" Reuben asked incredulously.

"Afraid not."

"Then you are one lucky motherfucker. You gotta start watchin' your back, man. Big time."

"Thanks for the advice. You heard anything about why he's put out the word on me?"

"I don't know. That dude is fucked up."

And I had him, out on the sidewalk in front of our office, with a patrol car approaching, and I let him walk away. Now Kristi is

178

dead and I've got a contract on my head.

"McCall?"

I tried to kick-start my brain again. "How long has this contract been out there?" I noticed Malone perk up at the word "contract."

"Brand new today."

"You sure?"

"'Course I'm sure. I'm in the traffic, man."

Then this did not explain the ambush at George Heatherly's on Friday. That was someone else, not the brand new hit man or men or, what the hell, women. Life was just getting better—and harder to follow—every hour.

"Okay. You being in the traffic and all, have you learned anything about where I can find Guth?"

"Maybe."

Well, that was good news. "You want to share?"

"Okay—but you didn't get it from me. There's a house on Fairlawn a couple blocks off King his girls just started using for private time with the johns. That's what I heard, anyway. It would be a good place for him to hole up since most people don't know about it yet. But, McCall, you get killed for sure you show up there. Not the best 'hood for white private cops, you know what I mean."

Nevertheless he went on to give me a description of the house and its location. "I appreciate the information," I said, "and the advice. I'll take the information."

"Play it your way, McCall. You always do."

"One other question. The girl Guth was looking for. You hear anything about her being in trouble besides that? Something Guth might have on her that could send her to jail?"

"Nah, I ain't heard nothin' 'cept about him."

"Okay. Take it easy."

We disconnected and I turned to Malone, who was giving me her best glare.

"So," she said. "Who wants to kill us now?"

179

CHAPTER FORTY-SEVEN

The air from the car heater was warming up and the rain was coming down much harder, a downpour with aspirations to become a deluge.

"Actually, the contract is just on me, according to Reuben. Guth, naturally."

Her lips formed a little moue. "I'm offended."

Mine formed a little smile, despite the seriousness of the situation. "I'm not surprised."

"Well," she said, "no question now which case has the higher priority. We need to get Malcolm Guth before he gets you. And, am I to understand we might know where he is?"

"We might," I replied as I started the car and got the windshield wipers going.

It was going to be another long trip, from the east end of Holgate to the north end of Martin Luther King Boulevard, but I stuck to surface streets anyway. You can pretty much count on at least one fatal accident on a Portland metro freeway every time there's a big storm. The way things had been going for me lately, I thought I should be especially careful. Wouldn't do to get accidentally killed by a stranger before all the people who intended to kill me had their chance.

I took 82nd to Burnside, then east to MLK and turned north. We must have passed fifty fast food places on the way, but Malone didn't say a word about being hungry—a sure sign that she considered the situation really serious.

I slowed to a crawl as I turned onto Fairlawn, or it might be more accurate to say "to a drift" since the Outback was moving through water up to the hubcaps. The sewers were apparently not very efficient in this neighborhood.

As Reuben had said, the house was the third on the left: green clapboard faded almost to gray, the color even more washed out by the overcast and heavy rain. The yard was all dirt (now muddy swamp), with a huge ancient willow drooping down to conceal the roof and windows opaque with filth. Had it been an illustration in a children's book, it would have been where the evil gnome lived.

I drove a half-block further and pulled over to the curb. We sat for a moment checking out the street. Reuben's warning had been unnecessary. There was no one out in this storm to see that a couple of white private detectives had appeared in the neighborhood.

"You're going to get very wet," I announced. I shrugged off my sport coat and reached back to the rear seat for the waterproof hooded parka that I stored there during the fall and winter. It should keep me dry, warm, and anonymous as I approached the house. Malone didn't even have a hood on her jacket.

"I've been wet before," she said with an eyebrow cocked in my direction. "I'm not a weather wimp."

Ignoring her implied insult, I unclipped my belt-holster from the small of my back and moved it to a spot just beneath where the right-hand pocket of the garment would be. The lining of that pocket was cut out to provide access to the Smith and Wesson. I wriggled into the parka and zipped it up, then dropped my cell phone into the left pocket and pulled the hood over my head.

My partner snorted. "You sufficiently protected now? Want to spray some waterproofing on your face?"

"No," I said. "I'm fine now. You'll regret your sarcasm when that cold rain has soaked your hair and is running down your back."

"Wimp."

I opened the door and looked down at the urban river coursing by just below my floorboard. Too bad I hadn't put some galoshes in the back of the rig. Crap. I was going to be cold and clammy right along with Malone, at least up to my knees.

We bailed out of the car, forded the street, and headed down the sidewalk toward the house.

We hadn't taken more than a few squishy steps in that direction when a blue Honda Civic pulled to a hesitant stop right in front of our destination. I could make out two people in the front seat and I put a hand on Malone's arm to slow our already casual pace, hoping the two new arrivals would move on before we got there.

Instead, the driver and passenger doors popped open and the two got out. Neither had rain gear or umbrella. The passenger was a pasty young woman protected from the elements only by a minidress and thin denim jacket. The driver was a paunchy middle-aged balding guy wearing an overcoat. Not too difficult to guess what they were doing here, though I was somewhat surprised that they'd managed to hook up (as it were) in this weather. The girl must have been really desperate to go trolling on a Sunday afternoon in a gully-washer. Ditto her customer.

She came around the car and urged her companion into a dash for the front door. Of a single mind, Malone and I covered the remaining distance down the sidewalk and dashed just a few feet behind them. Strangers are coming and going at a house like this all the time. I didn't expect us to be questioned and we weren't. The girl actually held the door open for us, said hello, and went on with the business of showing her client to a bedroom. He kept his face turned away.

I pushed my hood back and let the surroundings sink in. The damp and chilly house smelled of mold, lust and cigarette smoke. The incoming daylight, already overcast and heavily filtered by the dirty windows, revealed cracked linoleum and peeling wallpaper. We were standing in a small room with two ratty armchairs and a card table; a hallway directly ahead led to the rest of the house where the other two had already disappeared. The house was silent except for what sounded like a cartoon playing at the far end of the hall. I was glad it was cold, since I intended to keep my hands in my pockets until I found out who was watching those cartoons.

"I love what they've done with the place," Malone muttered dryly.

From where we were standing, I could see three closed and one open door along the hallway. The girl and her client were behind the second closed door on the left. The open door was furthest down on the right and seemed to be the source of the soundtrack.

183

The hallway didn't dead end there, though; at that point it appeared to angle left to parts unknown. We'd have to keep our eyes on that.

Without another word, we moved down the corridor quickly but quietly and stopped just short of the open doorway.

The Smith and Wesson firmly in hand under my parka, I peeked around the edge of the doorframe. Malcolm Guth was sitting in an old overstuffed chair turned three-quarters away from me. He was leaning forward over a small, rickety folding table that held a half-eaten frozen dinner. He was chewing thoughtfully, fork paused halfway between mouth and tray, as he stared intently with a slight frown at the Bugs Bunny cartoon unfolding on the screen. He appeared to be having trouble understanding it.

I stepped back and gestured for Malone to take a look while I checked around the corner to our left. Another hallway with closed doors. No one in sight. I then moved forward again to look over her shoulder into the room.

Guth swallowed audibly and picked up a bottle of beer with his left hand. The fork in the right hand continued to hang out in mid-air as he tilted his head back to take a deep gulp, his eyes never leaving the screen. Didn't want to miss a vital plot point, I guess.

There was no weapon in sight and he was wearing a simple sweat suit that probably didn't conceal one, so it seemed like a good time to step in and say hello.

I nudged Malone again and we both stepped through the doorway. "Hello," I said.

A satisfying spray of beer hit the TV and a fork clattered on the floor as he jerked around in our direction.

"Motherfu...!" The obscenity was interrupted by a choking fit. Apparently not all the beer had escaped.

His thin, sharply etched features were suffused with crimson by the time he recovered and eased back in the chair, head turned to glower at the two of us. He rested his elbows on the arms of the chair, palms up and fingers splayed. He knew why my right hand was still in my pocket and he couldn't miss that Malone's was on her gun as well.

"We're here to see about canceling a contract," I said. "I wouldn't mind canceling you at the same time, so just be very still."

The scowl didn't waver. "I don't know what you're talkin' about, McCall."

I retrieved my cell phone with my left hand and thumbed it on. "And I don't have time for your bullshit, Guth. Tell it to the cops."

His head turned even further in our direction and I knew the second his eyes focused between and past us that we were in trouble.

CHAPTER FORTY-EIGHT

Guth wasn't nearly talented enough to fake the attempt to conceal his surprise, so I knew someone was behind us. My hand inside the parka tensed on my weapon as torrents of adrenaline flooded my system. In my peripheral vision I could see Malone registering the danger.

"Freeze. Drop the phone, motherfucker." It was a young voice, just a couple of feet behind us, a little tremolo undercutting the fierce delivery. Which was too bad: you'd need unadulterated fierceness to get away with a line like that even if it didn't contain an obvious contradiction.

"Which?" I asked while holding myself otherwise absolutely still.

"What? Which what?"

"Do you want me to freeze or to drop the phone? For that matter, what do you want her to do?" Malone snorted very softly.

"Uhhh, fuck. Drop the fucking phone and both of you freeze. You think I'm stupid?"

Considering the very good odds that the guy had a gun, I chose not answer that question. If he did, and his trigger finger was as shaky as his voice, it would be wise not to provoke him further. I dropped the phone—and heard it shatter on the floor. Must be concrete underneath that linoleum.

"Get on in the room," he said. "Both of you." Still ambivalent about the freezing part, apparently.

We stepped further into the room, as instructed. I noted that Guth was staying put and not looking a great deal more comfortable than I was feeling.

He was keeping his eyes fixed on the party-crasher. "What are you doing here, kid?" he asked carefully as I edged to my left and turned slightly to look back over my shoulder. Malone was mirroring me to her right.

It was a kid indeed, a shrimpy little white guy who didn't look a day over sixteen. Greasy hair hanging down over his ears, acne covering his forehead, tatty black leather jacket over threadbare sweatshirt and jeans. He was holding a pistol that looked older than he did; I could actually see some rust on the side of the barrel. His wide, glistening eyes were jumping from Malone to me to Guth, apparently not even registering that Malone and I both still had one hand in a pocket. He seemed to be either drooling or dripping snot, maybe both. I got the impression he wasn't in any shape to notice much.

He did finally acknowledge the question. "I came to talk to a guy named Guth," he said to Guth. "Who the fuck are you?"

"I'm Guth."

"Oh, okay. And who are these fuckers?"

"McCall and Malone," Guth responded with a growl.

"Private cops."

The young man paled and his eyes grew even wider as he stared at me. "No *shit*. Fuck me! Is that the guy I'm supposed to kill? You gonna kill him yourself now? I need that money, dude!"

Dude?

I exchanged a glance with Malone whose eyebrows were up near her hairline. This snot-nosed kid was going to need a lot of luck to walk out of here alive.

Guth's face, meanwhile, was a mask of incomprehension. "You're here about the contract?"

Our newest arrival was standing stiff-legged and had started shifting his weight back and forth as if he were on some kind of skateboard. Maybe, in his universe, he was. Again his response was very slow: "Yeah, sure."

Guth's attention went back to the pistol in the kid's hand. "What is that for if you didn't know McCall was here?"

"I heard this guy say he was gonna call the cops. I didn't know what was going on. I pulled the gun just in case. What the fuck *is* going on?"

188

"We was havin' a talk," Guth said.

The kid was looking more confused and angry all the time. The room was awash in bewilderment. And the motion of his body was faster now, almost a jerk. "Shit. You friends now? You don't want him dead after all?"

Guth scowled and slowly leaned forward. "Listen, dumb fuck. We ain't friends. I want him dead—and her, too, now I think about it. But not *here*. Not *now*. Not while I'm sittin' here watchin' the whole thing! I put out the word so the cops couldn't pull me into it. I get their blood spatter on me, that kind of defeats the purpose. You fucking *understand?*"

"Hey," Malone interjected, "you could have picked a better time to start including me."

Guth sneered at her. Meanwhile, the kid's face was progressively flushing bright red, an artery pulsing visibly in his neck. In addition to being young, stupid, high, and otherwise uncoordinated, he obviously had a very bad temper.

The gun was moving back and forth among the three of us as fast as his weight was moving from foot to foot. "You got no cause to call me names, to insult me! I come here to tell you I'm your man and you...disrespect me? Fuck you! Fuck all of you!" He was screeching now. "What am I supposed to do now, goddamn it? Just walk away? I don't think so! I got him right here where you can see I got him. I don't need to prove it was me did it. You can see!"

He was going to completely lose it and shoot all of us in a minute.

Guth was tensing and I could see Malone's hand moving in her pocket. I was easing my own gun out of its holster. Amazingly, the stupid punk still didn't see that we each had one hand out of sight. My hope was that Guth would distract the kid, thinking we were going to shoot him; no doubt that's what he would have done in our position.

And maybe we would have to shoot the youngster, damn it. It would depend on how it all came down.

Even as I was getting a better grip on my gun, I was inching my left foot around and relaxing my knees ready to drop into a kicking stance.

The kid sensed the shift in my body and focused his attention on me. Guth chose that moment to use the simplest approach possible: "Hey dumb fuck!" he boomed. "Look at me!"

The kid looked at him.

I brought a roundhouse kick up from the floor that struck the pistol just as it twitched back in my direction. It went off, a deafening bang in the small room, and I was showered with plaster from the ceiling as I watched the weapon sail back over the kid's shoulder. He twisted around, making a futile grab to catch it, and then screamed in anger and frustration as Malone stepped up behind him, clamped one arm under his chin, and jammed the barrel of her Glock into the side of his head.

"Settle down or die," she said.

He settled down.

I saw then that Guth was no longer in his chair and I remembered I'd caught a flash of motion toward the door as I was focused on the kid and Malone. Crap.

"You got him?" I asked Malone.

"I've got him."

I spun around and took off down the hall in the direction Guth had disappeared.

"Disappeared" turned out to be the operative word. There was no sign of him in the front room or on the street outside the house. Ditto around back. The skinny little bastard could scamper.

I hurried back into the house to find the young woman who'd held the front door for me peeking out the door of her bedroom. She had wrapped an old bathrobe around herself and looked remarkably calm for someone who'd just heard a gunshot in a nearby room.

She held her ground when she saw me coming. "What's happening?" she asked. "You a cop?"

It could have been my quiet air of authority but more likely it was the gun still in my hand. "Private," I answered. I holstered the weapon.

Behind her in the bedroom I could see her paunchy customer desperately hopping around, trying to get his pants zipped. He was muttering to himself, a steady drone, "Gotta get out of here. Gotta get out of here."

"Was that Mal got shot?" the woman asked me.

"Nobody got shot," I said. "Just a bullet in the ceiling."

She looked disappointed. "Oh."

I glanced down the hall, beginning to feel some urgency to make sure Malone still had everything under control. "Get some clothes on," I said, "and get your client out of here before Portland PD shows up."

She shrugged. "They ain't comin'. Not for one gunshot in this neighborhood, not 'less somebody's dead."

I headed down the corridor, talking back over my shoulder. "That may be true, but I'm about to give them a call if my partner hasn't already. They'll come—and you probably want to be gone when they get here. I know your customer does."

"Yeah, okay," she said with a sigh and turned back to the room.

When I got back to the scene of the action the kid was sitting on the floor glaring at Malone with beady-eyed hatred. She had her gun trained on him with one hand and her cell phone was in the other.

"You lost him?" she asked.

"I did. You called the cops?"

"I did. And you know what else I'm going to do after we finish all the paperwork on this one?"

"What?"

"I'm taking the rest of the fucking weekend off."

CHAPTER FORTY-NINE

As Devon Malone approached the door of LeAnn Hannaford's apartment, she was wondering if maybe she should have called ahead after all. It was a Sunday morning. She glanced at her watch. Even though it was after ten, maybe they were sleeping in. She imagined one of the old detectives answering the door in his pajamas—or even less. She should have called. Ah well. Too late now.

She knocked and waited to see what she would see.

She'd told McCall she was taking the weekend off and at the time she'd meant it. After she left him explaining one last time to Mike Whitehall how they'd gotten involved in yet another shooting, she'd tried to relax by going to a nice restaurant and then a movie. But the whole time her mind was bouncing back and forth between the dead ends of their current investigations and her laughable efforts to overcome her own resistance to intimacy with Clint. She remembered little about the meal and less about the movie. It was a totally wasted evening, followed by a restless sleep.

What had she said to him? Something about fucking like bunnies? After getting twitchy just because he'd put his damned hand on her back? She was beginning to sound nuts, even to herself; God knew what he must think. He had no idea how difficult it was for her to let someone in, but it wasn't his problem—and she had the option of explaining it to him. Which was more fucking intimate than she could manage right now. She didn't have to share everything. Nobody shares everything....

Johnny Crew answered the door, wearing slacks and a sweater to Malone's relief. He invited her in. The old detective was looking almost fully recovered from his recent fight with Malcolm Guth. His nose was still a little discolored but he seemed to have good energy. LeAnn on the other hand was semi-sprawled on the couch, looking exhausted, sullen and haggard. She too was fully clothed, an old gray sweat suit in her case. It matched her apparent mood perfectly.

Hap stuck his head in from the corridor and said hello to Malone. He asked if she'd like any coffee and she said no, she was fine. He disappeared again and she realized she could smell bacon cooking. They hadn't been up for long.

"Clint's not with you?" Johnny asked.

"No. I need to talk to LeAnn if that's okay."

He shrugged. "Fine with me. I'll give you guys some space." He hurried off in the same direction Hap had gone.

Malone stayed put in the middle of the living room floor and gave the young woman a long, quiet look, trying to ease the hostility a little. "We've got to talk," she said finally.

"Fuck you and McCall both."

"We've got to talk," Malone said again. "If Clint and I are going to get Malcolm Guth for killing Kristi and keep him from hurting you—and we do plan to do both of those things—we need to know everything you know about the situation. Especially we need to know what Guth has on you, why you're worried about going to prison."

LeAnn jerked upright and stared at Malone in shock. "Colleen told you! That bitch!"

At that, Malone stepped over to the couch, moved LeAnn's one leg that was in the way, and sat down next to her. "Colleen told her father because she's a friend of yours, because she cares about you. We are all trying to help you—and you have to help us."

LeAnn slowly shifted her weight, easing her legs together so that she was sitting perfectly upright, her face a mask of indecisiveness. Then: "I can't," she said softly.

"Whatever it is, we won't use it against you. Believe me. It's Guth you have to worry about, not any of us. The only way you get hurt is by remaining silent."

LeAnn turned and looked at Malone, maintaining eye contact for what seemed like a full minute. Tears were beginning to spill down her cheeks.

"It's murder," she finally said, so softly that Malone could barely hear her.

"Murder. You killed somebody?"

"No." She wiped her eyes with one hand and straightened up.
"No, but he can make it look like I did."

"Tell me what happened."

Having made the decision, LeAnn now seemed fully com-
posed, almost business-like as she began to reply.

"A few weeks ago I picked up a john downtown and took him
over to the motel room I usually use. We got into a...kind of dispute."

"What kind of dispute?"

"I don't like johns to go down on me. One time a guy left some
bubble gum stuck down there and it was really gross. So now if
they want to do that, I make them do it through plastic wrap."

"Plastic wrap?" Malone asked incredulously.

"Yeah," responded the younger woman as if nothing were out
of the ordinary, "I carry some with me in my purse and if the guy
wants to go down on me I cover myself down there with plastic
wrap first."

"Okay. And the guy got angry about that?"

"He was pretty pissed but it's not like he was going to hurt me
or anything. He was just cussing about it, you know, calling me
names and shit. Then all of a sudden Mal crashes into the room
and shoots him!"

"Just like that?"

"He must have been listening outside. The door blasts open
and he's standing there with a gun. He slams the door behind him
and shoots the guy. Just like that. Didn't say a word to him."

"Then what?"

"He says he killed the john to protect me, which is bullshit, and
tells me to hold the gun while he's wrapping the guy up in the bed-
spread. We manage to get him out to the car and put him in the

195

trunk, then Mal takes me back in the room and tells me that my prints are on the gun and his aren't, because he's wearing gloves, and if I ever tell what happened or try to leave him or anything like that, he'll make sure the cops find the gun and the body and I'll be up for murder."

Malone couldn't decide if she believed this cockamamie story or not.

"Why do you think he killed the guy?"

"I don't know. Mal's crazy."

"All this happened in Portland? I don't remember hearing anything about a guy going missing in the last couple of weeks. Nothing about a bloodstained motel room."

"Mal made me help him clean up the room. It wasn't hard. Most of the blood was on the sheets. So it looks like we stole some sheets and a mattress cover. That won't be on the news."

"And nobody missed this guy?"

"He was a traveling salesman. He said he was supposed to be up in Seattle. That's probably where they're looking for him."

"Why was he in Portland?"

"Shit, I don't know. He didn't have time to tell me his life story. He was just a john, okay?"

She was still looking Malone in the eye, about half hostility and half bravado.

"Can you help me?" she asked, never wavering.

Malone was having more than a little trouble with all this. "Are you sure you need help?" she asked. "You did leave him and he hasn't done what he said he would."

"He will! He says he doesn't want me to go up for murder; he wants me to come back...but he isn't going to wait much longer!" She was either a fantastic actress or Guth had her convinced.

Malone decided, very tentatively, to believe her. It was too weird to be a lie. Plastic wrap, for Christ's sake. But there had to be more.

"We'll do what we can," she said. "Do you know why Guth

killed Kristi? Was it because she wanted to leave him?"

LeAnn shook her head. "I don't know. I really don't. He's always saying he's going to kill any girl who tries to leave—and a lot of them believe it, at least at first. But girls do leave. He never killed one before that I know of. He never killed anybody before the john that I know of."

"Could there be any connection between Kristi and the salesman? Maybe he'd been with her too?"

More head shaking, bewilderment. "I don't know. I don't think so. She didn't say anything. Mal is getting crazier all the time. And...truthfully, he doesn't care that much for black people. Maybe that was part of it."

"He killed her because she's black?"

A tiny shrug, almost a tremble. "It might have been easier than if she was white."

Well, Malone thought to herself, *at least we know now that there's a weapon and a body out there somewhere and Guth probably knows where they are.*

But we still don't have the whole story, not even close.

She shook her own head. Crazy and racist might have contributed. Clearly they were both true. But, in her mind, it just wasn't enough.

CHAPTER FIFTY

Hawthorne Street Electronics is just around the corner from my house and down the block from the Pen and Pastry. I knew I could find a replacement for my cell phone there—and plenty of help getting it programmed correctly. The young couple who own the place have created a small nerd paradise in the middle of my neighbourhood —computer repair, video game advice, all the latest toys.

I was there promptly at nine when they opened Monday and was soon outfitted, programmed, and back in touch with the world. My test call was to George Heatherly, who'd left me a voicemail the evening before saying he was going to return to work this morning. It was the only message I'd missed.

His wife Shanna said he'd already left; I reassured her as best I could that he was likely to come back at the end of the day. I disconnected, paid for the phone, and headed downtown.

As I expected, Malone was already in the office when I arrived. Less expected: "You're late," were her first words before I was even fully in the door. She had an odd expression on her face; I couldn't read it.

"I stopped to get a replacement cell phone. The store didn't open until nine." I explained as I hung up my jacket. I stowed my gun in the drawer and sat down. "And how are you this morning? Did you enjoy your Sunday off?"

"I did. I enjoyed it quite a bit."

Her tone of voice suddenly clued me in on that facial expression. She was smirking. I'd never in all our time together seen Devon Malone smirk. Something was definitely afoot. Maybe she had a date that she really "enjoyed." Wouldn't that be a bummer?

I wasn't sure I wanted to hear whatever it was. I looked at the phone on the desk, noting that the message lights were all dark. I gestured at it. "Anything come in this morning?"

"A couple of idle inquiries. A few more media. Mike Whitehall called to say that kid who wanted Guth's contract would be undergoing psychiatric evaluation today. I'm predicting that the diagnosis will be drugged-out and dumb."

Still the smirk. Crap. Might as well bite the bullet. I sat back and gave her a look. "What else? Clearly you have something to share besides that."

She let the moment drag out and finally nodded her head. "I had a very productive talk with LeAnn yesterday."

I immediately felt a surge of irritation—at her for not including me and at me for my stupid worry that it might have been a date. "You were going to take the day off," I said in a mildly accusatory tone.

"I intended to take the day off. Then I got restless and didn't. Would you like to hear what I learned or do you want to pout a little more first?"

I took a deep breath and let it go. "What did you learn?"

"That Guth is threatening to frame her for a murder that he committed," she began, and she laid it all out over the next ten minutes or so. I couldn't help being impressed, nor could I help being a little dubious.

"It's fantastic that you got her to talk," I said. "But do you believe her? That's quite a story, involving as it does everything from plastic-wrapped genitalia to a missing corpse. And it still leaves unexplained why Guth doesn't just kill her rather than frame her."

Malone nodded again. "Oh, it leaves all kinds of things unexplained. I believe that, at the very least, Guth killed a man in LeAnn's presence and is using the evidence as some kind of leverage. My take is that she just doesn't have the imagination to come up with that on her own."

I spent a few moments looking out the window while processing. The morning had turned sunny and there was a lot of foot traffic on Stark, the shoppers in light jackets or sweaters. Looked like it might hit the fifties out there. That would be a nice change.

I turned back to Malone. "I agree," I said, "though he could have lied to her about keeping the gun and the body. There'd be less risk for him and he'd still have the leverage."

"That would be the smart thing to do—so it's a fair bet he still has the gun and the body."

"One way or the other, we have to find out. If he does have the weapon, corpse, or both stashed somewhere there has to be a clever way to use that against him. If he doesn't, we can deal with him some other way and prove to LeAnn that she's off the hook."

For the moment, however, nothing clever was occurring to me as I watched the ebb and flow of pedestrians and vehicles on the street below. We had to keep moving, though. If there's nothing clever, go with the routine. I swiveled back to look at Malone.

"Have you been able to confirm anything about her story?"

She nodded, looking extremely self-satisfied again. "First thing this morning. I've got contacts up in Seattle from my days with missing persons and a salesman was indeed reported missing about that time. You aren't going to believe his name: Morgan Klodpusser."

"You're right. I don't believe his name. Nor could I spell it."

"Well, it's legit. According to the detective I talked to, Mr. Klodpusser's wife—who had retained her maiden name of Alicia Roman for some reason—reported it but did not seem particularly distraught. She and his company both confirmed that he was supposed to be in Seattle at the time he went missing. He was the Northwest regional rep for a small-time diamond importer that operates only in the western states."

"Diamonds. That's interesting. You planning to stay on that?"

She shrugged. "Unless you want to trade. The contract is on you, after all. I could pursue the Heatherly case. One way or the other, I think we should split up for now."

"I agree and I don't need to trade. You're on it, so keep going. Get everything you can on Klodpusser. He had a reason to be in Portland rather than Seattle and it probably wasn't to pick up a prostitute. Might be relevant, might not, but it would be good to know."

"And I'll look for connections between him and Guth," she said. "Could be a long shot, but it also seems unlikely that Guth would bust in a door and blow away a john just because the guy mouthed off to LeAnn. And, like you say: diamonds. Could be something."

"I agree with that, too, but don't forget we're yet again dealing with a major nutcase. We can't assume there's any kind of rational connection."

She let go a little sigh. "I know. Maybe in the future we should consider rejecting cases involving crazy people."

I had to chuckle at that. "We'll talk about it. It might work if we're both willing to take other jobs on the side. How are you at re-tail?"

"Hah. Lousy. I'm going to hit the street now."

She grabbed her jacket and her gun and departed.

CHAPTER FIFTY-ONE

I retrieved my own gun and holster from the drawer, snapped it to my belt, covered it with the sport coat, locked the office, and set off on foot in the direction of Pioneer Square. If the Heatherly case was all mine for the moment, it seemed like a good time to do a little jewelry shopping.

I needed to talk to Max Overton, assuming he was back at work today. I wanted a lot more detail about the shooting. And, it occurred to me, I wanted to ask him if he knew a diamond import rep named Morgan Klodpusser. Separate cases, so the odds weren't good, but what the hell?

I enjoyed the sunny and almost warm walk. I wasn't going to hide out just because a bunch of people were out to kill me. Still, as I opened the door under the red and gold City Jewelers marquee, I could probably have described every person and vehicle that I had passed on the way. Nothing wrong with paying attention.

I saw Overton immediately, at the far end of the store behind the counter, showing some merchandise to a well-dressed, white-haired lady. Even in selling mode, he looked nervous and bashful, his expression almost beseeching as he held out the bauble for his customer's inspection.

Then he saw me.

His already doughy face went as white as school paste and he let out a small *yip* as if I'd just stepped on his foot rather than into his shop.

The woman, nearly as startled by him as he was by me, turned to look in my direction. I tried to appear innocent and non-threatening, but once she had glanced again at Overton's terrified expression she apparently decided that shopping might be more fruitful elsewhere. She skirted me widely on her way out.

There were no other clerks or customers in evidence, so the store was still for several moments as the jeweler pulled himself together—which, among other things, involved carefully replacing the item in the display case, adjusting his wire-rim glasses, tugging on his gold chain, pulling out a handkerchief and wiping a sheen of sweat from his bald spot.... It was a little like watching a silent movie as he slowly transformed himself from intimidated to irritated.

He finally made eye contact, brow furrowed in a determined frown. "I was in the middle of a sale," he said sharply—or as sharply as he could in a voice that barely carried across the room. "You ruined it."

"Sorry about that," I said as I crossed the intervening space. He backed away as I approached but couldn't go far; there was only about three feet between the counter and the wall. I stopped, put both hands palm-down on the glass, and leaned forward. "Tell me about getting shot."

He reached across his body and touched his upper left arm. He was wearing a long-sleeve shirt to cover the bandage but the shirt was white and lightweight; you could see the wrapping in there underneath his fingers.

"It was...I was...I don't have to tell you anything."

I leaned a little further forward. "Look, Mr. Overton, we're working on this case and we're not going to stop. If you think our investigation is the reason you were shot, your best bet is to help us find out what's going on so we can end the threat. You don't want to see anyone else get hurt, do you?"

"No." Long pause. "I...I was in the rose garden."

"You have a rose garden?"

"No, no, *the* Rose Garden, in Washington Park."

There are a number of rose gardens in Portland, which calls itself the Rose City after all, but Overton was talking about the International Rose Test Gardens maintained by the Portland Rose Society. Thousands of visitors come every year to see the four-hundred-plus varieties of roses. But not usually in March.

"Why were you there?"

"Stan called and asked me to meet him there."

"Your friend Nakagawa, the banker?"

"Yes."

"Why?"

"I don't know."

"Well, what did he say?"

"Nothing! It was a voice message. We didn't actually talk. He asked me to meet him and I drove up there."

"Okay then, what has he said...."

I was interrupted by the cell phone squealing at me from my sport coat pocket. I almost reached in and just shut it off but—given everything that was going on—decided I'd better look to see who was calling.

It was Mike Whitehall's direct line at the Justice Center. Uh oh. I excused myself to Overton, punched the button and put the phone to my ear.

"What's up, Mike?" I asked as I turned away from the counter for some privacy.

"They just pulled Stanley Nakagawa's body out of a dumpster in the warehouse district. I think we need to have a little chat."

CHAPTER FIFTY-TWO

Devon Malone savored her last bite of the massive Home Run Big Burger. She'd no more than hit the sidewalk when she decided to have an early lunch before visiting Guth's regular haunts again and checking with a few of her old informants.

Her table was next to the front window and she'd seen Clint leave just a minute after she sat down. She had an impulse to jump up, run outside, and see if he wanted to join her before going wherever he was going. She ignored it.

Devon carefully retrieved the last French fry from the pool of ketchup on her plate and considered her options. She had to get out on the street because that's how she would find Guth, if he could be found, but maybe the first thing to do was see what she could learn from Alicia Roman, Morgan Klodpusser's wife. Devon had gotten the woman's contact information from her source in Seattle but had put off calling her. She hadn't shared with the Seattle cop that Klodpusser had been in Portland or that he was probably a murder victim and she didn't want to share the latter with his wife, either—but she wasn't looking forward to lying about it.

Still, it would be good to have all the info she could before tracking Guth down.

She took another swig of her Coke and pulled out her cell phone. The number in Ellensburg, Washington, rang only twice before it was picked up.

A woman's reedy voice. "Morgan?"

"Is this Alicia Roman?"

A sigh. "Yes. Who's is this?"

"My name is Devon Malone. I'm a private investigator in Portland, Oregon, and I'm calling about your husband."

"Portland, Oregon?" It was practically a squeak. "A private investigator? What's happened? Why are you in Portland?"

Because I live and work here, you hysterical female, is what Malone

207

thought. "I have reason to believe that this is where your husband disappeared," is what she said.

"In Portland? That can't be. He was supposed to be in Seattle. Who did you say you were?"

Malone bit her lip and then spoke very slowly. "My name is Devon Malone and I'm a private...."

"Yes, yes, okay, what are you saying about Morgan? He was in Portland? Why was he in Portland? What's happened to him?"

"I was hoping to find out from you why he might have been in Portland, Mrs...er...Ms. Roman."

"Yes, Roman. No one who knows me calls me Mrs. Klodpusser. Surely you understand. Actually I tried to get Morgan to take my last name but he rejected the idea. Morgan Roman. That's a nice name, don't you think?" Her voice kept getting thinner and her words faster as she spoke. Malone began to worry that the woman was going to lose it completely. Alicia Roman knew as well as Malone did that her last question had not been answered.

"I don't know what's happened to your husband, Alicia." Technically it was true. LeAnn Hannaford could be lying. "But I do know he was here in Portland and he seems to have disappeared here. Do you have any idea why he would be here rather than in Seattle? Was this part of his territory? Did he have any friends here?"

"He had the whole Northwest, so Portland was on his route— but not this trip. I don't know if he had friends there. He would have buyers, so I suppose some of them could be his friends too. But...how do you know he was in Portland if you don't know what's happened to him? Do you know what's happened to him?"

"No," Malone repeated, "I don't. But I do have reliable information that he was here and it's related to a case I'm working on, which is why I'm calling you."

"Why should I care about your case if you can't help me find my husband?"

"That's my point. I might well find your husband in the course of working this case, because they seem to be related." *Or your husband's body, anyway.* "Has your husband had any problems lately? Received any threats? Been acting oddly? Anything like that?"

"No, no.... Well, like I already told the police, we were having some problems, some financial problems because of his gambling."

Ah ha. "Your husband's a gambler?"

"Yes. It's a sickness, or so they say. He was doing good for a long time but I just found out recently he'd gone back to it and lost a lot of our money. Do you think that's why he was in Portland?"

"I don't know. It's possible."

"Do you think I drove him away? I try to be supportive but he can be very difficult, you know, and...."

"This is helpful, Alicia, and I'll do everything I can to find out where your husband is now."

"Uh, thank you. Should I tell the police here that you're working on it?"

"I already talked to them. Just try to take care of yourself and wait for news, okay?"

They said their goodbyes and Malone punched off the phone. A guy who needed money and had access to diamonds is shot to death by a local pimp who might have access to buyers. That was good information to take with her to the street.

As she started to put her phone away she noticed it was blinking. Another call had come in while she was talking to Alicia Roman. From an unidentified cell phone number. She called it back and Merritt the Ferret answered.

"Malone. I got new info and I need some help, too. I'm downtown looking to buy a present for my niece's birthday. You got any idea where I can get a plastic AK-47?"

CHAPTER FIFTY-THREE

The civilian behind the bulletproof glass at the front desk of the Police Bureau knew me, so it took only a minute to get a visitor's pass.

I had had plenty of time to think as I walked the eleven blocks from City Jewelers to the Justice Center, but my brain was still on overdrive as the elevator took me up to the Detective Division on the thirteenth floor.

I confess that I fled from Overton's store without telling him what the call had been about. I didn't ask him about Klodpusser, either, of course. I just said something had come up and I had to leave. His look of relief was far superior to the look of horrified accusation I'm sure I would have gotten if he had heard another board member was dead.

He'd know before the day was over anyway and I'd have to deal with his reaction sometime—but at this point I was having enough trouble dealing with my own.

Was our investigation getting all these people killed? Was there something we missed, something we could have done to prevent the deaths? Most important: could we prevent more?

No doubt Mike Whitehall had some of the same questions.

The Portland Police Bureau's Homicide Detail is to the left in the back of the Detective Division and looks nothing like what you see on television. There are a half-dozen low-walled cubicles with lots of light coming through the big picture windows. Reproductions of famous paintings hang on the walls and the workspaces are well-decorated with colorful family mementos and other tchotchkes, just like any modern office space you might find in the city. It was probably a little more colorful than average; you do everything you can to keep your spirits up when your job is dealing with murdered people and their killers.

Whitehall was sitting at his desk in his office off to the side, talking on the phone. He motioned me to sit down and it quickly became apparent that he was getting an update from whoever had been the scene investigator for Nakagawa's body.

"Anything in the dumpster that the killer could have used?" he asked, absently running a hand over his short-cropped brown hair. Wearing white shirt and tie, sitting next to his desktop PC with Garfield screensaver running, he might have been an extremely fit junior executive in a corporate office. A corporation that happened to search dumpsters for murder weapons.

He listened a moment more, hung up, and reached over the desk to shake hands. "How ya doin', Clint?"

So we were going to be a little formal for this talk. At least I could be pretty confident he didn't think I was the murderer.

"About as well as could be expected," I said. "How did Naka-gawa die?"

"Prelim indicates he was strangled. Of course, being as it's the warehouse district, the dumpster is full of twine, plastic cord, wire, you name it. They're just going to haul the whole thing down here. Probably take a couple of days to go through it all."

"Exactly where was it?"

"The dumpster? Behind the Pacific Foods warehouse, the big one, their central shipping facility."

"Yeah, I know where that is."

"One of the garbage guys took a look inside before they went to empty it. God knows why, maybe there's something the company throws out that he collects, but it's a good thing or our banker would have been somewhere in the landfill before the end of the day." He paused. "You know what's really interesting about all this?"

"What?"

"Well, assuming these attacks on Lifestream board members are all related, we've got a blow to the back of the head, a shooting, and a strangulation. I'm thinking I should stake out places that sell poison now."

"The media might call our guy 'The Eclectic Killer' if they could spell or pronounce it."

He grinned. "You sure it's a guy?"

"Not at all. I've got two female board members who are un-harmed—so far—but no particular reason to suspect either one."

He patted a copy of *The Oregonian* that was lying on his desk. "We've been lucky. Nobody's asked about Carter and Nakagawa being on the same board. Wouldn't be unusual for two guys like that to be associated with the same charity...except that they've both been murdered in the same week. Somebody happens on the incident report for Overton, puts two and one together, and we've got a red ball; the media will be all over it and the mayor's office all over our asses. It's a pretty big story already, two such respectable citizens offed in the same week."

"I know."

"There's no sniffing around your investigation as far as I've heard. Your buddy Alison Roberts must be falling down on the job."

"Good thing that potshot at me wasn't in front of a board member's house. She'd have already put it together."

"Hmm," said Whitehall. "Whose house *was* that in front of?"

My turn to grin. "Yes, it was my client. George Heatherly, by name, as you could easily find out from the report."

"Already did. You know I respect your desire to keep investigations confidential but I've got two dead, wealthy citizens and it's time to share."

CHAPTER FIFTY-FOUR

The Ferret not only wanted advice about where to buy a plastic AK-47, he wanted to meet at a downtown strip club. Devon Malone's thought as she stepped around the red partition to the interior of Mary's Club was that the little twerp's new information had better be really good.

Mary's Club is a Portland institution of sorts, the oldest strip club in the city, dating from the fifties, and located at the north end of Broadway near Burnside—and far too close to the central downtown area for the more proper city fathers and mothers. It's dark and loud and reeks of stale beer and unrequited lust but it's popular with both locals and tourists for reasons that were beyond Devon's comprehension.

She paused to survey the room as best she could in the dim light. It was well-populated for so early in the day, just past the lunch hour. A dozen or so nondescript males sat either on stools at the bar or at the little round tables. None of them appeared to be connected, all sitting alone. There were no women except for the stocky young bartender with dirty blond hair and a very thin, not-so-young brunette stripper performing a desultory pole dance. Her music was old-fashioned hard rock and her remaining costume was sparkly green pasties.

Merritt the Ferret was sitting by himself, like everyone else, at a table in the far corner.

She stopped at the bar to order a beer, then walked across the room and took the other chair at the table, across from him. He was dressed in brown and gray as usual, though today his cravat was blue.

Devon launched right in. "Your niece wants an assault rifle for her birthday? How old is she?"

The Ferret grimaced. "Hi. How are you? I'm fine. Good to see you."

"I'm fine, too, but I'm more concerned about your niece."

"She's eight and it's a toy assault rifle she wants, not a real one." He grinned. "She specified an AK-47, though. Isn't that something? I think she kind of takes after you."

"Huh. I don't think that's a compliment to either one of us, Merritt. I didn't have toy guns when I was a little kid."

"Bet you didn't have many dolls, either."

"No, not many, but let's get down to business. You called me. I can't help you with your shopping and, honestly, I hope nobody else does. Can you help me with my investigating?"

The little man frowned. "That's not very nice. Here I offer to help you out...."

"Merritt."

"Okay, okay. The thing is, I got curious and asked around some more about this asshole Guth and, I swear to God, it sounds like he thinks he really does love that girl you were talking about before, the one he wants back."

"You said that wasn't possible."

He shrugged. "So I was wrong for the first time in my life. It's not like 'whatever you want, dear' kind of love. It's more like, 'I love my car.' Not that I love mine. It's a piece of shit...."

"So you're saying it's part of his whole control thing."

"Yeah, but more than that. He's told people that she's special and that he loves her—whatever the fuck that means to the sick motherfucker." He sat back, finishing the dregs of his own beer. "I thought you might want to know, you comin' all the way out to my place to ask about Guth before."

Devon took the second and last sip of her own. It tasted only a little better than the air smelled. "That's interesting," she said. "How about this? Have you heard anything about Guth connecting buyers with a guy selling diamonds?"

That gave the Ferret pause. He frowned, apparently thinking it over. "Diamonds? No. Drugs, for sure. Guns, maybe. Where would he hook up with stolen diamonds?"

"Good question. Well, if you do any more asking around, keep that in mind."

"Okay."

She slipped him two twenties across the table. "Don't spend it on a goddamned plastic gun. If your niece isn't a girly-girl, buy her a chemistry set or something."

The money disappeared into his jacket. "I'll think about that. She's not really the scientist type."

Devon got up, as did the Ferret. "Maybe that's because nobody ever gave her a chemistry set," she said.

They headed together toward the front entrance. As they walked along the length of the bar, a man sitting on one of the stools suddenly swung around and grabbed her arm. He was middle-aged, balding, dressed like a day laborer, with a goofy drunken grin and severe halitosis.

"You leavin', little lady?" he slurred.

Devon looked at him. "I'm not little," she said just loudly enough to be heard over the music, "I'm not a lady, and if you don't take your hand off my arm I'll take it off your arm."

His hand instantly popped open but for a very long moment it was as if he couldn't fully understand what she'd said—until finally the grin faded, to be replaced by resignation. "Ookay," he responded finally, and woozily swiveled back to the bar.

She urged the Ferret on toward the exit. Meanwhile he had started grinning. "You really are kind of small," he said.

"Look who's talking," she said, and shoved past him to exit the place first.

CHAPTER FIFTY-FIVE

Whitehall was right. It was time. So I shared. I told him about the phone calls George Heatherly had gotten accusing his wife's uncle of some unspecified wrongdoing, the incoherent call I got that might have been from the same person, my impressions of the board members (living and dead) from my interviews with them, and the information—or more accurately the gossip—I'd gotten from young Crystal Schilling.

Like me, Whitehall was unable to deduce a single damned thing that might be of use from it all. He did conclude that he was going to have a talk of his own with Albright; he promised that he would share.

Before I left, I got the rest of Overton's story about the shooting. According to the police report, the jeweler had walked only a short way into the Rose Garden when he was struck by the bullet. Didn't see who fired. Wasn't even sure he'd heard the shot. He ran for his car and didn't know if there had been any more shots. So far investigators had not found any evidence of where or who the shooter had been. No shell casings, no suspicious footprints, nothing.

When detectives went to talk to Nakagawa, his wife told them he'd been gone since early morning and she hadn't heard from him. She didn't know where he'd gone or why, except that he'd said he had to meet someone.

I hoped he and his wife had had a pleasant goodbye.

Walking back to the office, I tried not to think so hard. I watched the other pedestrians and the drive-bys...er, cars...just as I had on the way to the Justice Center, but otherwise I gave my brain a break. Nakagawa invited Overton into a trap at the Rose Garden and ended up dead himself in the warehouse district? It made no sense. Better to enjoy the unseasonably warm March air and simply be alert.

Malone's Jeep was not in the parking lot, so before going up to the office I stopped at the Home Run for a hot, juicy hamburger with everything on it accompanied by seasoned fries and a beer. As I ate I watched a half-hour of soccer on the nearest TV monitor, losing myself in the vision of incredibly athletic and fleet-footed young men chasing a ball back and forth. Which was all I knew about soccer.

When I came out I saw that now Malone's vehicle was in its accustomed spot. Maybe she had something. Certainly I had a lot to tell her, especially if she hadn't been listening to her police scanner. I hurried across the street, around the corner, and up the stairs.

CHAPTER FIFTY-SIX

She was on her side of the desk watching the door when I opened it. I don't know if she'd heard me coming or was simply waiting for my arrival. I said hello, sat down, and enjoyed a good whiff of her cinnamon-scented shampoo. I sometimes think that it is enhanced when she's excited about something, which she clearly was now.

"I've got some good stuff," she said.

I noted that my message light was blinking but I let it go. "And I've got some bad stuff."

That stopped her for a second. "Really? Okay, you first."

"Stanley Nakagawa is dead."

"Shit! How did I miss that?"

"You must have been away from your scanner at the time."

"What happened?"

I laid it out for her, what I'd learned from Whitehall as well as what I'd shared with him. I added in my conversation with Max Overton, then sat back. "And how was your day?"

"Well, I learned from Klodpusser's wife—who, by the way, won't touch his last name with a twenty-foot pole—that he had a gambling problem and was badly in need of money. That could be a motive for him being in Portland and a possible connection with Guth."

"Certainly worth thinking about."

"And I heard from my buddy Merritt the Ferret."

I had to smile. "And you still claim you're not making him up."

"Nope. I'm sure you'll have the misfortune of meeting him someday and then you'll know I'm completely truthful."

"I look forward to it. So, what did the tiny little mammal have to say?"

"He claims that Guth has been telling people he loves LeAnn Hannaford and that's why he wants her back. Or, to be more realis-

221

tic, why he's trying to coerce her back."

"Huh. So he frames her for murder and kills her best friend to prove his love? That's a tough one to believe."

"Even Merritt conceded that it was not exactly a chivalrous love."

"Huh, again. I've got to think on that one for a minute. Let me check and see what this message is meanwhile."

It was a voicemail message from Reuben Keys, coincidentally about our current subject of discussion. "If you still alive, give me a call," he rasped. "Guth is tryin' to cancel the contract now. I think we gonna need a straitjacket for that fucker real soon."

I gave Malone a look and held up one finger. "Give me another minute. I've got to call Reuben back."

She gave *me* a look; she's not a big fan of Portland's most flamboyant pimp.

Reuben answered right away and I confirmed that he was hearing word on the street Guth had apparently decided he didn't want me killed after all—at least not by anyone else. Maybe now that he'd seen the quality of applicant, he'd thought better of farming out the job. Or maybe he was just getting more fucking crackbrained by the minute, which was Reuben's analysis.

I was fairly certain that the latter had at least some truth to it and I had a new idea by the time I hung up.

I reported the gist of what he'd said to my partner and then went on, "How about I have Reuben put out the word that LeAnn wants to talk to Guth? If he takes the bait, she tells him she's not coming back because she doesn't believe he really kept the body or the gun. She thinks he's too much of a coward. She wants him to stop bluffing and leave her alone. She's adamant and doesn't back off even a little bit."

"So then he has to prove to her he has the body and the gun."

"You got it."

Slight frown. "Do you think she's got it in her? Can she pull it off?"

"I think so. I'll let Johnny and Hap do the persuading; they've spent a lot more time with her. And of course they'll be with her for support."

A shrug. "What the hell. Give it a try. It would be good to have a body and a gun."

CHAPTER FIFTY-SEVEN

Reuben agreed to put out the word on condition that I not ask him for any favors that would put him directly in Guth's way.

"You're okay for a private cop," he noted, "but I don't like you anywhere near that fuckin' much."

I allowed as how that was probably true and promised to keep him out of it.

Johnny Crew answered the phone at LeAnn's apartment and I asked him to tell Hap to pick up the extension. I wanted to make sure they were both aware of the young lady's latest story. They were, minus the more exotic details having to do with plastic wrap —which was too bad, because Johnny at least would have loved them.

"All right," I continued. "This is the plan. I'm having Reuben Keys put out word that LeAnn wants to talk to Guth. So she should be the one answering the phone at the apartment from now on. You guys need to persuade her to do that and then be there for her." I laid out the details of what I wanted her to say, and how. "She needs to be confident she can handle it," I went on, "before she gets on the phone with Guth, okay?" I also told Johnny to be on the extension with her if the plan came to fruition. I wanted his version of what Guth said.

"Yeah," Johnny responded. "I understand. She blows it and we could all be fucked."

"Talk to her and let me know," I said, and we hung up.

"That sounded good," Malone said. She held up her own finger. "And we don't want to forget the other victim in all this. Given what we know now, you remember what Kristi said to us—or started to say to us—on the street? About something else going on? I'm wondering if she knew about Klodpusser's murder or maybe overheard something about the deal Guth had with him."

"Could be," I said. "As long as we get him for one of the murders, he'll be off the street. But don't worry; I'm not going to forget Kristi."

"Good."

"Meanwhile, I think we should go talk to Heatherly again. He might not know about Nakagawa's murder yet, but he certainly will soon. His wife told me this morning he had returned to work at *The Portland Bulletin*. A newspaper office is a pretty good place to catch the news."

"It would be interesting to get his reaction," Malone agreed.

We were getting ourselves together when the phone rang again.

"She'll do it," were Johnny's first words. "She's rarin' to go and we've got her back."

"The Guth plan is a go," I told Malone as I put the handset back in its cradle. "Now let's just hope he calls."

CHAPTER FIFTY-EIGHT

I made one more call before we were on our way. The guy who answered the phone at the *Bulletin* said George Heatherly had just left the office in a big hurry. He didn't know why, only that George seemed really upset, maybe some problem at home.

I was certain, as I locked our office door behind me, that at least one of Heatherly's problems was a young wife at home who was going to be greatly worried when she heard there'd been another murder. Definitely time for that face-to-face. Both she and her husband were going to need some reassurance from the private detectives they'd hired to help them out.

Not least because we didn't seem to be doing such a great job so far.

I voiced some of those thoughts as I drove us toward southwest Terwilliger Boulevard.

"I just hope George and Shanna don't have to deal with more bullets hitting their house," Malone said as we were on Broadway. "There's no guarantee every aspiring hit man has already heard about that contract being cancelled—and whoever took the potshot the last time we were there is still at large."

"I know," I said, "but the odds are fairly good that we can spend a few minutes at our client's home without any violence occurring."

"Fairly," was her only response.

I couldn't help taking a good long look down the street at Duniway Park as we got out of the car. Nobody in sight who appeared to be carrying a rifle. No one ducking behind a tree. We walked up to the split-level's front door and I knocked.

George and Shanna Heatherly answered the door together, looking very young. It occurred to me only then that we'd made the trip entirely on the assumption that George was rushing home and I'd find them both here. I could only wish all our guesses were so

227

good.

George looked even thinner than when I'd seen him last and apparently had given up completely on combing his thatch of dark brown hair. He was wearing black slacks and a white dress-shirt, collar open, no tie. His brownish-gray eyes, behind the wire-rimmed glasses, grew wide with welcome when he recognized us.

"Mr. McCall! Miss Malone! What are you...? It's good to see you! Come in, come in."

His wife's small, oval face looked pinched without its customary broad smile. She wore tan slacks and blouse that complemented her cropped dark hair. She said nothing as they led us down to the family room where we'd talked before. I suspected that we'd arrived hard on the news from George that Stanley Nakagawa was dead.

She found her voice after Malone and I were seated on the couch. "We have fresh coffee...."

"No, thank you" I said. "I don't need anything." Malone said the same.

Shanna sat in one of the overstuffed chairs and George perched on the arm; they clearly didn't want to be far apart.

"I'll tell you what I need to know," George said without preliminary, leaning forward as his wife put her hand on his knee. "Were Mr. Carter and Mr. Nakagawa murdered because I started this investigation? Is it my fault they're dead?"

I wasn't surprised by the question. He seemed like the type to worry about such things.

"No, it is absolutely not your fault," I replied firmly.

He sat back a little but then thought again. "That doesn't answer both my questions."

I scooted forward to the edge of the couch, elbows on my knees and hands open, outstretched.

"Look," I said, "murderers don't kill because a private detective starts asking questions. They kill because they're killers. You asked us to find out if your uncle was in any kind of trouble, possibly doing something illegal. A question we still haven't answered, by the

228

way. You take any group of people and start asking questions, a thousand different things can happen. Murder will be one of them only if there's a killer around. This investigation might be the *occasion* of these deaths—and I emphasize "might"—but they aren't your fault or ours. Do you understand?"

He slumped a little, maybe with relief. "Yes. Yes, I guess so."

"What if that isn't the problem?" asked Shanna. Her voice was firm now, though she was still clutching his knee.

"What do you mean?" asked Malone.

"George blaming himself. What if that isn't the problem? Whoever is killing these people, the killer probably doesn't think it's his own fault. Maybe he blames George. What if he wants to kill George now?"

Her husband pressed a hand over his eyes. "We can't keep hiding here at home," he groaned.

"You can't forever, no," Malone said before Shanna could respond, "but your wife is right. We don't know the killer's motives or reasoning. You could be in danger whether you deserve it or not. It's best to lay as low as possible for the time being."

He raised his hand slightly and gave us both a resigned stare. "This is not good," he said.

"No," I agreed, "it's not. But these are the cards we're holding right now and we have to play the hand as best we can." Even as I spouted the cliché, I realized there was one more card I could draw. "I'll tell you what," I said. "I'm going to ask an associate of mine, another private detective, to stay with you for a short while and provide extra security."

Shanna's eyes widened. "Like a bodyguard?"

I could just imagine her thinking to herself that she might be the first librarian in history to have a bodyguard. If she did get around to having such a fantasy, Hap Harbaugh would probably be a disappointment to her.

"Yes," I said nevertheless, "like that."

They both had their mouths open to ask more questions when

the phone on a side table near my chair rang. Shanna started, then hurried over to pick it up. She listened for a moment with a frown and held the phone out. "It's for you," she said.

I started to reach for the handset and then froze for a second with the realization that this was very wrong, extraordinarily wrong. No one knew where I was. No one knew the name of my client, not even Eleanor. No one could be calling me here.

But someone was.

CHAPTER FIFTY-NINE

I took the phone from her and put it cautiously to my ear. "This is McCall."

"I can't wait any longer. I need to talk to you right now." The voice was tight with stress, as though forced from the throat of the speaker.

I recognized it immediately: the soft, tension-filled male voice that had left the message about parties and guilt at my office. I did not want to lose this call and I wanted Malone on an extension if the Heatherlys had one.

"Give me a minute to find some privacy," I said to the caller. "I'm in the middle of a meeting...."

"I know exactly where you are—and I need to talk to you face to face. Right now."

That stopped me again. "How do we do that? How do you know where I am?"

I could hear some of the stress release in his voice as he replied, making a sound that could have been a very dry chuckle.

"Easily," he said, "on both counts. I'm standing by your vehicle in front of the house. Come out and see me."

I punched off the phone and looked at my partner. "Our mysterious caller is out front and wants to talk to us," I said.

Her eyebrows went up but otherwise no reaction. "The party guy?"

"That's the one."

"Well, this will be interesting."

I told George and Shanna to stay put in the family room and we took the stairs to the landing, drawing our weapons before we got to the front door. I pressed against the wall to the right of the entrance and Malone to the left. I turned the doorknob slowly, pulling the door open just a crack. No gunfire in response. I heard a vehicle passing by, but otherwise it was quiet outside.

I edged forward, peering around the doorframe.

There was indeed a man leaning back against the Subaru, arms crossed, an expectant expression on his face as he looked up toward the house. He had the body and casually confident poise of an ex-wrestler, a short and slightly stocky man with a square jaw and high cheekbones, probably in his late forties. Brown hair cut short, a neatly trimmed moustache. He wore dark dress slacks and sport coat over a white tee shirt and possibly a holster nestled at his back like mine. White canvas tennis shoes completed the ensemble. He did not look anything like the voice I'd been hearing on the phone.

He saw me and casually raised his hands as he smiled. "Don't shoot," he called.

I half-lowered my gun and stepped cautiously outside, joined immediately by Malone, who closed the door behind us. Neither of us holstered our weapons until we'd taken a good look all around us. Nobody lurking. The guy was holding a cell phone in his right hand. He was my caller, all right.

I took in more details as we approached. Within the square outline of the jaw were soft, full lips that jibed more with the voice than the rest of his image. Aquiline nose and light blue eyes. The slacks and jacket looked expensive; the tee shirt and shoes clearly were not.

He held out his hand as we came up to him and we shook. His grip was firm. "I'm Tony Zahl," he said as he offered his hand to Malone, who took it cautiously.

So at last we had a name for the mysterious caller, though not one that meant anything to me. "Why don't we go down to our office to talk?" I suggested. No way was I going to invite him into the Heatherlys' house.

He leaned back against the car and crossed his arms again. "Actually that's why I'm here, because I wanted to meet with you in your office."

"We're not big fans of riddles," Malone said.

He grinned. "Really? I would have thought a detective would like riddles." He shrugged and went on in a more business-like tone. "I was on my way to your office and looking for a place to park when I saw you pulling out of the lot. I went around the block and luckily was able to catch up, then followed you. When I saw you going in here, I called a friend of mine who has a reverse directory to get the number. Nothing too difficult."

"What were you driving?" I asked. I was not thrilled to learn I'd had an amateur tail all the way over here without spotting it.

His eyebrows lifted in surprise and he pointed at a dark blue vehicle just down the street. "Ford Explorer."

That helped. Probably I'd been followed from downtown out Terwilliger by a dozen SUVs, half of them Explorers. On the other hand, assuming whoever had taken a shot at me here last Friday had also followed me, that was twice. Maybe I'd better report to George Heatherly by phone from now on.

"What do you want to talk to us about?" Malone inquired while I was still mentally kicking myself.

Zahl pursed his lips and seemed to consider for a moment.

"I'm afraid I started all this. I had no idea...."

"You were the one who called George Heatherly and told him Norman Albright could be dirty," I guessed.

"Yes."

"So, is Albright dirty?"

"I don't know. I doubt it."

"You doubt it."

He shrugged, his crossed arms going up and down with his shoulders. "Norm isn't the type for financial impropriety, plus he doesn't need it. He's filthy rich already."

I was glad the skies were clear and the weather relatively warm. This was sounding like it might be a long conversation before we ever got to the office.

"Why did you make the calls, then, and what was with the party references?" Malone asked.

An odd little smile. "Ah, the parties to which I was not invited. Those aren't really important. The reason I made the calls? I guess you could say, unrequited love."

I guessed I could say that I was rapidly becoming impatient. "Stop with the riddles, Mr. Zahl, and tell us whatever it is you have to tell us. If you don't want to tell us about the parties, tell us about your supposedly false accusation. Why did you do it?"

His expression became serious. "Norm and I had a relationship for a while—not a very long while. I was his little adventure on the dark side, no more than that it turned out, an adventure for which his courage failed rather quickly. To me, it was a great deal more. Were you ever rejected by the love of your life, Mr. McCall?"

"I wouldn't say so." I managed not to even glance at my partner, though of course she wasn't.... Never mind.

He gave me an appraising look. "But perhaps only because it's not my business?"

I nodded. "That, I would say. What are you trying to tell us? You wanted to hurt Albright because he rejected you? Didn't invite you to some parties? That's quite a reaction. And what do you mean by 'the dark side'?"

"I wanted to hurt him, yes. But not badly—and I certainly didn't want anyone killed." He pushed off from the car and stood up straight. "My business.... Well, let's just say that it offers me many connections with people who are not entirely reputable. That was what, I think, intrigued Norm at first—and put him off finally. I was angry, hurt, resentful that he considered himself better than all that, better than me. I wanted to bring him down, just down enough that he wouldn't consider himself above me...and maybe would consider taking me back."

"So you think one of your 'connections' might be killing the board members?" asked Malone.

His eyes went wide and his hand came up to his throat in his first and only overtly effeminate gesture. "No! No, not at all. My intention was no more than to pass on a little gossip and let the chips fall. I heard, through my connections, that there might be some financial hanky panky with the board, some money going places it shouldn't. No names, no details, just vague rumor. I was certain it wasn't Norm, but he is the chairman of the board and would bear some responsibility. If there were any improprieties, they would tarnish him. Perhaps enough for my purposes."

He grimaced and looked away from me for a moment. "I see now that it was completely silly. Far worse than silly. I'm afraid these people have died, at least indirectly, because I called George Heatherly."

Malone followed up. "So maybe your accusations weren't entirely false, just misdirected?"

"Yes. Maybe."

I was having a hard time buying any of this. "Why Heatherly? Why not *The Oregonian*? Or the police?"

"I keep telling you: I wanted to hurt him only a little bit. Keep it in the family, a low-key investigation by a small weekly paper at worst." He leaned back again and laughed, a short bark of a laugh that had no humor in it. "I guess you could call that a miscalculation as well as a misdirection."

CHAPTER SIXTY

We got nothing more out of him. His story was that he had needed to confess and now he'd done so. Assuming for the moment that he was telling the whole truth, about which I was highly dubious, he'd known nothing of real substance about the board to begin with and had learned nothing since. As far as he actually knew, Shanna Heatherly's Uncle Norman had done nothing wrong at all. Which would have closed our client's case except for the dead people scattered about.

We parted from Zahl on his two promises that he would cause Albright no more trouble and call us if he learned anything that might be helpful—not that I believed either one.

I left Malone out front to watch for anyone else who might show up, armed or otherwise, as I checked back in briefly with the Heatherlys. They'd watched us through the front window and neither had recognized Zahl, which left his story of an affair with Albright unsupported. Despite their pleading, I didn't share his tale of incrimination and regret with them because I wanted some kind of confirmation first. One of our first chores when we got back to the office would be to get whatever background we could on our newest mystery guest. Then it would be time to chat once again with Uncle Norman. After that maybe I'd give the Heatherlys a more complete report—by phone.

It appeared, one way or the other, that we now had two nutcases vainly—not to mention insanely—pursuing their true loves. Guth was willing to kill and for all I knew Tony Zahl was equally dangerous. Lucky, lucky us.

I had two calls to make before we got to work on Zahl's background; the first one was to get Hap over to the Heatherlys, a plan that seemed even wiser now that Zahl had shown up at their house.

LeAnn answered the phone, so my trap-Guth plan had gotten at least that far. I confirmed with her that she'd agreed—not too eagerly, I gathered—to see if she could provoke some hint of where his "evidence" might be. He hadn't called yet. I didn't blame her for asking me if I really felt it was necessary. I told her I did and got her to pass the phone to Hap.

"Clint? You wanna talk to me?"

I could hear the puzzlement in his voice. He and Johnny had been partners since their early days as detectives in the Portland Police Bureau and Johnny had always been the primary. Hap was as strong, steady, and dependable as they come, but it was usually Johnny people wanted to speak to when they called.

"Yeah," I said. "I've got a job for you."

"Really? Well, you know, I'm not sure we should leave LeAnn alone...."

"Johnny can stay with her and I'll get someone else to back him up. This one's just for you."

"Dang! What is it?" There was definitely a little excitement mixed with the puzzlement now—excitement that increased as I explained I wanted him to provide protection for the Heatherlys. My thinking was that, old and retired as he might be, Hap was a very big and intimidating presence. The guy who looked scary was probably better for them.

"Yeah," responded Hap. "Yeah, I can do that. I'll get right over there. That'll be great. I'll just tell Johnny and head right out. Thanks, Clint."

He hung up in a downright cheery mood and I could imagine him shlumping hurriedly to find his partner and get his things together. Of course, I hadn't mentioned that the Heatherlys certainly would not let him smoke in their house. That news would restore his normally querulous disposition.

My next call was to Roger Arbuckle, to see if he'd be willing to back up Johnny again—and not let the old detective send him home this time. He readily agreed.

While I'd been making my calls, which took just a couple of minutes, Malone had been fielding voicemails and sorting through the snail mail. She reported that neither offered anything of immediate use or even interest.

"I have a bad feeling about Tony Zahl," she announced then.

I sat back and considered her sour expression. "You think it was all bullshit?"

"Maybe not all, but something was way off. Didn't you think so?"

"Yeah, actually I did. Got a recommendation of who we should talk to about him?" As a recent Portland police detective herself, she knew a lot more than I did about Bureau's sources

She thought for a moment and then frowned, deeply, a whole different degree of sour. "Ray Fletcher, I guess."

"You sure? You don't look like he's the best choice."

"Ray's with the drugs and vice squad. Not one of my favorite people, but he goes back a long way and knows all the players on the street. That's who I'd call. Put it on speaker but don't tell him I'm listening in."

"Okay. I take it you're not one of his favorite people, either."

"We had the occasional disagreement."

I could only imagine. I put the phone on speaker, dialed the Justice Center, and asked to speak to Detective Ray Fletcher.

He answered his extension on the first ring and I identified myself. He was not excited about the opportunity to help a local private detective, but grudgingly allowed me a moment of his time.

I got right to the point. "Ever heard the name Tony Zahl?"

"Oh yeah, the phantom of the opera."

"Is that what they call him?"

"That's what we call him, because he deals only with the opera crowd and we can't get anything on him—nothing that would stand up in court against high-priced shysters, anyway."

"What does he do for the opera crowd?"

"Designer drugs, stolen art, smuggled artifacts, high-end stuff like that. You want the real thing from the Louvre, rather than a copy, you go through Tony."

He pronounced it "louver," like the transom, but I knew what he meant. Hopefully he hadn't heard Malone's soft chortle.

"Ever hear of any violence in connection with his operation?"

A grunt. "Nah. Tony's a queer. You know, hasn't got the balls for it."

And with that I could understand Malone's reaction. Ray Fletcher was a bigoted asshole. As police departments go the Portland Bureau is socially liberal, but there are some Neanderthals remaining among the officers and Ray Fletcher was clearly one of them. It was a good bet that he and Mike Whitehall were not close friends, either.

My partner was rolling her eyes like crazy as I thanked Fletcher for the information, and hung up.

CHAPTER SIXTY-ONE

While listening to a short commentary from Devon Malone on the character and likely genetic antecedents of Detective Ray Fletcher, I checked the time. Five minutes after three. As soon as she was done, I made another quick call confirming that Albright was home and willing to see us.

Eighteen minutes later I drove through the open gate of the wrought-iron fence and pulled in behind Albright's black Corvette. This time it was parked in a slightly different place at a slightly different angle, so apparently he did drive it.

Looking as he always did, like he'd just stepped out of a Victorian novel, Albright opened the front door on the second *clank* of the ornate knocker. A shot of something—looked like rum—already in hand, he greeted us with a big display of his perfect white teeth and escorted us into the library. He was again wearing a smoking jacket, this time in a shade of tan that nicely complemented his pompadour and the slightly darker brown pants.

After we declined his offer of a drink, all three of us settled into a grouping of chairs and he took a sip from his glass. Obviously he was feeling more relaxed than last time when I told him about the phone calls. I wondered how he'd feel when he learned who'd been making them—if he didn't know already.

"The police have been here," he said. "A homicide detective named Mike Whitehall wanted to know all about Jesse and Stan and the other board members. I told him what I could." He swirled the remaining rum in the glass, observing it with some interest. "You two know Detective Lieutenant Whitehall. He's a friend of yours, isn't he?" That last was directed specifically at me.

"Yes," I replied. "Did he mention me?" I found it hard to believe he would have.

"No, but I've been doing some detective work of my own." He smiled a little smugly. "There's a nice archive of news stories about you two. Some of them talk about the karate studio where you teach, Mr. McCall—and the Portland homicide detective who shares the teaching duties."

Malone spoke up, abruptly redirecting the conversation. "Speaking of friends," she said, "tell us about Tony Zahl."

Albright's smile faded as his eyebrows went up. He set his drink carefully on the side table. "Ah," he said finally. "I was afraid Tony might have something to do with this."

"You thought he might be the one making the phone calls?" she followed up.

"Yes, that occurred to me—but only because Tony is the only person I know who *might* be involved. He is the one, then?"

"So he says," I responded.

"You talked to him."

"He came to us, yes."

"Then...did he kill Jesse and Stan?"

"What do you think?"

He picked up the glass and downed the rest of his drink, then got up heading for the liquor cabinet. "Sure you don't want something? Neither of you?"

"Absolutely," I answered and Malone agreed.

"Do you think Zahl killed them?" she asked our host.

"No. I don't know." He splashed more amber liquid into the glass. "Now I don't think he did. There was a time I thought he might have killed Jesse out of misplaced jealousy. There was never anything between Jesse and me. He was heterosexual as far as I know and a loner to boot, but Tony did ask me about him once. Any young, rich male who doesn't have a woman on his arm generates rumors in this homophobic society of ours; Tony had heard them. But now...now that Stan is gone too.... I have no idea why Tony would kill Stan." He glanced at us almost sheepishly as he went back to his chair. "I...I really didn't know him that well. Tony, I mean."

I was sure Zahl would be thrilled to hear himself dismissed that

242

way by the man he claimed to be obsessing about. Certainly could be a motive for something.

"You did have a relationship with him," Malone continued.

"Briefly, very briefly. Two months or so at most. He...was not my type. Extremely volatile, and I didn't care for some of his friends."

I took my turn again. "Then why get involved with him at all? I've heard you are 'very selective and discreet.'"

He smiled ruefully. "I must thank Tanya for the compliment." He paused and finally said with a sigh, "It seemed like it might be something different." A shrug. "And I do like some variety. Tony can be charming and can make his...ah, business...sound quite refined and upper class. I suppose it *is* upper class in that we're his clientele, but most of his associates are dubious at best." He took another sip and set the glass on the side table. "That, along with a growing sense that he could be a violent man, just made me too uneasy to continue. He was too much, simply put, too difficult to deal with."

"I see."

Albright leaned forward and looked closely at me, his expression suddenly almost mischievous. "Detective Whitehall is quite an attractive man. Do you know if he has a partner?"

Oh crap. An almost inaudible gasp came from the direction of Devon Malone. "I assume you don't mean a partner on the job."

"That's correct. Speaking of variety."

"Ah. Yes, he does have a partner. Besides, it's unlikely he'd go out with someone he's interviewing for an ongoing investigation. I'm afraid you're out of luck."

Albright smiled, just a little smile, and sipped his drink. "That's too bad."

Glad to have that out of the way, I went on. "Zahl says he heard from those friends of his that there are financial improprieties associated with the Lifestream Foundation. I asked you before and I'll ask you again: You know anything about that?"

Albright's smile disappeared and he pulled back. "I told you before and I'll tell you again: Absolutely not. There are no financial irregularities that I'm aware of. I don't believe there are any at all. Tony is just trying to make trouble, though I don't know what he thinks he can gain by it."

"You," said Malone.

Albright jumped slightly. "What? What do you mean?"

"He claims he wanted to bring you down to his level so that the two of you could get back together."

Albright sat there looking from one of us to the other as if she'd just told him he was being courted by a Martian. Then he cocked his head back and let go a long peal of laughter. "That...that is absurd!" he exploded when he was able to catch his breath. "I can believe he wanted to hurt me, but not that he expected...." He went off into another giggling fit.

I thought about Malcolm Guth, who apparently believed he could win his lady fair's love by killing a man and threatening to send her to Death Row for it.

"You never know," I offered as the laughter finally tailed off into silence.

We talked for another quarter-hour and we came away with a few more tidbits about Tony Zahl, such as his MBA from Berkeley and a predilection for ropes of velvet. Apparently he presented himself in the living room as just another businessman with a slightly unusual trade and in the bedroom as just another lover with slightly unusual tastes. He wanted to be a regular guy, our Tony, and couldn't quite pull it off; that was Norman Albright's ultimate take on his ex-boyfriend.

CHAPTER SIXTY-TWO

As for me, I needed some time to clear my head. We had a whole new player in the Heatherly case and still no clue what was actually going on, most notably why board members were biting the dust. Guth was putting out contracts on me and canceling them the next day; for all I knew, there could be another one in effect by now. It seemed as if the complications were beginning to consume my life.

So I suggested to Malone that we take a walk. The weather was relatively good and I needed a change of perspective. She thought that the walk—not the change of perspective—was a rather odd idea, which it was at the moment, but agreed.

With Albright's permission, I left the Subaru in his driveway while my partner and I headed for the nearby Mount Tabor Park. It being a weekday, the park was nearly deserted except for elderly hikers and young parents, mostly female but not all, pushing strollers. The March flora presented few colors besides green and brown, but the day had remained clear and the late-afternoon views of the city, Mount St. Helens, and Mount Hood were spectacular. For the first few minutes we just ambled around, neither of us speaking—though I could almost hear Malone wondering what I had in mind. Maybe she feared I was going to propose? Eh. Probably not.

"Here's what I'm thinking," I finally said, just to let her off the hook. "First one of Portland's lowest scumbags is claiming the barely-ex whore under our protection as his one true love. Then one of the city's higher-level scumbags nominates our client's uncle-in-law as the love of his life. And now said uncle-in-law has the hots for our good friend and my fellow black belt who happens to be the primary on two murders that are probably related to our client."

"Maybe we should just forget the whole private detective business and open a lonely hearts club instead."

"Not helpful." We'd come to a stop near the basketball court. Never was my game. I'm way too short.

"Well, how about this?" Malone offered. "We both know Albright was holding something, maybe a lot, back. We need to re-interview Tanya Petosky, Max Overton, and Barbara Schilling to see what they can tell us about Tony Zahl and Albright. We don't have it all figured out yet, but I think we're closer."

By unspoken mutual consent, we started back toward the car. "You thought this walk was going to be about us, didn't you?"

Just a hint of a hesitation. "It is about us. Solving mysteries is what we do, right?"

And a hint of a sigh from me. "Right, partner. That's what we do."

CHAPTER SIXTY-THREE

However, once we got to the car and compared notes on how tired and frustrated we both were, we agreed that tomorrow would be soon enough to solve further mysteries. I dropped Malone off at her Jeep, we cautioned one another to watch our respective backs, and I headed home.

It being just past five o'clock, the drive back over to the Hawthorne District was mostly stop-and-go. (Why don't they call it "slow hour"? No one is able to rush.) I almost stopped by the do-jang to work off a little of the frustration but decided that quiet time at home with the cats would do me more good.

I pulled into my driveway at five-thirty and picked up the mail on my way into the house. Stella greeted me at the door as always. Maxine, also as always, hung back to make absolutely sure that I was alone. Then they both dashed for the kitchen to inform me that their bowls were empty, which of course actually meant that there was a hole in the middle of the remaining kibble. I dutifully filled the holes and they eagerly set about recreating them.

I was just deciding which frozen meal to pop into the microwave when the phone rang. It was Johnny Crew, calling from the Pen and Pastry. He said he had news and I said I'd be there in a minute.

I retrieved my Smith and Wesson, shrugged on my jacket, and walked around the corner to the café. The darkening day was getting colder and cloudy; it felt like there would be rain before the night was over.

The warm light of the café washed out onto the sidewalk through the storefront windows. The dinner crowd was only beginning to gather, fewer than half the twenty tables occupied. The place would be packed later, when the main feature at the neighborhood theater next door let out.

I observed through the front window that one of the tables in back was occupied by my daughter, Johnny Crew, and LeAnn Hannaford. Apparently LeAnn had forgiven Colleen for ratting her out. Sitting at a table across the room was Roger Arbuckle.

I stepped through the entrance and savored the aromas of warm pastry, hot roll-ups, and strong coffee. I spotted proprietress Veronica Fortune chatting with several patrons at a table to my left. She was wearing a plain white blouse and gray mid-calf skirt, nevertheless attracting a lot of male attention as usual.

She saw me and smiled as I nodded hello and then headed for Johnny's table.

Colleen came around to give me a hug. Johnny leaned across the table to shake hands. LeAnn, who had remained seated, offered a small wave but no smile. I was assuming she'd heard from Mal Guth since they had felt free to leave the apartment.

"Hap wanted to be here," Johnny said as he resumed his own seat, "but he's still holding down your client's fort."

I took a seat as I answered Johnny. "Hap doing okay at the Heatherly's?"

"Having the time of his life, far as I can tell, 'cept for having to go outside to smoke. It seems Mrs. Heatherly is a very good cook."

I had to chuckle as I sat down. "That's great."

Maureen Loori, Veronica's chief lieutenant and café den mother, was already at my shoulder, asking if I wanted to order dinner, which I did.

I turned then to LeAnn. "You talked to Guth?"

She grimaced and cast a sideways glance at my daughter. "God, I hated it. He scares the shit out of me. I wouldn't have had to do it if...."

"Yes," I interrupted, knowing she was thinking of Colleen's ratting her out, "and you might be dead instead. Since it sounds like you *did* do it, why don't you—one of you—tell me how it went."

Johnny put a hand on LeAnn's arm and took up the burden of story-telling. "The asshole didn't exactly blurt out the location of the body or the gun," he growled, "but there's some possibilities."

"I didn't hear any possibilities," LeAnn said miserably. "He was just making fun—and scaring the shit out of me."

Johnny squeezed her arm gently. "Nah, there was more to it than that." He focused on me. "She did good, Clint, and we might have got something. She told him she didn't believe he still had the stuff—or the stiff—like you wanted, said she thought he'd never kept the body and probably thrown the gun in the river; that was my idea. There was a couple of times I covered up my extension and whispered stuff for her to say, just trying to provoke the son of a bitch some more.

"Anyway, he came back with all kinds of shit, threats and other crap, denied throwing anything in the river, but almost jokey-sounding if you know what I mean, telling her she couldn't get away, that he had her cold. That's what he said, 'I've got you cold.' I cued her to tell him again she thought the gun and the body was probably with the fishes and he got a big kick out of that, saying she was right, that that was why she'd never get away from him. I'm sure he's still got something, at least the gun with her prints on it. He was having way too good a time."

A waitress appeared at that moment with my beef roll-ups and coffee. I waited until she'd gone, processing in the meantime what Johnny had told me. I had an idea of what he thought we'd gotten. "What else?" I asked him then.

"He was playing with her; that's what I think. You could hear it in his voice. Twice he laughed out loud. Once when he said that line about having her cold and the other time when he agreed that the stuff was with the fishes. He really got a charge out of that one —only he said 'fish,' not 'fishes,' when he repeated it back. That was on purpose. The motherfucker was dropping hints."

LeAnn's expression was somewhere between confusion and disbelief. "Why would he give me hints?" she asked.

"Because he wouldn't expect you to hear them," Johnny replied. "He was just having some fun for himself. Wouldn't have done it if he'd known a cop was listening."

LeAnn looked at me. "What do you think?"

"I think there's a good chance Johnny's right. 'I've got you cold' doesn't sound like Guth and there's no reason for him to say the gun or the body is 'with the fish' after he's denied throwing any-thing in the river."

"These guys," chimed in Colleen, indicating Johnny and me, "don't listen the same way as other people. Believe me," she grinned at LeAnn, "you wouldn't want a detective for a father when you were trying to get away with something."

LeAnn produced another small, albeit forgiving, smile for Colleen and then turned her attention to me. "But what does it all mean?"

I shrugged. "That we've got some things to think about. Maybe the body's in a freezer somewhere. That would make sense —or an aquarium, which wouldn't so much. We can try to find out whether Guth is renting a big freezer or has access to one. We take it a step at a time." I reached over and gave her hand a pat. "You did a good, brave thing," I said, "and now we have another direc-tion to go. Thank you."

CHAPTER SIXTY-FOUR

The sirens woke me at three-fifteen, already winding down as I came to consciousness. They were behind the house somewhere; I staggered into the kitchen, almost tripping over Stella along the way, and looked out the back door.

There was a dim glow beyond the back fence toward Hawthorne Street, a glimmering red against the black night sky. It wasn't on the corner. It wasn't the theater. It looked like it was the Pen and Pastry.

I hurried back to the bedroom, wide-awake now but holding my growing fear tightly in check. I got pants, shirt, and shoes on as quickly as I could and grabbed my jacket on the way out. Both cats were crouched under the dining table by then, clearly picking up on my distress. As I dashed past, I called to them that it was okay and I would be back. Which probably didn't reassure them but made me feel a little better.

I hadn't noticed it was raining when I looked out the back door, but I was sopping wet by the time I rounded the corner to find the fire trucks in front of the café.

I was halted by the barricades just being set up to keep the gathering neighborhood crowd at bay. I realized only then that I was way underdressed for standing in the cold March rain. Not much to do about it but try to keep the shivering to a minimum.

Smoke was billowing from the smashed front windows of the Pen and Pastry, the flickering of flames in the dining room barely visible through black-gray clouds. The air was heavy with the stink of smoke and damp, charred wood and plaster.

There were three fire trucks and two police cars, the latter blocking off the street at each end of the block, the rain creating a surreal blur of flashing lights and glinting wet metal. I realized, with a small measure of relief, that the red glow I'd seen from my kitchen must have been more the lights than the fire.

251

I yelled at the nearest fireman, "Was anyone in there?"

He frowned. "No, sir. No sign of anyone. Was somebody supposed to be in there?"

I shook my head. "No, I was just checking. A friend of mine is the owner."

He stepped a little closer. "Oh? Who is that?"

"Her name is Veronica Fortune. No one has called her?"

"Probably, but I'll go tell the boss just in case." He moved off toward the trucks.

I was just thinking about going back to my place for my own cell phone and some rain gear when I heard Veronica's voice. Obviously she had been called right away.

I quickly worked my way over to where she was talking with one of the firefighters, an older guy who was probably "the boss." She was far more disheveled than I'd ever seen her before, in jeans and sweatshirt and not even a jacket, her long red hair draped in strings across her face and down her back. She looked deathly pale in the flashing lights.

I put my hand on her shoulder and she glanced over, seeming not to recognize me for a second. Then she did, and turned into me with a wracking sob. I could feel my stomach twisting around an empty place in the middle of my gut. What were the odds that this devastation of her livelihood had nothing to do with me and my latest great idea to provoke Malcolm Guth?

I lowered my head to hers and whispered "I'm sorry" into her smoke-scented hair.

Maureen Loori showed up ten minutes later dressed in what looked like a woolen muumuu and a scarf. She practically tackled Veronica, her stout black arms bringing her friend into a tight hug even as she mournfully hoped aloud that it wasn't anything she'd left on in the kitchen.

I'd had a chance to visit with another of the firefighters in the meantime and could reassure them both that the kitchen was relatively undamaged. He'd told me it looked to him like the fire started with material thrown through the front window, but that was just unofficial speculation; he didn't want to step on the investigators' toes.

I invited both Veronica and Maureen back to my house, to dry out and have some coffee. It was about four-fifteen by then. The fire seemed to be out and we had confirmation that overall the damage wasn't too bad. The rain had helped keep the roof in one piece and the fire itself had been confined to the dining area near the front.

We were back on the fire line with a thermos by five. The two women were far too worried and antsy about the café to sit around my kitchen, even though it was warm and dry. Outside it was still dark and drizzling, but we were immediately surrounded by café regulars vying with one another to hug Veronica and wanting to know what they could do to help. Several of the early-shift waitresses had already joined Maureen in surveying the damage and watching the firefighters begin to stow their hoses. There was plenty of manpower available for clean-up, but that would have to wait awhile. I could see one of the Bureau's arson investigators already poking around inside, his powerful flashlight scanning the floor.

As the three of us stood watching him, I felt a tap on my arm. There was something about the abruptness and force of the tap that told me who I was going to see before I even turned my head.

I was half right. Devon Malone was standing there by my side but she wasn't alone.

The floodlight attached to a television camera came on as soon as I turned, a harsh glare that silhouetted Malone and almost blinded me. Still, I didn't have to see clearly to recognize the young woman who was attempting to insert herself between me and my partner.

"Who was trying to get you this time, McCall?" asked Alison Roberts in her best on-air voice, thrusting the microphone in my face.

"Fuck off," I replied in my best you-can't-air-this-sound-bite voice. Malone leaned over Roberts' shoulder and made a braying sound into the microphone, which didn't improve the quality of the interview.

Roberts hesitated, then lowered the mike. "Shit. Okay, kill it, Murray." She stepped closer and lowered her voice. "Give me a break, McCall. The second I heard on the scanner where this 'suspicious' fire was, I knew it had to have something to do with you two. And here you both are, standing in front of the place. I *am* going with a story whether you cooperate or not. Might as well help me out here."

Her face flickered in and out of shadow as the lights atop the few remaining fire and police vehicles revolved. She was dressed in a pull-over sweater and station-logo blazer that would show on camera along with blue jeans and sneakers that would not. I was thinking that I was getting too old; she looked eighteen to me, maybe younger, rather than late twenties.

"We are standing here with our friend Veronica Fortune, who owns the place. It caught on fire. We're here to offer what comfort we can. That's all there is to it."

Roberts' mouth twisted. "Right." She looked at Malone. "You're a friend of hers as well?"

Malone pointed at me. "Of his," was all she said. I decided I could wait a while to get the real explanation of what she was doing here. Heard it on her scanner, probably.

Roberts turned somewhat desperately to Veronica. "Well, then, maybe I'll do the story about you. Have you heard yet how the fire started? I see there's an arson investigator in there. It's already been called a suspicious fire. Somebody from *your* old days, maybe?"

I knew Roberts was just trying to provoke one of us. Otherwise she would have told her faithful ex-hippie cameraman Murray Kravitz to start recording again before she asked the question.

Veronica must have had the same realization. "Leave me alone," she said simply and turned her attention back to the ruined storefront. Roberts muttered something under her breath and motioned Kravitz to follow her.

My young nemesis wasn't kidding about doing the story anyway. She did a stand-up about fifteen feet away, the camera positioned to show the smashed plate-glass windows behind her. At one point Kravitz panned over to get a long shot of our little group standing together. I resisted the temptation to offer a middle finger in reply.

CHAPTER SIXTY-FIVE

Around seven, Malone and I went back to my house. I needed to get properly cleaned up for work and we both needed some more coffee.

Veronica and the rest of her crew stayed behind to begin their own clean-up. The Pen and Pastry, much more than her best-selling book, represented to her the distance she'd put between her present and her former life. Seeing it so damaged, she'd told me, felt like losing her center, being suddenly at risk of returning to all that went before. She needed to get the café open again as soon as possible.

"And we," I said to Malone after showering and dressing, over a last cup of coffee in the kitchen, "need to end this crap with Guth before he does any more damage."

"We're sure it was him?"

I nodded. "One of the cops on the scene told me that they'd found a witness who saw a car slow down in front of the café. The driver threw two Molotov cocktails through the front windows. The car was nondescript, maybe tan, probably late-80s, an American-made sedan, license plate not illuminated. Which doesn't help us, but the vehicle that followed right behind, also slowing as if to make sure the fire got a good start, was a bright red Lincoln Continental low-rider—of which there is exactly one in town as far as we know."

"Owned by Malcolm Guth. So you're right: it's time to put a period on that asshole."

I chuckled and downed another good slug of coffee. "I wouldn't have used such a wonderfully unattractive image, but yes, it is."

There was something about sitting across my own kitchen table from Devon Malone, drinking coffee early in the morning, catching a whiff of her cinnamon-scented hair now that I'd showered away

257

my own smoke smell, that tugged at my heart and apparently loosened my tongue.

"You never kid me about my age," I found myself saying out of nowhere.

Her cup stopped halfway up to her mouth and she cocked an eye at me. "Your age? Why would I kid you about your age?"

I set my cup down, committed now—to what, I wasn't sure. "You've given me a hard time about almost everything else at some point or other, but never my age. I'm fifty-three years old and you're, what, mid-thirties? Why don't I know when your birthday is, by the way? Anyway, you've never hassled me about my age."

She was looking at me seriously now. "So?"

"It makes me wonder if you really do think I'm too old."

She took what seemed like a long time to respond. "Too old for what?"

Okay, she was going to make me work for this. "For a relationship. We've been talking about a relationship, but not much more than talking. I wondered...."

"Your friend Veronica is pretty spectacular," she interrupted. "What is she, mid- to late-forties?"

It was my turn to take a long moment. "So?"

"Just sayin'. Age sure as hell hasn't hurt her any. Beautiful woman, best-selling author, sex expert, a successful café full of male customers drooling more over her than the food. You've known her a long time, right?"

"As a matter of fact, she was my first client after I set up the agency. What does she have to do with anything?"

"You never talked about a relationship with her? Or did more than talk?"

"No, never. I'll confess that I did my share of drooling when she first walked in the door but then she was my client—and after that my friend, more like a sister, Colleen's aunt. I ask again: What's your point?"

She took another sip of coffee. "Eh. If you can be insecure

258

about your age, I can be insecure about your friend. So then we're both stupid. Does that make you feel better?"

I put down my own cup and stood. "Yes," I said as I came around the table to her side. "Yes, it does make me feel better." I leaned down as she looked up at me and our lips met. It was a long kiss this time. I don't know how long because I completely lost myself in it, only realizing when I finally pulled away that Devon Malone had been kissing me every bit as much as I was kissing her.

"You didn't run away this time," I said. Her eyes were softer than I had ever seen them, but they also sparked with amusement.

"Neither did you," she said.

I glanced around the kitchen. "It's my house. I've got nowhere to run."

And she punched me in the arm.

CHAPTER SIXTY-SIX

We spent several more pleasant minutes in the kitchen but mutually decided there were too many distractions—not the least of which was the lingering smell of smoke from the Pen and Pastry arson. I had to really make an effort to shift from feeling great relief to feeling threatened again. But I managed.

Another mutual agreement was that matters were too urgent for us to bother hitting the office before taking some kind of action.

Warnings first. I'd made three phone calls by eight, one to LeAnn's apartment, one to Hap at the Heatherlys, and one to Colleen. Everyone but Colleen agreed to stay put until they heard from me again; my daughter announced she was coming down immediately to help Veronica and hung up on my protests. I let it go. Like father like daughter.

Malone finished what must have been her fourth or fifth cup of coffee and stood. "Do you want to stay here until Colleen is with Veronica? We need to get moving pretty soon. None of them will be safe until we have Guth."

"I know," I answered, "and, no, we don't need to wait for Colleen. I doubt that Guth will go after her between her place and the café. He probably went to ground, at least for a while, after last night's adventure. And I think I know who might be able to tell us where."

She grimaced. "Reuben."

"And we could use the extra backup."

Much bigger grimace. "You want the pimp who dresses in pink and chartreuse as backup? I'm insulted. I don't think I'll kiss you anymore. And didn't you promise not to put him in Guth's way?"

"I'm thinking that Reuben will change his mind when he hears about the café. He's still very fond of Veronica. And he's one tough mother. You know that. He couldn't get away with dressing the way

261

he does if he wasn't. We know that Guth wasn't alone on the arson job. If we're going to finish this now, I'd like as many guns as possible."

"So why not call Mike?"

"Reuben's not going to tell us anything if cops are involved and who knows how long it would take to set up a SWAT team or whatever approach was decided on...."

"You just want to do it yourself."

"Well, yes, there's that."

"Okay, then. Let's go."

I retrieved some extra clips for my Smith and Wesson from my gun safe while Malone got some for her Glock from her Jeep parked at the corner. We met up at my Outback. Just before backing out of my driveway I tried Reuben Keys' cell phone and got no answer; it went straight to voicemail but I didn't leave a message. This early in the morning he would be sound asleep and the only way to talk to him was to roust him out. That's exactly what I planned to do.

As I drove down Hawthorne, Malone checked the office voicemail and reported that there were no messages, not even any media. Which was good. No new clients we'd have to ignore, no weird voices making incoherent threats, no questions from the Heatherlys about their case which I was going to totally neglect until we settled with Mal Guth.

Reuben currently lived about a mile east of the Burnside Bridge in a two-story apartment building near the corner of 21st and Ash. I parked on the street a couple of doors down. I could see his ride in the off-street parking in front of the building that many years ago had been painted in tones of peach and Burgundy.

The rain had finally paused but the sky remained a solid gray and the wind chilly. We took the outside metal stairway up to the second floor balcony that ran the length of the building and I knocked on the door of apartment 2B. Repeatedly.

It was a good minute-and-a-half before I heard a muffled

"What the fuck!" on the other side of the door. Obviously Reuben was a little surprised to see us through the peephole.

He opened the door and glowered at both of us equally. He was wearing dirty blue boxers and loosely holding what looked like a .38 down at his right side. There were even more scars on his torso than on his face and throat. I felt, more than saw, Malone react to the gun and put a hand on her arm to ensure that she didn't draw her own weapon.

"What you fuckers want?" Reuben growled as he motioned us into the room with his free hand. Apparently he hadn't even noticed Malone's reaction. He did look like he was barely awake.

And apparently his housekeeping staff was still on vacation. I could see only two rooms, this small living room with a fold-out couch and a kitchen that barely qualified as a nook. Clothes, magazines, discarded fast food packaging, and a number of unidentifiable items cluttered every square foot. The unmistakable odors of pot and male pimp permeated the air.

"I want you to put that gun down, to start with," I said. "Otherwise Malone here is likely to blow you away."

"Oh," he muttered, looking at it as if wondering how it got in his hand. "Sure." He tossed it on the disheveled sofa bed. "What you doin' here?"

"We need you to find out where Mal Guth is right now."

I caught the glance toward the gun he'd just tossed away as his whole body tensed up. "How the fuck do I know where he's at?"

"He tried to burn down Veronica's café."

"Fuck me! When? Is she okay?"

"She's all right. It was the middle of last night. He had somebody firebomb the place."

"You sure it was him?"

"Positive."

He looked away and took a long, deep breath. "I'll make some calls."

It took only three. He hung up from the last one and turned to us with a satisfied expression. "Our white boy is back home."

"What do you mean?" I asked.

"He's hole up in a room upstairs above the Lounge."

"The Gentlemen's Lounge?" confirmed Malone. "You're kidding. He's back there again?"

"Upstairs, probably with some heat downstairs. You know how that is."

What I knew was that I found it just as hard to believe as Malone did. I was sure Malcolm Guth had never heard of a purloined letter, but I supposed he could have come up with the idea of hiding in plain sight on his own.

"How about you take me along," Reuben said.

Just as I had hoped. I looked at him standing there in his skivvies. "I thought you didn't want to confront Guth. That's exactly what we're about to do. There could be some bullets flying."

His eyebrows went way up and he cocked an eye at my partner even though he was speaking to me. "Then I'll bring my piece," he said. "The motherfucker went after Veronica."

I cocked my own eye at my partner, who was looking sour. "I guess," she said finally, "we could use another gun. But today only. Understood?"

Reuben nodded and reached for his pants. "Understood," he said.

CHAPTER SIXTY-SEVEN

The Gentlemen's Lounge opens at eleven on weekday mornings and we were there at two minutes past the hour.

I had been hoping to time it so that we didn't have to break in but before there were any customers. That's usually a very narrow window for a place like the Lounge. At least one desperately thirsty (or horny) morning drinker is likely to show up almost right away.

The three of us stopped just inside the door. The usually dim interior was almost pitch dark, the bartender still in the process of turning on lights. I could see her working her way toward the front from the stage area. No music yet. Probably there was at least one girl in back, getting ready for the first set. Which wouldn't be quite yet. We had successfully beaten everyone else to the place. Customers, anyway.

Even in the shadows you couldn't miss the two bruisers, a big white guy with shaved head and an even bigger black one with dreadlocks, sitting across from the bar that extended in an L-shape to our right. They occupied two of the little round tables, one on each side of a doorway in the far wall that revealed steps going up. That's where Guth would be. I was sure of it now. These guys were definitely *not* customers.

The bartender walked past them and flicked the last light switch. She continued on toward us, angling behind the bar. Young, stocky build, blond frizzy hair, jeans and work shirt with cuffs rolled up. She was the same woman I'd seen dispensing drinks when I was in here to confront Guth the first time.

She was giving us her full attention by this time, as were the two big boys. We didn't look like customers either.

As planned, Reuben took the lead, moving carefully around the corner of the bar toward the men. Malone and I stayed two steps behind and did our best to look harmless.

The two goons lumbered to their feet and came to meet us, initially focused on Reuben as we'd hoped. He at least looked like he might be a colleague of Guth's.

We all came to a stop with about four feet separating us. The black guy gave Reuben a long, cool look. "What you want, nigger?"

Reuben brought his hands up to show they were empty. "Gotta talk to the man upstairs."

Meanwhile the white guy was giving me and my partner the eye. "Who's the old man and the bitch, *nigger*?" he sneered, making it real clear that his use of the word was intended differently than that of his companion.

I could feel Malone at my side practically vibrating with hostility as Reuben replied with not much more diplomacy than she would have used, his chin jutting and chest thrusting, one hand gesturing toward us. "These two know some stuff Mal's gonna want to hear." He paused, glaring right at the smaller man. "Just goes to show you white folks ain't *all* ignorant fucks."

Okay, so this wasn't going well. It had been fifty-fifty at best that Reuben could talk us past the lookouts anyway; launching immediately into an insult contest had reduced the odds to one in a hundred. This wasn't the one.

Mr. Dreadlocks reached for his buddy's arm as the guy stepped toward Reuben. "Let it go, Carl...," he said.

"Fuck that!" Dome Head yelled as he shook off the restraining grip. "Hands on the bar, boy," he growled at Reuben, "and spread 'em. We gotta see if you're carryin'--and I hope you fucking are." He gave me and Malone a quick beady glare. "You two stay put." By now his partner was looking like he'd just as soon be someplace else.

Reuben and I made eye contact as he turned and leaned to put his hands on the bar. He knew he'd blown it but appeared ready to deal with the consequences. Nobody was paying much attention to Malone or me, apparently believing that the white folks were not currently a threat, so I shifted my left foot back a few inches and lowered my stance slightly. I felt Malone making a similar move. I was still hoping we could do this part without any gunfire.

Since Reuben had simply stashed his gun in his jacket pocket, the pat-down found it immediately. The bruiser let out a short, harsh laugh and reached around to hold the weapon in Reuben's face, almost shoving it up his nose.

"This what you want Mal to hear?"

Dreadlocks took a step forward. "Carl, just...."

Too late. Carl jerked Reuben back from the bar and swung at his head with the gun. Reuben ducked underneath the swing, grabbed two handfuls of shirt-front, and tossed the off-balance white guy in our direction as he went for the black partner.

Perfect. All I had to do was plant a solid side kick on Dome Head's jaw as he staggered toward me. He did a nice pirouette as he was going down. There was no doubt that he would be staying down for a while. I did hope he'd had a spare split-second to appreciate that the old man could still kick above shoulder-height.

Malone, meanwhile, had drawn her Glock as Reuben flailed through the air back into the further reaches of the seating area and crashed down among the tables and chairs. Apparently the big black guy was much better than his buddy at throwing people around. Also, his hand was moving in the direction of the holster I'd just seen on his belt nestled in the small of his back.

"Don't do it!" Malone shouted. "Take it out easy and drop it." He froze, then slowly withdrew his hand from behind his back holding a .38 revolver with thumb and forefinger. He leaned slightly forward so that it wouldn't fall too far and then raised his hands.

He looked at Malone, then me, then at the unconscious figure on the floor, and his mouth twisted in a half-grin. "Dumb shit," he muttered.

"You...you just hold it right there," came a quavering female voice from my right. I glanced over to find that the bartender had come up with another weapon from behind the bar, a snub-nosed . 32, by the look of it, wavering back and forth between Malone and me.

"Put that down before you hurt somebody," I said to her as I focused back on the black guy. "We're private detectives and we're after Guth. He's upstairs, isn't he?"

Long pause. "Maybe," she answered.

"You want to go to jail for shooting two people to protect him?"

The weapon made a solid metallic thud as she placed it firmly on the bar.

"Good choice," I said.

About then Reuben came limping and groaning into the light from where he'd landed. He didn't look good; he could barely walk, his left arm was hanging limply, and there was blood running down the side of his face.

"How bad?" I asked.

He glowered at me as he hobbled around the bigger black guy, giving him plenty of space. "No fucking problem at all. What the fuck does it look like? My knee is killing me, I think my arm's broken, and I've got one motherfucker of a headache. You're gonna owe me for this one, you honky fucks." He dropped into a nearby chair with a grand moan.

His pistol had landed right at Malone's feet when the smaller thug went down. She crouched carefully to pick it up and then edged sideways to hand it to him as I kept my own trained on the bruiser still standing. "We'll get you some help as soon as we can," she said. "Your good arm good enough to keep this on our friends here until then?"

He gave her a sour look, snatched the gun from her hand, and leveled it at the upright bad guy and then at the one still on the floor—who was flailing a little as he began to come around. "Don't need no help," Reuben said.

I holstered my weapon and stepped over to the bar. "Have you called the police?" I asked the bartender quietly.

"No," she said and started to turn to the phone behind her.

I put my hand on her arm. She hadn't tried to shoot us and my

268

gut told me she was no more a fan of Guth and his crew than any other sane young woman would be. I was going to trust her.

"Not yet," I said. "My partner and I are going to go up those steps and I don't want to hear sirens before we get to the top. Five minutes. If you haven't heard or seen anything by then, make the call. Tell them what happened and that you need paramedics." I picked up her .32 and handed it back to her. "Don't point this at anybody unless you need to defend yourself." I gestured back at Reuben. "Especially don't point it at him. If you hear shots upstairs, go ahead and call the cops right then. Understand?"

Apparently the bartender was recovering just fine from her initial fright. She gave a little shrug and said "Sure," as if I'd ordered a draft beer. And then she indicated Malone. "That's your partner?"

"Yep," I said, tossing a little smile over my shoulder at the person in question, "that's her."

"Huh." I guess she wasn't accustomed to the idea of female private eyes.

We rounded up the guns belonging to the bodyguards and put them on Reuben's table. Meanwhile, he was instructing the now-conscious bald guy to join his buddy—by crawling, if necessary.

As we turned to go up the stairs, Reuben hissed at me. "What if cops show up? They see me holdin' this gun and I ain't gonna have time to explain what I'm doin' here—and what the fuck would I say about that anyway?"

Good point. "If you hear sirens out front," I suggested, "wait until they're at the door and put your gun down with the others on the table. Let the bartender over there cover these guys until the cops are inside. She can be the hero."

He glanced over at her. "You handle that?" he called. She nodded almost imperceptibly. Her hands rested lightly on the glossy surface of the bar, one on either side of her gun. She seemed steady enough now.

He looked at our two captives. "If I gotta put it down," he said to them, "I can pick it up again real quick."

Then to me out of the corner of his mouth: "Don't take too fuckin' long up there."

CHAPTER SIXTY-EIGHT

I drew my gun again, as did Malone, and we started slowly up the stairs. It was a narrow, dimly lit single flight leading to a small landing at the top. I could see two doors when we got there, the one on the right closed and the one directly ahead open with a light on in the room beyond. The stairwell smelled of cigarettes, piss, and vomit. At least the construction was good; none of the bare wooden steps made noise as we edged our way up.

Unless he was very stoned or an unusually sound sleeper, Guth must have heard the commotion downstairs. It struck me that we hadn't checked the outside of the building to see if there was a usable fire escape from the second floor. He could be gone already. Crap.

The room beyond the open door gradually revealed itself as we rose step by step. A big-screen TV (no cartoons this time), an easy chair (empty), side table with what looked like a half-finished glass of beer, a ratty brown couch against the far wall with a closed window above it. He hadn't gone out that way, but the beer looked newly abandoned. Somewhere up here was either an open window or a nasty guy looking to blow both our heads off.

We paused on the landing and Malone carefully put her ear against the closed door. Shook her head. Nothing. She motioned that I should keep my eye on the open door while she checked further. So I stood ready while she turned the knob and eased that door open. The room beyond was dark but she reached around and clicked on the light, then stepped partway inside. After a moment she backed out and shook her head again. Apparently she was satisfied that the room was clear.

That left the door ahead of us. Decisions, decisions. From what I could see now that we were on the landing, there was a kitchen area to the left of the living room furniture, set off by a divider of waist-high cabinetry or shelves. We were going to have to check it out. Malone came up beside me and we moved forward.

And hit the first creaky board just inside the doorway.

Guth sprang into view from behind the kitchen-living room divider, firing his first shot as he was still rising. I heard wood splinter in the doorway above and behind my head.

Malone dived to the left and I crouched down where I was. Guth was getting both feet planted for a second try, which gave me a nice stable target. I fired. He cried out and jerked sideways, the weapon flying from his hand. I'd aimed for his arm and it looked like a good shot.

He recovered his balance and his cry of pain became a scream of rage as he charged full-tilt across the room, both arms raised as if to batter me down, blood pouring from his right bicep. His greasy pale blond hair was wild, as were the eyes blazing above his knife-sharp nose. He may have been ingesting more than beer before my arrival because a bullet wound wasn't slowing him in the slightest.

A second bullet wound, this one in his leg courtesy of my partner, did the trick. He cried out again, spun around, and his forward momentum carried him right to my feet where he slid to a stop, glaring up at me with bulging eyes.

I stepped a little back from Guth as Malone got up and rejoined me. We both stood looking down at him. His face had taken on a bluish tinge. He seemed to be having a hard time taking a breath, I suspected from fury more than pain.

"Batshit crazy right to the end," commented Malone.

That was apparently too much for Guth, that or the blood loss. His eyes glazed over and his eyelids drooped shut.

I heard sirens in the distance, growing louder. "You didn't hit his femoral artery, did you?" I asked Malone.

She leaned over and nudged his bloody leg. "Nah. He's not going to bleed out before they get here." She stood up. "Unfortunately."

While she was checking his wound, I'd been doing a quick survey of the living room and kitchen areas. Something was nagging at me, something it felt like I was looking at but not seeing....

The refrigerator in the kitchen.

Not a normal refrigerator, but an over-sized combination freezer-refrigerator. I went over and jerked open the upper, freezer compartment. The sirens were very close now. I was looking at...fish. Twenty, maybe thirty boxes of frozen fish portions. The temperature had been set unusually low and the stacks of boxes were frozen solid in place. The sirens were pulling up in front. I knocked the boxes loose with a couple of straight palm strikes.

Malone joined me in front of the appliance. "What the hell are you doing?" she asked.

"Check it out."

Toward the back, among the boxes of frozen fish, were two plastic bags. One contained a revolver, which didn't surprise me. The other contained a hand, severed raggedly at the wrist.

"What the hell is that?" Malone asked.

"Looks like a hand to me."

Snort. "I can see it's a hand, Clint, but what the hell is it doing here?"

"Well, chances are that gun has LeAnn Hannaford's fingerprints on it—and the hand has the missing salesman's fingerprints. I don't even want to speculate about what Guth thought he might do with it."

I could hear shouting downstairs now.

"So we take the gun and leave the cannoli, uh, I mean, hand?" she said.

"Right," I replied with a chuckle and tore the bag containing the gun loose from the bottom of the freezer, then tucked it in my belt at the small of my back under the jacket, right next to my own weapon. The cops wouldn't search me after we showed them our ID and handed over our guns.

"I'm sure the crime scene guys will be thrilled to find a severed hand in the fridge." Malone reached and poked the boxes around

273

some more to cover the fact that there had been two bags originally. "That should keep Guth off the streets for a while. And yuck."

She'd just finished knocking stacks of frozen fish around and slammed the freezer shut when the first officer, gun drawn, appeared at the top of the stairs and told us to...freeze.

CHAPTER SIXTY-NINE

My spine was already well on the way to frozen with the ice-cold metal of the concealed handgun pressing against my back. Luckily, the ID and our weapons were sufficient as I'd expected. There was no pat-down, for me or Malone. We were still the good guys.

Three police cruisers and two ambulances sat outside, all with lights flashing. Traffic was stopped and a lunch-time crowd had gathered to see the action. A disturbing sense of déjà vu rippled through me. This was happening way too often lately.

Reuben was sitting in the rear of the ambulance, paramedics just finishing a field splint on his arm. His head was bandaged and I could tell from watching his mouth that he was cussing nonstop. When I caught his eye, he raised the volume enough for me to confirm that. Two more cops stood just outside the open rear doors of the vehicle, one watching Reuben, the other the crowd.

Guth's downstairs lookouts occupied backseats in two of the patrol cars. The man himself was brought out strapped to a stretcher carried by paramedics and accompanied by several officers. I watched them load him in the second ambulance, which drove off immediately with lights and siren. I hoped his wounds hurt like hell.

Finally I saw another friendly face: an old-timer I'd known since my apprenticeship at the Crew and Harbaugh agency. With his fireplug body, shaved head and bushy eyebrows he looked like every career non-com Marine you've ever seen in the movies. Even had the same kind of name: Sergeant Brady Grant. He appeared to be in charge of the scene, much to my relief. I needed to get Reuben off the hook and us out of here.

I pointed him out to my partner and we headed that way the moment he seemed to be free. "Hey Sarge," I said as we walked up.

"McCall! And Devon Malone! What are you two doing in the

middle of this shit?"

"We tracked Guth here."

"And brought him down, looks like. One each?"

"Yeah."

He clapped me on the shoulder. "Good teamwork!" The clap transitioned smoothly to a grasp. "That means you gotta go down-town, though, both of you. Reports and stuff. You know."

"I know." I gestured at the remaining ambulance. "That's Reuben Keys. He's with us."

Gant dropped his hand and grimaced. "I know who he is. What do you mean, he's with you?"

"I mean he helped us find Guth and was here to watch our backs."

"Really. You guys that hard up for help?"

"Today we were." I didn't look to Malone for agreement about that, didn't even glance in her direction because I could imagine her sour expression.

"Crap. Then maybe we won't keep him too long. I was kind of looking forward to putting him away."

CHAPTER SEVENTY

I stashed the handgun from the freezer under the seat of my vehicle as we drove to the Justice Center and we kept it short and sweet once we got there. We had gone to the Gentlemen's Lounge because we had information from Reuben Keys that a person of interest in a case we were working on might be there. His name was Malcolm Guth and he also happened to be a wanted fugitive. It turned out he was indeed there. We defended ourselves when attacked. Then the police arrived. That was it.

The two detectives who were taking our statements had just turned off the recorder when Mike Whitehall opened the door and came in. He explained to his colleagues that he needed to talk to us about "another matter" and sent them on their way.

He sat down across from us, leaned forward with his hands clasped on the table, and got right to the point. "I've been watching through the two-way. One of you want to tell me what you didn't tell them?"

"Why do you think there's something we haven't told them?" asked Malone.

"Let's say we found some unusual evidence at the scene. Evidence of a possible murder. And some diamonds. I'm just wondering if you two know about any of that."

Whoa. "Diamonds?" I asked.

"They were in the freezer, a little bag of diamonds off in the corner behind a bunch of frozen fish. Oh, and there was a hand in there, too. We're trying right now to identify who it might belong to. Any ideas?"

I exchanged a glance with Malone. We'd missed the diamonds. I was glad that the CSU guys found them. That explained a lot.

"Well," I said, "We did hear a vague rumor that Guth might have killed a traveling salesman a few weeks ago, some guy who was in Portland when he was supposed to be in Seattle. Selling diamonds."

Whitehall sat back, grinned, and ran a hand through his blond hair. "Gee, that's a very helpful—and specific—vague rumor you've got there. I don't suppose you're going to tell me where you heard it."

"Ah, you know. We just hear things. It's nothing either one of us could testify to."

"Right."

Malone spoke up again. "Is your 'unusual evidence' enough to convict him?"

"So we could leave your source out of it? Don't know yet. Probably. If both the hand and the diamonds turn out to belong to that missing salesman, that should be enough. And maybe then I can get him to confess to the young woman's murder as well. Kristi, she called herself? Her real name was Lenore Stuyvesant, by the way. We found her family."

"That would be good. That is good."

"If the evidence isn't enough, we'll have to talk about this again. With the recorder on."

"We understand that," I said.

He gave me an appraising look. "You guys really were using Reuben Keys as backup?"

I had to chuckle. "Yeah, life gets a little strange sometimes."

He grimaced. "No shit."

"How's he doing?"

"He was interviewed at the hospital and released—by them and us. It's not against the law to get beat up while assisting a couple of private eyes. He's got a fractured forearm and some cuts and bruises, no big deal."

"Glad to hear it," I said.

I ignored the grimace from my partner.

We drove straight back to the office, where I sealed Guth's gun in a manila envelope and filed it for the time being in the back of the bottom file cabinet drawer. One of these days, when I was sure

I didn't need it any more, we'd go for a long drive in the country. Maybe take a swim.

While Malone checked messages and went through the mail, I called LeAnn's apartment. Johnny Crew answered the phone and I gave him the good news that Malcolm Guth was no longer a threat.

"Hot damn!" he yelled. "All right!" His voice went away from the phone. "You can relax, sweetie. The cops have Guth and Clint has the gun." He came back. "How's Veronica doing? We haven't been able to get a hold of her."

"She's okay. I imagine she's at the café, putting things back together."

"I'll stop by and see if I can lend a hand before I go home. God, it will be good to sleep in my own bed again." He suddenly laughed. "Roger's already headed for the door. Good working with you!" he called out. Then: "Oh, here's somebody wants to talk to you."

It was LeAnn, words tumbling out before she got the receiver to her ear. "Mr. McCall! You really have the gun? And the police have Mal? I'm okay?"

"Yes, it looks like you're okay."

"Thank you, oh, thank you!" Sounded like she was bouncing up and down.

I told her she was welcome and got off the phone, leaving them to their celebration. "She's a happy young woman," I reported to Malone. "Anything of interest in the mail or messages?"

"Not bad this time," she responded. Two potential new jobs and some info we needed to close the file on an old one."

"What old one?"

"Mrs. Leadbetter?"

"Ah yes. You mean we finally got a response from that place in Boise?"

She waved a sheet of paper at me, looking smug. "According to this letter from the Rising Sun Motel, Mr. and Mrs. Arlow Leadbetter were registered guests on the tenth and eleventh of last month."

"When the wife was in fact at home here in Portland. She talked mostly to you. You want to do the report and prepare the bill?"

"No problem. 'Dear Mrs. Leadbetter. Your husband is a cheating, slime-dripping scumbag. That will be five hundred dollars. Thank you for your business.'"

I had to chuckle. "You might try to sound a little more sympathetic."

"I can do that."

"We'll have to worry about taking on new clients after we settle the Heatherly case. We've been neglecting that again and I'm sure Hap would like to get home as well."

Malone looked at her watch and stood. "First things first," she said. "You realize it's pushing two and we haven't eaten lunch yet?"

I hadn't realized that but, now that she mentioned it, my stomach was growling—and it also explained why she was growling. Malone missing lunch by two hours had to be like most people starving for a full day. I stood up as well.

"Let's get over to the Home Run while you can still walk," I said.

"Fuck you," she said.

I really did kind of love my partner.

CHAPTER SEVENTY-ONE

"So, what do you make of this Tony Zahl character?" Malone asked after she'd polished off her second burger and helping of fries. She'd done little besides eat for the last forty minutes and I was glad to hear she now had the strength to refocus on the case.

"I don't know," I said. "He claims to be motivated by unrequited love and that the mysterious voicemail message was his initial effort to confess. I don't buy that, at least not that it's the whole story. How about you?"

I noticed that she seemed to have her eye on the nearest waitress. Thinking about dessert? But then she brought her attention back to me and shrugged. "It's possible for someone to be a bad guy and also an emotional wreck, I guess. Possible. But we need more information. Whatever's going on is motivating murder—Carter, Nakagawa, and the attempt on Overton so far. Is any of that Zahl? And, if so, why?"

"No question," I agreed, "we need a lot more information." I checked my watch. A little after three. "How about we talk again to Petosky, Overton, and Schilling to see what they can tell us about Zahl and Albright?"

"Sounds like a plan to me."

We paid our bills, went back to the office, and made some calls —to no avail, as it turned out.

Barbara Schilling's voicemail told me she'd be back this evening. Max Overton's told Malone he was very sorry he couldn't come to the phone. Tanya Petosky's wished me a wonderful day and said she was looking forward to talking to me. In all three cases we asked them to call back at their earliest convenience.

By four-thirty we were both feeling frustrated and irritable, ready to head home and try again tomorrow. We were, in fact, headed for the door when my cell phone signaled a call.

Tanya Petosky's strong contralto voice responded after I an-

281

swered. "You said you needed to talk to me?"

I punched on the speakerphone and held it out between me and Malone. "I'm glad you returned my call," I said. "Are you free this evening?" I asked. "My partner and I would like to see you."

"No," she said to my disappointment, "I can't meet with you this evening. But I'll tell you what: I'm volunteering at the shelter tomorrow, so just stop by there like you did before. Any time. Has something else happened?"

"There have been some developments, but no more attacks on board members if that's what you mean."

"Good. That is what I meant. Anything else right now?"

"Not unless Max Overton is still at your place," I said with a quick glance at my partner to confirm.

She laughed. "No, he didn't even stay for dinner Sunday evening. Finally got tired of moaning about his arm and went home."

"All right then, We'll see you tomorrow."

"I look forward to it."

"I'll just bet she does," offered Malone after I'd ended the call.

CHAPTER SEVENTY-TWO

Malone called it a day soon after and I was left sitting at the desk, contemplating my own evening. It was free. I hadn't been spending nearly enough time in the dojang lately. So that's where I would go.

I passed two small storefront delis on the three-block walk and paused both times, wondering if I should have more nourishment before working out for a couple of hours. After all, I'd had only one lunch. But it was a late one and I wasn't that hungry.

Daisy Mansfield and Carmen Gonzales were already dressed out and sparring when I arrived. I didn't expect to see Roger so soon after his long stint of watching LeAnn Hannaford and I had no idea whether Mike Whitehall or his partner Bobby Brewster would show up.

I said hello to the two young women, who paused from punching and kicking one another to greet me back. In our single, necessarily unisex bathroom I doffed my street clothes and work worries, replacing them with white dobak (traditional loose-fitting pants and jacket), black belt, and headband displaying the Korean and American flags.

It was destined to be a shorter evening than I'd intended. By the time I'd warmed up, stretched, and sparred once with each of the women, I was feeling more fuzzy than fit—and beginning to suspect that I would pay a price for standing underdressed in the rain in the middle of a March night watching firefighters at work.

I never get sick, I told myself.

You're coming down with a bad cold, my stomach and head replied.

It was still just the three of us at that point and I confess that I made an excuse about having another appointment. No way was I going to admit to these youngsters that I was feeling old and creaky.

Back in the bathroom, I got dressed and checked my cell

phone. I'd missed a call from Mike and there was a voicemail. I retrieved it with some trepidation, devoutly hoping that it didn't require me to go somewhere besides home to bed.

Whitehall's voice was slightly muffled by the sounds of car engine and traffic: "This is Mike. Somebody fired a shot through Barbara Schilling's front window earlier this evening. I was just over there. She and her daughter were cut by flying glass but had no other injuries. The media's onto it already, though. That red ball we were talking about? We've got it now. Talk to you soon."

I just sat on the toilet seat for a minute. There was nothing I could do this evening. I wasn't even going to call Malone to let her know. She might as well get a good night's sleep, even if I didn't.

Little did I know that that plan wouldn't work out either.

CHAPTER SEVENTY-THREE

Just after ten that evening I settled on the couch with Maxine, feeling stuffed-up and generally crappy, wondering whether I should dig around the medicine cabinet for some kind of sleeping aid. The cat suddenly alerted and then growled. Since she was looking toward the front door, I knew from experience that someone was approaching. Maybe I couldn't hear them yet, but Maxine could.

I was so fuzzy that for a moment I couldn't remember where I'd put my Smith and Wesson when I got home. It came to me after a couple of seconds but by then somebody was knocking on my front door.

If they were knocking, they probably weren't a threat. In any event, I didn't feel like trying to get to the bedroom and back. I shuffled to the front door. If whoever it was shot me, at least it would put a stop to the nausea and sniffling.

Before I even had a chance to check through the peephole, I heard Malone's voice on the other side calling my name. What the hell was she doing here this late in the evening? Had something else happened? Was I going to have to pull myself together and go out again? Was I going to have to pull myself together and be romantic? God, I hoped not—on both counts.

I opened the door just as her fist was raised to pound on it again. "Hello," I said.

She lowered her arm and looked me up and down before replying. "You look like shit."

While it was true that I was barefoot in jeans and tee shirt, probably red-nosed and puffy-eyed as well, I was in no mood for my partner's color commentary.

"What's going on?" I inquired.

"Mike Whitehall called and told me that there'd been an attack on Barbara Schilling and her daughter. He said he'd already called

285

you—but you didn't call me about it. I was concerned."

"I have a cold or something. I was going to call you in the morning."

"Meanwhile, I was concerned. And now that I see you look like shit, I'm coming in."

I must have been feeling like I looked because I gave up and didn't even argue, though I really didn't feel like having company. She and Stella escorted me back to the couch. As always when I had a visitor, the cats had changed places. Maxine had exhausted her guard cat routine with the growl and was hiding somewhere. Stella wanted to thoroughly check out the new arrival.

Malone got me settled, determined that I hadn't made myself any dinner, and headed for the kitchen. By then I was feeling more light-headed from her being back in my house than I was from having a cold. On top of that, I couldn't believe she actually managed to find a can of chicken soup in one of my cabinets. I didn't remember buying it and for some reason felt embarrassed that she was prepared to heat it up for me.

I struggled back up off the couch and stood in the kitchen doorway. "You don't need to do that," I said.

She dumped the soup into a pan and looked over at me, a smile playing over her lips. "You're right. I don't." She held up the empty can and inquired if I had a recycle bin. I did, beneath the sink. It is Oregon, after all. She tossed the can and began to stir the soup. "You should go sit back down." She gave me an appraising look. "Now I can see why you have to bundle up so much when you're going out in the wet and cold. Poor baby."

That did it. My bewilderment gave way to irritation. "Give me a break, here. I just have the sniffles. I appreciate your coming over to make me soup and all, but you don't need to insult me while you're doing it."

That damned little smile stayed on her lips. "No need to get defensive. I completely understand. Older people are more prone to these things...."

That stood me up straight. "You're trying to piss me off, aren't you?"

She laughed out loud at that. "And it's working, isn't it? Adrenaline is good for a cold. Go sit down. You can simmer on the couch while this soup simmers on the stove."

Sitting on the couch waiting for my soup, I did a little exercise in meditative concentration, trying to focus my thought processes. I had to either get better in a hurry or learn to function while sick. Someone was still out to kill members of the Lifestream Foundation board and we had an obligation to stop them.

Malone brought in two bowls of soup on a tray she'd found somewhere in there and set them on the coffee table in front of me. Rather than seating herself on the couch beside me, she folded her legs and sat on the floor opposite.

I shifted forward so that I could eat my soup. Stella jumped up beside me to investigate the unusual eating arrangement. Maxine was still nowhere in sight. I inhaled a good sip of the savory concoction. Not bad. Warm couch, curious cat, chicken soup, and a caring (even if insulting) partner: What more could a person want? I had to admit that I was feeling a little better already.

Malone looked up at me after spooning some soup of her own. "You notice that the attack on the Schillings breaks the pattern?"

"Pattern?"

"Well, the pattern of not having a pattern. Carter was hit in the head, Overton shot, Nakagawa strangled, but now we have another shooting."

"Ah ha. Yeah, Mike and I talked about that variety the other day. Maybe the killer has impulse control issues—or is trying to throw us off."

"Maybe. Maybe it's not all the same person."

I sipped some more soup. "And maybe we don't have a fucking clue."

Malone waved her spoon at me. "But we're working on it—or

287

at least I will be, if you're still sick in the morning."

That was just before we turned on the TV to see what the local news had to say. The shooting at Barbara Schilling's house was among the lead stories, as Mike had anticipated, but they hadn't made the connection to the two dead Board members yet. And thank goodness there was no mention of us. After a commercial break, however, we were confronted with an Alison Roberts promo:

"Portland's most newsworthy private eye brings down one of the city's most notorious pimps and killers! Could it be related to recent attacks on a respected Portland charity? Clint McCall is on the case again! Tune in tomorrow afternoon!"

My already-distressed stomach seized up even more as I exchanged a look with Malone. Goddamn. So, somehow, she'd discovered a possible connection to the Lifestream Foundation, a connection the rest of the media was sure to pick up on now. Great. Just great.

CHAPTER SEVENTY-FOUR

Somehow I managed to get a good night's sleep, possibly because Devon Malone was still here when I drifted off. Not in my bed, alas, but planning to sleep on the living room couch. She didn't even kiss me goodnight because, she said, one of us had to stay healthy. Which was fine given how crappy I felt anyway. It was all so new and iffy between us that I didn't even know yet if kisses goodnight were to be expected. I hoped so.

Anyway, I awoke a little after seven feeling pretty perky compared to the evening before. I didn't hop out of bed, but I did manage to arise smoothly and make my way to the bathroom without any dizziness or nausea, not even much in the way of sniffles. Was there such a thing as a twelve-hour cold? Or perhaps chicken soup and a concerned partner really did work miracles.

At my first stirring, Stella had jumped off the bed and headed for the kitchen. I didn't see Maxine and hoped she hadn't felt the need to hide away all night.

After I'd splashed water on my face and accomplished my other ablutions, I headed for the living room to see if my guest was up —or, come to think of it, if she'd really stayed the night as she'd said she was going to.

She had. She was sprawled the length of the couch, no cover, no pillow, but still sound asleep. Even more amazing, quite astounding actually, Maxine was snuggled firmly in between Malone's knees and just as sound asleep. Someone had finally obtained the blessing of the fat, furry Queen of Asociality.

I dropped to my knees beside the couch and kissed them both on the forehead—first Maxine, then Malone. That, I decided, would substitute nicely for my usual morning meditation. They both woke immediately and grumpily. The cat departed in the direction of the kitchen and my partner grimaced up at me.

"If you just gave me that cold, I'm going to kick your ass," she announced in a slightly raspy voice.

I sat on my heels and grinned at her groggy face. "I'm feeling much better this morning, thanks to you and some soup. Whatever it was, it seems to be passing, so you're probably safe."

She sat up and shook her head. "I'd better be. What's for breakfast?"

"Unless you want to settle for dry cereal and coffee, we should plan to stop somewhere before we get going on the work day."

"I'll settle for coffee before we go anywhere. I also want to stop at my place for some clean clothes. Then breakfast and, after that, how about we see what's happening at the Schilling residence? I wouldn't be surprised if they were more interested in talking now."

"Sounds like a plan to me," I said, and kissed her again—on the lips this time. She must have believed me about the cold because she very firmly kissed me back.

CHAPTER SEVENTY-FIVE

At least we managed to get Malone's fresh clothing and a good breakfast behind us without encountering any media. We both knew that there would be a lot more scrutiny now that our old buddy Alison had begun to connect the dots.

I called Barbara Schilling right after breakfast. It was nearly nine by then and she reluctantly agreed that we could come on over. Not surprisingly, she still sounded shaken.

A boarded-up front window is a starkly jarring note on a Lake Oswego mansion, like a bright red zit on a fashion model.

Schilling apparently agreed because her first words upon opening the massive front door and inviting us in were, "The window will be fixed today." Her voice was brittle.

I'd recognized it as the big picture window belonging to the living room, where she now led us as she had on our previous visit. She showed us to a couple of well-padded chairs and offered coffee, which Malone accepted and I declined.

Neither the lady herself nor her surroundings looked quite as put together as they had during my first visit. She wore a simple blue dress with beige flats, definitely not a match, and no jewelry at all; wayward strands of her short blond hair were visible in the light from several lamps needed because of the wood-covered window frame. There were a number of small bandages on her forearms. The furniture was slightly askew and the lamps weren't centered on their round side tables as they had been. I could see glints in the rug where small pieces of glass had yet to be cleaned up.

She placed herself stiffly in a plush chair opposite ours and motioned minimally around the room without really looking at it. "The maids will finish when we're through talking," she announced.

I was wondering if I should politely reassure her that we didn't give a damn when Crystal Schilling appeared in the archway and hurried to her mother's side. She was wearing flip flops, what looked like men's light green boxers, and a white tee shirt; she had clearly just gotten out of bed. She had a small bandage on her forehead.

"I'm sorry," she said as she crossed the room, "I couldn't seem to wake up." She leaned down and kissed her mother on the cheek. "Are you all right?"

Mrs. Schilling gave her a quick, tight smile. "Yes, dear. I'm fine."

"Bullshit you are," replied her daughter, and flopped onto the end of the couch nearest her mother's chair. "Hello, Mr. McCall, Miss Malone," she sneered.

I'd been wondering until the expletive and the pretend-politeness whether this was the same sullen and rebellious young woman I'd come to know but not love. Close enough. The latest trauma hadn't changed her attitude that much.

The elder Schilling, meanwhile, ignored the younger's evaluation of her self-assessment and turned her attention to us. "You insisted on seeing us this morning, Mr. McCall. This is a very stressful time. I hope we can keep this short."

"I'll do my best," I said. "My partner and I need to know what happened."

Very slight shrug. "We already told the police. Can't you get it from them?"

"I'm sorry. We need to hear it first-hand—and we have a few other questions."

A sigh. "All right. Perhaps you have resources the police don't. I hope someone can put a stop to this." She paused, suddenly looking older than her mid-forties. "We were both in the room last evening around quarter past seven. Crystal was on that couch, lying down, and I'd just come in to ask if she was going to join me for dinner. I was standing at the other end of the couch, facing the window...when it shattered." Her face twisted with the memory. "There was a horrible noise. I didn't know what had happened...."

Crystal sat forward and interrupted. "Mother jumped on top

of me," she said. Her voice held an element of wonder in it. "She jumped *toward* the window to get on top of me."

"I didn't know what I was doing."

"She protected me."

They were both silent for a moment, looking at one another, both their faces open and vulnerable for just that moment. Then they both turned back to us.

"There's nothing else I can tell you," Barbara Schilling said. "According to the police, there was a single gunshot." She gestured across the room. "You can go look at the hole in the wall if you wish."

"Can you think of *any* reason someone would take a shot at you?" Malone asked.

Mrs. Schilling shook her head. "No. I've told you both before, I know nothing about any problem with the board finances. And certainly there's no one else...." She threw up her hands and looked suddenly on the verge of tears. "Whatever it is you're investigating, I wish you had left us alone—all of us."

Crystal reached over to put a hand on her arm. "Mom...."

"I'm really very sorry," I said, "and I hope that none of this is our fault."

The older woman patted her daughter's hand and then straightened her shoulders. "If it is, I'm hoping you can fix it."

"We'll do our best," I said. "I have one final question: Have you ever heard the name Tony Zahl?"

Barbara Schilling thought for a moment and then shook her head. "No," she said. "Who is he?"

"A friend of one of the other board members," I replied discreetly. "He seems to have some connection to what's going on."

Crystal perked up. "Tanya's friend Tony?" she asked.

Whoa. "Do you know him?" Malone asked, looking every bit as surprised as I felt.

Crystal sat forward again. "I've never met him, but I've talked to him on the phone a few times when he called Tanya at the

293

Foundation."

"And he said he was Tony Zahl?" Malone followed up. "She might have more than one friend named Tony and we need to be sure."

The younger woman's brow furrowed. "No...he never said his last name. He always says, 'Tell her it's her good friend Tony.' That's why I thought of him right away, because he always says that."

"Any idea what they talked about?" I asked.

She shrugged. "No, you'll have to ask her. Sometimes she wasn't happy to hear from him, I'll say that. She would shout at him. I could hear it out in the lobby."

"But you couldn't hear what she was saying."

"No. Why not ask her? She already told you about him, right?"

"She didn't mention those particular conversations. I'll follow up. Thanks." I looked at my watch and started to get to my feet. "You got anything else?" I asked Malone.

"No," she said and stood up. "We have another appointment coming up." I knew exactly what she meant: with Tanya Petosky, as fast as we could get our butts downtown.

The rest of us also stood and Barbara Schilling put her arm around Crystal who had moved close by her side. I wondered when was the last time they'd stood like that. Mrs. Schilling looked from me to Malone and back.

"Mr. McCall, Miss Malone, you understand that we're very frightened. My daughter.... I don't want to see anything happen to Crystal, you understand. I...I don't know anything about private detectives except what I read in novels. *Do* you have resources the police don't have? Perhaps you didn't start all this...but can you end it? We need your help."

"We do, Mrs. Schilling," I said, "and believe me we're going to do everything we can."

She nodded. "I know we aren't your clients, but please keep us posted."

"We will," Malone assured her, and we all walked together to the door.

As it closed behind us and Malone and I continued down the walkway, I said, "If those two survive all this, it could turn out to be the best thing that's happened to them in a long time."

"If," was all Malone said. Ever the optimist.

Then I pointed the Subaru downtown and we started talking about how to handle Tanya Petosky.

CHAPTER SEVENTY-SIX

We had a tentative plan by the time we entered the orange-carpeted lobby of Lifestream House. There was a young woman sitting behind the wooden reception desk that I hadn't seen before.

I guessed that she was a last-minute replacement for Crystal because she didn't look comfortable with her surroundings. Mid-twenties, nicely dressed but cheaply made-up, hair peroxide blond and bigger than you usually see on women that age nowadays. She'd been doing her bright red nails when we appeared and she eyed our approach, taking deep breaths, as if about to face some major challenge. Where, I wondered, did the Foundation get this one from? She would have looked more at home in the reception area of a lap-dancing establishment.

"Welcome to Lifestream House. How can I help you?" The words ran together as if she'd rehearsed them too often.

"Is Tanya Petosky here?" I asked.

She brightened and the tension vanished from her shoulders. I'd given her something she could handle. "Yeah," she said as she picked up the phone, "Tanya's in back. I'll tell her you want to see her. Uh, who are you?"

"Clint McCall and Devon Malone."

"Okay." She punched a couple of numbers. "Tanya? There's a couple of people here to see you, named Clint McCall and...Malone. I will." She put down the phone. "She says she'll be right out." And went back to her nails, apparently feeling no need to apologize for forgetting Malone's first name.

Tanya Petosky came through the door behind the desk at full tilt just as she had on our first visit, her shoulder-length dark hair billowing behind. She was again decked out in a custom-fitted business suit and an array of gold jewelry. She swept around the corner of the desk, a woman very comfortable in her short but substantial body, and smiled as she held out her hand.

"Mr. McCall," her low voice purred, "it's good to see you again. And you, Miss Malone. Come on back."

She led us down the short hallway, through the conference room with the huge old table, and into the same small, plainly furnished office where we'd talked before. She settled behind the desk, while Malone and I took the visitor's chairs.

"Have you talked to Barbara?" she asked. "Is she all right?"

"We were just at her house," Malone replied. "All things considered, she's fine. You haven't talked to her?"

She shook her head. "No. I tried calling when I saw the story on TV last night, but they weren't picking up. Then this morning Crystal called to say she wouldn't be in, which didn't surprise me. I'd already recruited an emergency replacement."

"The girl out front. Is she one of Lifestream's clients?" I asked.

Petosky actually giggled. "Not exactly. I know her through another organization I work with. Another social agency. She's doing her best."

"How's Max Overton?" I went on. "Have you talked to him lately?"

That sobered her up. "Not in the last day or so. I think the last time was Monday afternoon. His arm was feeling better and he was planning to go down to the store."

She leaned forward. "What's going on? We've lost Jesse and Stan. Somebody's taken shots at Max and Barbara. It was also on the news last night that you two shot somebody. They didn't say anything about us in the story, but...was he the one?" I exchanged a glance with Malone. Apparently Petosky had been watching a different news show. The media attention was going to get really bad, really fast, if this kept up.

At least she hadn't been watching the newscast that contained Alison Roberts' promo. "No," I said, "that was another case we've been working on. He has nothing to do with the board."

"Damn. Then who's doing this--and why? Am I next? Or Norm Albright? You're the detective. Don't you have anything?"

What about the police?"

"The police are working on it, just like we are," said Malone. She paused. "We have a name."

Petosky's eyes widened as she sat back. "You know who's doing it?" she asked incredulously.

"No," I responded, "but there is a name that's come up, someone who might be involved or have further information. Do you know an ex-boyfriend of Norman Albright's named Tony Zahl?"

Tanya Petosky was very good, but at this moment she became the victim of a common misconception: that when you don't want to give yourself away, you don't react. Normally the body is constantly reacting—unconscious gestures, shifts, twitches, blinks. For the space of two seconds, the mention of Tony Zahl's name interrupted all those little signs of life in Petosky's body. She could have passed for an unusually zaftig department store mannequin.

Then she took a breath, went nonchalant on us, and sat back as if I'd said nothing of any interest at all. "I think I've heard the name," she said thoughtfully. "Norm was going out for a while with some gangster type. Is that the guy?"

"Yes, that's probably Zahl. You know anything about him?"

Eyes wide now in innocence. "Not a thing. I don't think Norm was with him for long and he didn't say much about it."

"That's too bad," Malone chimed in. "We know you want to do everything you can to help the investigation." She didn't even attempt to sound sincere.

Petosky gave her a little smile and leaned across the desk, stretching out her hand as though to put it on Malone's arm but couldn't reach. "I have a lot of faith in you two," she said softly. She dropped her hand to the desktop and the smile turned into a crooked grin. "I'm putting all my faith in you."

She didn't make any effort to sound sincere, either.

CHAPTER SEVENTY-SEVEN

"Well, that worked and it didn't," offered Malone as we stood in front of the Lifestream Foundation building, having bid Tanya Petosky goodbye soon after that last exchange. "We know she's lying but we don't know what the truth is."

"And what was with that last bit?" I wondered aloud. "She's putting all her faith in us?"

"I know. It almost sounded like she was trying to tell us something."

"But what?"

"Beats the fuck out of me. Maybe we can figure it out after we eat."

I glanced at my watch, then grinned at my partner. "You always know when it's close to lunch time," I said, "mostly because, for you, it's *always* close to lunch time."

Malone headed for the Subaru. "Nothing wrong with having a healthy appetite."

I went around to the driver's side and opened the door, giving her a quick inspection across the top of the car. "It's a mystery to me how you manage to stay so svelte."

She paused with her door half-open and gave me the eye right back. "Yeah, well, you can investigate the mystery of my svelte body some other time." Whereupon she got in and firmly closed the door behind her.

For some reason I had a hard time concentrating during our hurried consumption of hamburgers and fries at the Home Run. In any event, we didn't come up with any good theories about what Tanya Petosky might have been getting at.

Back in the office we had a voicemail from Shanna Heatherly, who'd heard about the latest attack and was concerned about her uncle Norman's safety. I called back and talked briefly with both her and her husband. All I could tell them was the same I'd told

301

Petosky, that the police and Malone and I were all working on it.

There was still no response from Max Overton to my call yesterday. I'd have to do some checking on him soon.

About that time there was a knock on the office door. In response to my invitation, Eleanor Ivory opened the door and leaned in.

"Just stopping by," she said. "My research hasn't produced anything else helpful."

"Your research?" I asked.

She shrugged. "Still checking on those board members. You never know with a set of names like that when you'll come up with good information. It's fun to try. There was a serial killer in North Dakota named Norman Albright, for instance—but don't worry; he's dead." She suddenly grinned. "And you should do a search just on the name 'Tanya' sometime. You'll find some interesting people. The funniest one I came up with was a Tanya who bailed out a local high-class hooker recently."

"That search thing gives you access to Justice Center records?" asked Malone, eyebrows going up.

"No, this was in a blog on the hooker's website. 'Tanya bailed me out,' it said."

Malone laughed. "The hooker has her own website? And a blog? Let's hear it for social media."

"Jesus," I said, feeling about a hundred years old. "Is her blog about her adventures as a prostitute?"

"Of course."

"I wonder if her customers know that."

Eleanor shrugged. "Well, since she apparently gets most of her customers through the website that prominently features the blog, I would imagine so." I noticed Malone looking at me like I was out of it. Which I guess I was.

"It's probably part of the thrill for them, Clint. Welcome to the current century."

"She only uses first names," Eleanor went on, "far as I can tell, so they're not in danger of being identified by their wives. But back to what I was saying about the research. There are all kinds of Tanyas and Schillings and the rest doing all kinds of things, but zilch I could tie to your board members."

"Thanks for trying, at least," I said.

"You're welcome," she replied as she got up. "I have to go get a quick lunch. Got another tax problem coming to see me at two. Don't work too hard, you guys." And she was gone.

I saw that Malone was looking at me with a thoughtful frown. "Are you thinking what I'm thinking?" she asked.

"That maybe we should look into the Tanya who bailed out the hooker?"

"Exactly. Think about what we know so far. Someone is attacking members of the Lifestream Foundation board. That has to be connected somehow to Norman Albright and Tony Zahl; no coincidence is *that* big. Tanya Petosky is lying, about Zahl and maybe more."

"And..." I started flipping through my notes on Guth. I paused on the encounter with LeAnn's friend Kristi outside our office Saturday afternoon. "What did Kristi say when we saw her out front? She said she wanted to work for an escort service called New Faith, which had the best girls in town and money to go with it."

"High class hookers, in other words. And who do we know...?"

"Who do we know that might be intrigued by an operation called New Faith?" I interrupted. Malone and I grinned at each other. "Maybe a woman who's into helping the downtrodden and left the Old Believers in the Russian community because she thinks of herself as a 'new believer'? A woman who was just telling us, with an ironic grin and odd emphasis, that she was putting all her *faith* in us?"

"And that young woman in the lobby, the replacement receptionist? She could easily be one of Tanya's rescues from this New Faith operation."

"That's what I thought, too. Great minds."

303

Which brought a typical Malone snort. "We're just equally per-verted; that's all." She paused for a thoughtful look out the window. "But, if so, why is she so secretive about it? Something to do with Zahl? Maybe he's running the escort service and isn't happy that she's helping girls get out of it. She did seem to be uneasy about him, if not actually frightened...."

"I think we're onto something," I said.

At which point the phone rang. I was quicker. The display showed Mike Whitehall's cell number, anyway. "McCall."

"Clint, it's Mike." Whitehall's voice was tense.

"What's up?"

"You're not going to believe this, but Mal Guth just escaped from the hospital."

CHAPTER SEVENTY-EIGHT

"Oh fuck," I said. "Hang on." I put the phone on speaker. "How did Guth escape from the damned hospital?" I heard a gasp from Malone—and that's exactly how I felt.

"He used Alison Roberts as a shield."

"What?"

"She talked her way past the guard I had posted and tried to interview Guth. He grabbed her and somehow used her to get himself some clothes and bluff his way out of the building, fucking bullet wounds and fucking all. I don't know the details yet. All I know for sure is that there's a cop named Haskins who's going to be busted all the way down to meter patrol, maybe lower."

"Does Guth still have Roberts?"

"No, he dumped her outside and hijacked a car. She's okay other than needing a goddamned brain. We don't know where he went after that, but believe me we're looking."

I hung up and immediately dialed the Pen and Pastry, suddenly filled with a fear that Malcolm Guth would go straight for Veronica and LeAnn.

Veronica answered the phone and I told her Guth was on the loose. I asked her to get LeAnn, Johnny and Hap all to the café if she could reach them. They would be safest together in a public place. We were on our way.

The rain that began as we crossed the Morrison Bridge turned into a downpour as I took MLK Jr. Boulevard over to Hawthorne. Portland drivers are notorious for being spooked by any kind of bad weather and traffic slowed to a crawl, only increasing the anger that had already been growing in my tortured gut.

Malone must have been feeling it, too. She hadn't said a word since agreeing that we needed to check at the café first, but now she grumbled, "I'm going to kick Roberts' ass clear up into her throat the next time I see her."

"He might well have escaped anyway. The son of a bitch is shot twice but still takes a hostage and hijacks a vehicle. He must have been pretty damned determined."

"But still...."

"I know. You'll have to take a number if you want to kick her ass."

Other than a momentary twitch of her lips into a smile, Malone offered no other response.

As for me, I needed to let the anger go so that I could focus on what needed to be done. I began to consciously relax my emphatic grip on the steering wheel. I controlled my breathing, slow two-stage inhalations, first into the pit of the stomach and then filling the chest cavity, just as when I sit zazen in the morning. I even tried watching the rain-splattered world outside the Subaru with a half-smile on my face. All the little tricks.

"I'll park at my place," I said as I approached the corner of Hawthorne and 37th.

"We're going to walk from there to the Pen and Pastry in this rain?" Malone inquired sarcastically. "That's almost a whole block. You'll get really wet."

I wasn't going to bite, not right now. "It won't be a problem," I said mildly.

"At least your relaxation routine worked."

Huh. Apparently she had noticed my little tricks. The woman never ceased to surprise me.

CHAPTER SEVENTY-NINE

I saw as we came in the front door of the Pen and Pastry that there were far fewer tables than normal but several of those that had survived were occupied by regulars with coffee cups, newspapers, and even food. The scent of hot pastry filled the air, masking the smoke odor that had dominated my last visit. The room was clean, some of the flame-scarred areas already repaired and freshly painted. The place was looking good considering that the fire had occurred only a little more than twenty-four hours ago.

Veronica swept out of the kitchen and over to us. "Any word on Guth?" she asked.

"Not that I've heard," I said. "You got ahold of everybody?"

"Johnny and Hap are picking LeAnn up at her apartment and coming straight here."

"Excellent." I gestured at some of the patrons. "You're certainly making progress."

She looked around with an air of pride. "Yes, the insurance is taken care of and I think we can get permission to open in just a few more days. The replacement tables and chairs are supposed to come tomorrow." She dropped her voice to a stage whisper. "If you happen to run into the fire marshal, these people aren't really customers. We were baking just to get a good smell back in the place and thought we might as well feed a few friends who dropped by while we were at it."

"Gotcha," I said.

Malone tapped me on the arm and pointed out the window at a passing patrol car. "That's the second one I've seen just since we got here," she said. "I'll bet Mike has something to do with that."

"Good for him," I said and made a note to myself to call and make sure it wasn't a coincidence. A regular patrol past the café sounded like a fine idea to me.

Just then Johnny and Hap escorted LeAnn in the front door.

307

The next couple of minutes were greetings all around and tables moved together. While everyone was settling I made a quick call to confirm that Whitehall had indeed increased patrols past the café. Then we got down to business.

"We can't stay," I said. "The Lifestream Foundation case is breaking, I think, and we've got to get on it. But I do have a question first." Veronica had joined us at the table and I looked at her and LeAnn sitting next to each other. "Tell us everything you know about the New Faith escort service. LeAnn, you must know something. Your friend Kristi told me she wanted to leave Guth and work for an outfit by that name. That may have been why she was killed."

LeAnn shuddered at the mention of her friend's name but didn't respond otherwise right away. I focused on Veronica. "Have you heard of it? It might be run by a guy named Tony Zahl."

LeAnn actually answered first. "All I know," she said, "is that Kristi heard about it from somebody else. The clients are really rich and the girls are taken care of. They have a lot of freedom. That's what she was told, anyway. None of the rest of us knew about it."

Veronica nodded. "That's the same as what I've heard. I've never met a girl who works there, that I know of. It's super discreet. No idea who runs it. I thought Tony Zahl was an up-market drug supplier."

Johnny Crew's deep voice broke in, a rumbling whisper across the table. "What I want to know is, what the fuck does a call girl operation have to do with your dead good Samaritans?"

"That's an excellent question," Malone answered him. "Maybe nothing. Maybe a lot. It's just an idea we're tossing around." She turned to Veronica and LeAnn. "Ever heard of a Tanya Petosky?"

After a moment, they both shook their heads. Veronica started to get up. "Before you go," she said as she pushed her chair back, "I'll make a couple of calls to see what I can find out." She paused. "If you think that might help."

"Go for it," I said. "Any information will be better than none."

308

She was gone a full fifteen minutes.

Malone, of course, waved down a waitress and had a snack while we waited. Johnny, collector of oddball news that he is, reported that a woman in Seattle had shot her husband after discovering he was the man she'd anonymously met in an Internet chat room. He was trying to talk her into getting together with him for sex. She of course discovered his identity by finally agreeing to do it. "Doesn't seem fucking fair," was Johnny's assessment.

I was getting pretty impatient by the time Veronica rejoined us, looking discouraged. "I couldn't find out much," she said as she sat down. "New Faith is a very, very private operation, apparently, only big money clients who've been thoroughly checked out in advance. Supposedly it's headquartered in Beaverton, but can provide girls throughout the metro area. No hint who's running it or that Tony Zahl is involved. I couldn't even get the names of any of the girls who are currently on call. The whole thing is tight as a drum." She threw up her hands. "Besides that, all I could get was rumors."

At this point, even rumors sounded good. "Which were?" I inquired.

She grimaced. "That there's some kind of trouble. Something is threatening New Faith; somebody's trying to take it over or maybe down, I don't know. That's it. No details. I'm sorry."

"No, that's good," I said. "That's an interesting rumor—and it fits with a theory we're working on."

My cell phone chirped at that moment and I pulled it out to check the Caller ID. Lifestream House. What a coincidence.

"I need to take this," I said to the table at large, and answered the call. Tanya Petosky's voice roared out of the speaker at me.

"McCall! Goddamn it, McCall, you've got to get your ass over here. Max Overton is here. He says he killed Jesse Carter and now he's supposed to kill me!"

"Have you called 9-1-1?" I asked.

"No! No police, not yet anyway. He's not going to do it, the little shit." Her voice lowered to a rasp, sounding to me more angry than fearful. "Max isn't the problem. Just get your butt over here and listen to what he has to say." She hung up with a bang.

I shoved the phone back into my pocket and looked at the set of startled faces surrounding the table. "I gather you all heard the first part of that?"

"The fucking jeweler?" exclaimed Malone, who was already getting to her feet.

"Let's go," I responded as I stood. "We'll keep you guys posted," I said to the others. "Stay put for now."

We sprinted for the door.

CHAPTER EIGHTY

"Are you sure we shouldn't call Mike anyway?" asked Malone as I drove back downtown as quickly as traffic would permit.

"I don't know. She seemed confident that she is in no real danger." I changed to a lane that was moving a little faster. "What do you think?"

"What the fuck. We go with the flow. You caught that she didn't mention Nakagawa? So Overton confessed to killing Carter but not Nakagawa?"

I changed lanes again and accelerated for a few car lengths. "Maybe she just forgot to mention it."

At least my parking karma was good when I needed it to be. I pulled into a space right around the corner from Lifestream House and we made it to the reception area within sixty seconds. The same young woman was there, fixing her make-up this time, and apparently unaware that a visitor in the back might be threatening mayhem.

She probably got a clue, however, from the fact that we both had our guns drawn when we burst in the door. She froze with a tube of lipstick halfway to her mouth.

"We're private detectives," I said to her as we headed straight for the door behind the desk, "and there may be some trouble back there. If you hear a gunshot or any commotion at all, I want you to call the police." I paused for just a second to address her open-mouthed stare. "Do you understand?"

She dropped the lipstick in her lap as she tried to get her jaw working. "Yes," she said, "call the police."

"Good girl."

Malone meanwhile had jerked the door open and took a look down the short hallway, waiting for me before going further. I stepped up and looked over her shoulder down the hallway. No one there. No sound from the large conference room beyond.

We started down the hallway and the door to the reception area closed behind us.

Halfway down the hall I heard low-pitched voices ahead and motioned Malone to pause. I couldn't make out the words, but the tone was reassuring; it didn't sound like either of the two speakers was about to kill the other. Nevertheless, we both kept a good grip on our guns as we approached the conference room doorway and looked in.

Tanya Petosky and Max Overton sat together at the far end of the scarred, oval-shaped table that filled most of the room. He was at the head of the table, pale and trembling, looking worse than just after he'd been shot. She was to his left, her face flushed, her long dark hair disheveled and her eyes glaring with fury. It appeared to me that if anyone was going to be killed, I'd been misled about the direction of the threat.

Petosky looked at us standing in the doorway. "You won't need the guns," she grated. "He's harmless. Now, anyway. Come on in and enjoy the show."

I put a hand on Malone's arm to hold us in place for another moment. "You're sure he doesn't have a weapon?" I asked. "You searched him?"

She nodded. "I'm absolutely sure. He had one." She gestured to a small table in the corner that had a single drawer. "It's in that drawer now."

I wasn't satisfied. "Why no police?"

She melodramatically reached over to put a hand on Overton's shoulder, at which he shrank down even further. "Because," she said, "this spineless little rat has been a friend of mine for a long time and I want to see what we can do to keep him out of jail."

She gestured to all the empty chairs. "Come on in. Have a seat."

"I think I'll stand," I said. "At least until I have a better idea what's going on." Malone and I both still had our guns out, held down at our sides now. My partner looked every bit as mystified as

I felt.

Tanya Petosky sat back and looked up at us. "What's going on is that this minuscule piece of crap came here to kill me, but decided to confess his sins instead."

I shifted my gaze to the slightly built jeweler hunched beside her. With his bulging eyes, Overton had the desperate look of a fish just pulled from water. His forehead was beaded with sweat and his long-sleeved white shirt was so damp from perspiration and rain that the bandage on his left arm was visible through the fabric.

I kept my voice carefully neutral. "You killed Carter and Naka-gawa? Why?"

He jerked back as if I'd shouted at him. "No, no. I only killed Jesse."

I was beginning to think he'd snapped completely, that this was all bullshit. The man looked about as much like a killer as my cats did—plus he wasn't making sense.

Malone edged a little further into the room, intent on the little man. "Really? You killed Jesse Carter...but you *didn't* murder Stan Nakagawa? Then who did?"

A chill shot down my spine as the reply came from behind us, a familiar male voice: "That would be me."

CHAPTER EIGHTY-ONE

Everybody went absolutely still. My first reaction was a flood of anger that we had let ourselves be surprised. Malone had been intent on Overton and I'd been intent on her. Nobody was watching our backs.

Tony Zahl spoke again. "I won't hesitate to shoot you both if you make any quick moves. Please drop your weapons and kick them back toward me. Now."

My mind was racing as Malone and I did as Zahl asked. I'd recognized the voice within the first few words, though he no longer sounded much like the soft-spoken, hesitant person I'd originally heard on the phone. No longer lovesick, maybe, or just in a different mood.

Anyway, he must have stepped into view as he spoke because neither Petosky nor Overton had shown any reaction until we heard his voice. Now they certainly did, Tanya looking even more angry and Max more miserable. As for me, I still couldn't believe Malone and I had both been standing there with our backs to the door.

"What did you do with the receptionist?" Malone growled, glancing back over her shoulder at him. I wanted to tell her to be cool, to not do anything rash, but figured that would just piss her off more.

He chuckled, though there was no humor in the sound. I sensed him step forward and kick the guns further away as he replied. "You mean the young woman sitting at the front desk? She bought my story that I was with you two, your backup. She even asked me if she should call the police now." Another chuckle. "I assured her that wouldn't be necessary. So she's still breathing. Which is good, because it wouldn't do to have a dead body out front while I'm back here. I'll take care of it on the way out."

"You're a fucking asshole, Tony," Malone replied fiercely, "you

315

know that?"

Yet again, the dry chuckle. "It's been mentioned a time or two. McCall, you and Malone can sit down now. The chairs next to Max, on the other side from Tanya, will be just right."

So, I thought to myself as we edged around the table and eased ourselves down into the chairs as instructed, Tanya Petosky isn't trying to bring down New Faith. She's the owner and Tony Zahl must be the one trying to take it from her. And here we sat in the middle of the whole damned mess, unarmed. My stomach, that was just beginning to feel better, was nearly nauseated again by the acrid odor of Max Overton's flop sweat.

I glanced over at Devon Malone who wasn't taking her eyes off of Zahl and found myself really wishing she hadn't come with me on this one. Found myself thinking that I really did love her and didn't want to see her hurt again. Nothing to be done about it. This was her chosen profession just as it was mine.

Zahl looked much as he had when we saw him last, outside the Heatherlys' house, though the .25-caliber semi-automatic with silencer added a sartorial edge to the sport coat and tee shirt combo. With his close-cut hair, narrow moustache, and short, stocky body, he now looked every bit the small town gangster.

Petosky spoke again, her voice beginning to betray some trepidation; it must have sunk in on her what Zahl said when he entered the room. "You killed Stan? Why? And how did you get this pathetic twerp to kill Jesse? That's got nothing to do with New Faith. I thought you might go after the girls, but this...."

She turned to Overton and backfisted his shoulder. "Why didn't you tell me this son of a bitch was behind it all?" she rasped at him. "I know he was; you wouldn't swat a fly on your own initiative. We sit here for ten minutes waiting for these two and *you don't tell me Tony Zahl might walk in with a gun?*"

"I didn't know!" howled the little man, his body quivering as he turned a beseeching expression from Petosky to Zahl. "I didn't say anything about you, Tony! I was going to cover for you! We're still good buddies. You gotta know that!"

Zahl's reply was edged with contempt: "Yeah, right. You killed Carter and...the tooth fairy did the rest. That would work." He waved Overton's pleas aside and looked at me. "Max was *supposed* to do it all, but he lost his nerve." A glare at the jeweler again. "You can be a real tough guy with Tanya's girls but not out here in the real world, huh, you pathetic little fuck." Back to me and Malone. "I had to kill Nakagawa and take the shot at Barbara Schilling. I can tell you why, if you care to know before you die."

"Oh goodie," muttered Malone. "Then I'll die happy."

"Easy," I muttered back while Zahl chuckled again. After all, our Mr. Zahl clearly considered himself to be a very cool guy and he'd probably be happy to play out the classic scene where the bad guy keeps talking until the good guys can think of something. Sounded like a plan to me. If we could think of something. "Let him talk," I said to my partner and hoped she'd get the idea. Apparently she did.

"Sure," she said, and we both looked at him receptively.

He in turn looked pleased and stepped over to the end of the conference table as if he were about to make a business presentation which, in his mind, I guess he was. But the gun didn't waver.

CHAPTER EIGHTY-TWO

"I've been planning a merger between Tanya's operation and mine," he began. "I have a very good clientele for my current products and services but Tanya has been filling one important need for them that I could not. It's always better and more profitable to offer one-stop shopping, don't you think?"

Malone and I both remained silent. I was certain that, like me, she was watching intently for the slightest sign that he was relaxing or distracted. I hoped she also agreed that we would have to wait a while. The table was about twelve feet long and he was at the opposite end from us. It would take a lot longer for either one of us to get there than for a bullet to get here.

"I made Tanya what I considered to be an excellent offer," he went on, "but she refused to even think about it. So eventually, even though I'm fond of her as a friend and colleague, I concluded she was an obstacle that would have to be removed."

Petosky grunted and muttered "Fuck you" loudly under her breath.

This seemed to amuse Zahl and his eyebrows went up again. "No, really, I have always viewed you as a worthy compatriot, my dear. We're both in the business of servicing the rich...though, I admit, your front is better than mine. Recruiting girls and supporting your business through the Lifestream House, right under the noses of the other board members, is a stroke of genius."

"Humph," was her only reply. Overton had pulled entirely within himself by now, quiet except for an occasional whimper.

"I couldn't take you out myself," Zahl went on. "It would be too obvious if I then immediately took over your operation. But fortunately," here he gestured at the little jeweler, "I had just the tool I needed at hand." He grimaced. "So I thought, anyway." Again he looked at Petosky. "Did you know he was embezzling money from the Lifestream Foundation to pay for your girls and my drugs, Tanya?"

Apparently he took her shocked glance at Overton as an answer. "I didn't think so." He cocked at eye at me. "You'd never guess Max was into domination, would you, McCall, not with *him* doing the domination anyway. But that's why I thought he might have it in him to do what I needed."

He shifted his attention to Malone. "Max wants the girls to be submissive. He likes to lord it over them, experience what it feels like to have some balls. I don't think he'd like you very much." Back to Overton. "Isn't that right, Maxie?"

Overton whimpered and Petosky spoke up again. "Leave him alone, asshole."

Zahl just smirked and went on. "I think your sympathy may be misplaced, Tanya. The income from Max's little bauble empire wasn't covering his expenses anymore, he couldn't replace the money he'd taken from the Foundation, and he came to me begging for a loan. The timing was perfect. I'd forgive his debt to me and make up the rest of the deficit, thus saving his life and reputation. In return he would kill Carter and then Nakagawa, stage an attempt on Barbara Schilling, and finally—this being the point—kill you." A little smile. "I didn't initially mention that he would have to be shot too, as an alibi. He had no enthusiasm for the project as it was. But he was desperate. And weak. Desperate and weak people always make good tools."

He appeared to be coming to the end of his story and I didn't have any ideas yet; it didn't look to me like Malone did, either. The gun was still twelve feet away and holding steady. "So," I interjected, "you set it up to look like somebody is out to kill all the board members when really the only target is Tanya. That's smart. But why the calls to George Heatherly about Albright?"

The smile disappeared. "Ah," he said. "That turned out to be not so smart, I admit. I was very angry at Norman and it struck me that if he was suspected of the embezzlement at the same time board members were being attacked, if he felt like he was in

320

enough danger, he might come back to me for help. I thought his nephew would just go to him with my accusations, but instead he went to you. Then my making those calls to try to misdirect everyone was even more stupid. Not my best day." He shrugged and, as he did so, the gun finally moved a little off-center. "At least George didn't go to the police."

"The police are certainly involved now," Malone piped up in a very clear "you're-an-idiot" tone. Not what I would have recommended. I was going to have to go for it, even though Zahl contemplating his lovelorn errors wasn't nearly enough distraction to get me down the length of the table from a sitting position. And now my partner was going out of her way to piss him off.

I began to prepare myself for the impact of a bullet. If Devon was alert enough to move a split second after I did, she might make it to him even if I didn't. Hell, if I had enough momentum when the bullet struck and it wasn't a really lucky shot, I might be able to help her take him down.

If. There wasn't much hope the gunfire would attract attention. A "silencer" never really silences a gun, but on a .25-caliber it would reduce the sound to something like a palm-slap on the tabletop. Hopefully there would be screams; that would do the trick.

Anyway, it didn't look to me like I had a choice: it was going to depend on where he hit me and how quick Malone was on the uptake.

I shifted slightly toward him as I asked my last question. "Why confess to us about the calls, then? We didn't even know you were involved until you showed up in front of Heatherly's house."

Another shrug, another waver of the gun. "That was exactly the point. And that wasn't the first time I'd met you in front of their house, you know. I'd hoped taking a shot at you would frighten you off, but I should have known better. You would eventually have found out who made the calls; there had to be an explanation. Why would I show up and confess if I was the killer—or the shooter, for that matter?" He grimaced at Overton as I began a slow, deep breath. "I was thrown off by Max's failure to follow through. I hadn't expected to do the dirty work myself and I found it...upsetting. But I'm getting used to it."

He was settling himself again and I braced myself for the charge.

"What we will have here, for instance," he went on, "is a triple-murder and suicide. The police will have no reason...."

I was within a split second of leaping from my chair when I saw a flash of movement in the doorway to Zahl's left.

CHAPTER EIGHT-THREE

Zahl must have caught a glimpse of it too because he jumped to his right, swinging the gun in that direction. I registered that now he was several feet closer—but at the same time I saw that we were not exactly rescued.

Malcolm Guth stood in the doorway waving a very large handgun back and forth between Zahl and the rest of us. "What the fuck?" he asked.

"You've got to be kidding me," my partner muttered, and I knew exactly how she felt. No doubt she was also wondering how the poor receptionist was faring by now.

Zahl and Guth were both apparently just as stunned as we were, having clearly recognized one another as not officers of the law.

Guth certainly wasn't looking like a cop. He must have taken the pants and shirt off an orderly, the shoes from the cop guarding his door, and then donned Alison Roberts' raincoat on top of it all. It was a motley combination. He was pale, slightly green, sweaty, trembling. He looked exactly like a guy who'd escaped from the hospital with multiple gunshot wounds. How he'd gotten across town without being picked up was beyond me. Likewise, how he happened to be here at all.

Guth's eyes darted around the room, then narrowed as they settled back on Zahl. "I know you," he said. "I've seen you around. What's happening here?"

Zahl held his eyes and his weapon on Guth, but was standing with his back against the wall now so that Malone and I were still in his peripheral vision. "Put the gun down," was all he said in reply to the question.

Guth seemed to be going a little bleary. He started to sag toward the doorframe as he deliberately swung the gun in my direction. "Fuck you," he grated. "I'm here to kill this motherfucker for

323

taking my woman and fucking up my big score. It ain't none of your business."

I watched Zahl's lips twist into a sardonic grin and I knew he'd come to a decision. I gathered myself for the best chance I was going to have. I could feel Malone doing the same, though I was determined to get there first.

It was time. Zahl's attention was almost entirely on Guth; if anything narrows your focus, it's the intent to kill.

"I'm sorry he stole your girlfriend," Zahl said very quietly, almost gently, not wanting the other weapon to come back on him too quickly. "I know all about losing someone you love. But I'm here to kill all of them myself and I don't want any witnesses."

I doubt that Guth had even understood the words before the silencer *popped* and I was flinging myself down the length of the table, horizontal to the surface, scrabbling on all fours. A second *pop* followed hard on the first, this one also intended for Guth, and I was halfway there, my eyes on the gun beginning to swing in my direction, aware of Malone plunging just behind me. She'd been every bit as alert as I hoped.

The room exploded into cacophony as Guth's weapon fired, an unsilenced blast. Screams did indeed fill the air, and Zahl roared either in fury or pain.

I was almost on him and reached out for his gun, feeling as if my left arm was pulling itself from my shoulder in the effort even as I pushed off one last time with my right hand on the table. My fingertips made contact with the hot silencer as I heard another *pop* and I thought the bullet missed me. Then I was on him, grabbing at the weapon as my weight slammed him back against the wall and carried us both to the floor.

Malone landed on top of us a split second later. Zahl was howling now and madly punching at me while trying to keep the gun away from us. I twisted so that I could knee him in the groin as I lurched for a better grip on his wrist and the howl became something else. Then I was on the floor beside him and Malone was on his chest pummeling his face as I pulled his gun hand over his head.

I twisted the gun from his hand, got a good grip on it, and pointed it at his head but it turned out to be unnecessary. My partner had already pounded him unconscious.

I sprawled on my back beside the two of them to try to catch my breath. The paint in the ceiling was badly cracked. Someone at the other end of the conference table was whimpering. There was a searing sensation on my upper right arm where Zahl hadn't missed after all.

Within minutes of Malone beating Zahl into submission the Lifestream Foundation was swarming with cops and medics. Obviously someone had heard the unsilenced gunshot and called 9-1-1. I hoped it was the receptionist. We still didn't know how Guth had gotten past her.

It was pretty chaotic for a while. Not only did we have an unconscious killer; we had a dead one. Zahl's two shots had been a perfect double-tap to Guth's chest.

Once the first responding officers tentatively sorted the good guys from the bad guys, Tanya Petosky, Max Overton, Malone and I were all escorted out of the conference room and told to stay put in the reception area. Where we discovered that the receptionist was woozy but alive. Guth had given her a mild concussion but she had come around in time to call the cops. She still had no idea how lucky she was to be alive.

A medic treated my left hand for burns from the silencer and my right arm for a minor bullet graze from that last *pop* of Zahl's gun. Then she left and an officer remained by the door to ensure our compliance.

Eventually Mike Whitehall retrieved Malone and me from the room and took us downtown to give our formal statements which, needless to say, were lengthy.

I managed to make a couple of necessary calls while we were there, to the Heatherlys to tell them that Uncle Norman was innocent and they had nothing further to worry about, to LeAnn at the

325

Pen and Pastry to tell her that Guth was dead and she was really safe now. We could prepare a formal report for our formal client later, including an explanation of Tony Zahl's role in it all.

Finally, we were done.

CHAPTER EIGHT-FOUR

It was six-fifteen before Malone and I got back to the office, both of us exhausted and sore. She hadn't required medical treatment but I knew she had to have some good bruises from tackling both me and Zahl. My first round of pain meds was already wearing off.

The building was empty and the corridor dimly lit as I unlocked the door and let us both in. I didn't even know what we were doing here; it was like we were on automatic, not wanting to go home but with nowhere else to be. The bad guys were dead or in custody and everybody was safe. So here we were in the office.

I flicked on the light, hung my jacket on the hall tree, dropped my holstered weapon in the upper right-hand drawer of the desk, and sat down. More like slumped down.

Malone was still standing by the door, looking at me. Our eyes met but I couldn't tell what she was thinking or feeling. She was just looking. Then she shrugged out of her own jacket, hung in on the hall tree next to mine, walked over to me, leaned down, and kissed me solidly on the lips.

That perked me right up.

I was still processing the kiss as she went to her side of the partner's desk, stowed her weapon in its drawer, and sat down with a very slight smile on her face.

"What was that?" I finally asked.

"You looked like you needed a pick-me-up."

"And that did the trick, but...what was that?"

"You mean why? Why right at this moment? Because you could have gotten yourself fucking killed today going after Zahl the way you did."

"I didn't think I had a choice. You were right with me."

"As I seem always to be."

I was still trying to plumb the deeper meaning of that statement, assuming there was one, when her shoulders twitched as if she were shaking something off and she sat forward, all business.

"At least Mike managed to keep the media off us."

Okay. "That won't last long. I'm surprised the phone isn't ringing already. Maybe Alison Roberts hasn't recovered from her latest adventure yet."

Malone snorted. "I hope not." She looked at her watch. "It's late. They wouldn't expect us to be here, anyway. Tanya's a real piece of work, isn't she?"

I mentally zigged to go with her zag. "At least we know now why she volunteered to man the Lifestream Foundation office so much. The escort service might have technically been operating out of Beaverton but she got her recruits and coordinated from the Foundation here in Portland."

"Like I say, a real piece of work."

I nodded in agreement. "People rationalize," I said. "My impression is that she wanted to believe New Faith was just another financial opportunity for women who needed to improve their lives."

"Which is bullshit—but what do you bet she walks? Wealthy, apparently reputable woman like that? She won't get jail time for running a high-class call girl operation. Probably be tough to find a judge who hasn't been a customer. She'll get a fine and a lot of fucking free publicity."

I shrugged. "Could be. Probably." And decided to take a zig of my own, as long as we are focusing on business. "How do you think Guth ended up there at that moment? Not that I'm not grateful."

Her turn to shrug. "We'll never know. My guess is that before she accidentally helped his escape Alison Roberts was questioning him about the Lifestream Foundation because she thought he was the one killing board members. Maybe she put it in his head that their office downtown would be a good place to start looking for us."

"Maybe. However it happened, I'll never again say I don't believe in coincidence."

"Yeah, you will." She grimaced. "And you do realize we can add more crazy fuckers to our list of crazy fuckers dealt with. I mean, did Guth really think that he was in love with LeAnn and could win her back by, what, killing her friend Kristi? Did Zahl really think he was in love with Albright and could...?" She stopped abruptly. "Oh, never mind. They are all crazy fuckers."

I had to chuckle. "Well, at least they weren't serial killers or outright psychopaths. Crazy in love isn't quite the same thing." Which was a good occasion to segue once more. I sat forward, leaning a little over the desktop toward her, putting on a big grin. "Now, about that kiss...."

She copied my posture but with a face suddenly serious. "You could have been killed, you stupid shit."

Whoa. I tried to keep it light. "Not the first time. Probably won't be the last."

Her expression didn't change and I felt like her eyes were boring straight into mine. "You could have been killed."

"Devon, you were right there with me. You landed on him just a split after I did. It could have been you just as easily as me."

Her expression softened. "I wasn't going to let you try to take him alone. Partners, right?"

"You know," I said, quite without consciously intending to, "I think I'm in love with you."

I expected her to jerk back, to frown, to blow it off in some typical Devon Malone way. As is so often the case, I was wrong.

She didn't even twitch. "I guess I love you, too."

So I was the one who sat back. Talk about too good to be true. But she'd said it, by damn, and the moment was here to be seized.

I leaned forward again. "Not ringing endorsements, on either side, but we should do something about it."

That pushed her back a bit, brought on a tiny frown. "You're not proposing, are you?"

Again I had to grin. "I'm proposing that we have sex. I'm dying over here."

"That's a relief." She matched my grin. "Not that you're dying." She grinned bigger. "My place or yours?"

THE END

ABOUT THE AUTHOR

Glenn Harris lives and writes in the middle of the Columbia Gorge National Scenic Area (Hood River, Oregon). Besides creating detective novels, short stories, and a monthly newspaper column, he acts and directs in community theater.

His former lives include college English teacher, private K-12 school director, graphic design business owner, weekly newspaper managing editor, corporate manager, and taekwondo instructor.

Want more McCall and Malone mysteries? Read *Grave Reckoning* next, and be sure to visit Glenn Harris' website (http://www.glennharris.us) and subscribe to the free e-mail newsletter so you're first in line for new books!

www.ingramcontent.com/pod-product-compliance
Lightning Source LLC
Chambersburg PA
CBHW070644180626
46817CB00006B/2234